CROSS & SAMPSON

BOOKS BY JAMES PATTERSON
FEATURING ALEX CROSS

Return of the Spider
The House of Cross
Alex Cross Must Die
Cross Down
Triple Cross
Fear No Evil
Deadly Cross
Criss Cross
Target: Alex Cross
The People vs. Alex Cross
Cross the Line
Cross Justice
Hope to Die
Cross My Heart
Alex Cross, Run
Merry Christmas, Alex Cross
Kill Alex Cross
Cross Fire
I, Alex Cross
Alex Cross's Trial
Cross Country
Double Cross
Cross (also published as *Alex Cross*)
Mary, Mary
London Bridges
The Big Bad Wolf
Four Blind Mice
Violets Are Blue
Roses Are Red
Pop Goes the Weasel
Cat and Mouse
Jack & Jill
Kiss the Girls
Along Came a Spider

For a preview of upcoming books and information about the author, visit JamesPatterson.com or find him on Facebook, X, Instagram, Substack, or TikTok.

CROSS & SAMPSON

JAMES PATTERSON
AND BRIAN SITTS

LITTLE, BROWN AND COMPANY
NEW YORK BOSTON LONDON

The characters and events in this book are fictitious. Any similarity to real persons, living or dead, is coincidental and not intended by the author.

Copyright © 2026 by James Patterson

Hachette Book Group supports the right to free expression and the value of copyright. The purpose of copyright is to encourage writers and artists to produce the creative works that enrich our culture.

The scanning, uploading, and distribution of this book without permission is a theft of the author's intellectual property. If you would like permission to use material from the book (other than for review purposes), please contact permissions@hbgusa.com. Thank you for your support of the author's rights.

Little, Brown and Company
Hachette Book Group
1290 Avenue of the Americas, New York, NY 10104
littlebrown.com

First Edition: February 2026

Little, Brown and Company is a division of Hachette Book Group, Inc. The Little, Brown name and logo are trademarks of Hachette Book Group, Inc.

ALEX CROSS is a trademark of JBP Business, LLC.

The publisher is not responsible for websites (or their content) that are not owned by the publisher.

The Hachette Speakers Bureau provides a wide range of authors for speaking events. To find out more, go to hachettespeakersbureau.com or email hachettespeakers@hbgusa.com.

Little, Brown and Company books may be purchased in bulk for business, educational, or promotional use. For information, please contact your local bookseller or the Hachette Book Group Special Markets Department at special.markets@hbgusa.com.

ISBN 9780316599849 (hc) / 9780316606288 (large print) / 9780316607278 (signed edition)
LCCN is available at the Library of Congress

Printing 1, 2025

LSC-H

Printed in the United States of America

CROSS & SAMPSON

Prologue

Sampson

MY BEST FRIEND, Alex Cross, has been my favorite ride-along ever since he joined the force, and that was a long time ago — before we both sported gray hair.

Tonight, we're cruising the streets of downtown DC in an unmarked patrol vehicle. It's the biggest SUV that I could pull from the Metro Police motor pool, but I'm six foot nine, so my head still scrapes the inside roof. I've got the scanner turned down low. I'm not even on duty. Just felt like a drive, and I needed the company.

"How's everybody at home, Alex?"

First thing I always ask. Nana Mama, Alex's grandmother, is a big part of his life — and mine. I was at their house so often as a kid, she basically raised me. The Cross family is practically my own.

"Good," he says. "Jannie's enjoying her classes and still focused on track. Damon seems to be settling in at UNC."

"Can't believe he's already in grad school. He likes it down there in Chapel Hill?"

"Loves it. He's in the clinical psychology graduate program, on his way to a PhD."

"And Ali?"

"Still doing well in school, still kicking up some good trouble. Bree and I have a ways to go before we're empty nesters."

"The house'll never be empty. What about Nana Mama?"

"Of course. Goes without saying. She's a permanent fixture."

Alex lobs a few questions back to me about my family. Doesn't take long, since it's just me and my young daughter, Willow.

"And how's Bree doing?" I ask.

Alex and I have seen each other through the pain of losing loved ones, and I was truly happy when he found Bree. She's a loving person and the sharpest investigator I've ever met.

Next to Alex, of course.

"You know Bree," says Alex. "She never lets up. Always working."

"You two should take a vacation. Fly off to Bermuda for a week."

Alex lets out a snort. "Right. You'll need to convince my wife. She's nonstop."

Who's he kidding? Alex and Bree are *both* workaholics. Crime-solving machines.

Made for each other. As a DC detective, I feel lucky whenever I'm on their team.

I ease past a four-car motorcade. From the level of security, I can tell that it's nobody too high up on the food chain. Probably some foreign ambassador or a federal official. I give the one-man motorcycle escort a salute as we pass.

Nothing shimmers quite like Washington at night. The landmarks are glowing as we drive along Constitution Avenue from the Capitol toward the White House. We pass the Smithsonian Castle and the National Museum of Natural History. Up ahead, I can see the Washington Monument.

It never gets old, none of it.

This might be the nation's capital, but it's also our hometown. Mine and Alex's. We were both raised here, and we've seen our share of pain and tragedy on these historic streets. I'm afraid we'll see more.

In the past year, we've dealt with suicide bombers, hate-group rallies, and homegrown terrorism. Hell, Alex got shot in the chest. Almost died.

He looks over at me. Must have been reading my mind.

"Enough with the family updates, John," he says. "What's bothering you? The city's peaceful tonight."

Alex knows me too well. We've been as close as brothers since we were kids. "You heard about the bombings out in Iowa?"

"The grain-tower explosions? Yeah. I thought those were solved."

"Yeah. They caught the guy. But I don't think that's the end of it. It's like a game of Whac-A-Mole these days—you knock the crazies down in one place, they pop up somewhere else."

Alex leans back in his seat and rubs his chin. "You know, John, there's something I took away from my recent near-death experience."

"What's that?"

"Don't go looking for trouble. It'll find you soon enough."

CHAPTER 1

Cross

ALEX CROSS SLOWLY SIPS his second cup of coffee and enjoys the sweet silence at his home on Fifth Street in Southeast DC. He's reading the *Post* and finishing the last of his scrambled eggs and toast, prepared by the Cross family's indispensable matriarch.

From the way his grandmother moves around the kitchen, it's hard to tell that Nana Mama is in her nineties. At the moment, she's busy cleaning and seasoning her cast-iron frying pan, the same one she's been using for decades. No one else in the Cross household would dare touch it. Not even Alex.

Across the table, Alex's wife, Bree, is working on her laptop, fingers flying, her hazel eyes focused on the screen. One of the rules Nana Mama enforces in the Cross household is that no electronics are allowed at the kitchen table until your meal is finished and your dishes cleared away. The rule applies to adults and children alike.

That means Bree usually eats quicker than Alex so she can get on her laptop and start her busy day. Retired from her previous jobs as a detective and FBI agent, Bree now works for the Bluestone Group, an international private security firm. She's one of their top investigators.

These days, Alex divides his time between consulting for the FBI as a forensic psychologist and writing books about the criminal mind. Every now and then, he lectures at his alma mater, Georgetown University, and he always packs the house.

With the two older Cross kids away at college—Janelle at Howard, Damon now in grad school at the University of North Carolina—and Ali off to middle school nearby, the day is starting quietly and peacefully in the warm, cozy kitchen.

Alex looks over at Bree. "What's getting you going this morning?"

"Just a sec, just a sec," Bree replies, not looking up.

Alex smiles. When Bree is working hard, "just a sec" could mean a minute, a half hour, or even an hour. She has an amazing capacity for blocking out distractions, including her husband.

No matter. Alex has his own project, going over the notes for a new book. The deadline is looming and his publisher is getting anxious. Time to bear down and—

Alex's iPhone rings, interrupting his thoughts.

He looks at the screen. The caller ID says UNC—Damon's school.

He puts the phone on speaker. "Hello?"

"Dr. Cross?" A woman's voice. Hesitant.

"Yes, this is Alex Cross. How can I help you?"

"This is Professor Clarisse Pope. I'm calling about your son Damon. He's in my Abnormal Psychology class, and I'm also his academic adviser."

Bree looks up from her work.

"Good morning, Professor. I've read some of your books, and Damon mentioned he really likes the course. What's he up to now?"

Damon's a dedicated student, but he's been known to miss a class here and there when he's doing something else that really matters to him. That used to be basketball but now it's more likely to be political activism, trying to save the world. A passion he shares with his younger brother, Ali.

"Go ahead, Professor," Alex says. "I have you on speaker. My wife, Bree, is here too. Is there an issue with Damon's academics?"

Pope's delivery is a bit halting: "No, no. Nothing like that. Damon's a great student. Very diligent. Always on top of things. Which is why I'm calling. I was just wondering...have you heard from him recently?"

Alex can see Nana Mama listening from across the kitchen, leaning in toward the conversation.

"No," says Alex, a cold sensation seeping into his gut. "At least, I haven't." He glances at his wife. Like a lot of college students, Damon is a sporadic communicator. It isn't unusual for him to be out of touch now and then. Alex and Bree have learned to give him some space.

"I got a text from him last week," says Bree, her jaw tensing. "He sent a cartoon—something about smart doctors who can't remember their own phone numbers."

"Right," says Alex. "I remember now. I got the same thing. I wrote back, telling him it wasn't as funny as he thought it was." He looks at the phone. "Professor Pope, is something wrong? What's going on?"

There's a quick intake of breath on the other end of the line.

"Dr. Cross, I'm not sure what it means, but Damon wasn't in class this week, and he missed our regular appointment. I checked with some other members of the faculty, and he hasn't shown up for their classes either. I called his cell phone, but it goes right to voicemail. He hasn't replied to my texts. I reached out to his girlfriend, Melissa, but I haven't heard back from her."

Alex locks eyes with Bree.

"Dr. Cross," the professor says, "I think your son is missing."

Nana drops her cast-iron pan to the floor, and a loud bang echoes in the kitchen.

CHAPTER 2

ALEX MOVES UP TO his attic office while continuing to talk with Clarisse Pope. During their conversation, he opens up his laptop and composes an email to Damon. Subject line: URGENT. Message: CALL HOME NOW!

"Professor Pope, are you sure about this?" Alex asks, trying to keep the fear out of his voice. "Maybe Damon's just been sick for a day or two."

"I don't think so. It's been three days now. I sent one of Damon's friends from class over to his apartment this morning to check on him, but his door was locked and the lights were out. Nobody answered."

"Have you contacted the police?" Alex asks. "Or campus security?"

"Actually, that's why I called," says Pope. "Damon is an adult, so a missing person report needs to be filed by a family member. But I'm worried, Dr. Cross."

"Me too," says Alex. He feels uneasy. His chest is tight and throbbing, reminding him that not so long ago he took a bullet in the line of duty and ended up in the ICU. He has his best friend and former police partner, John Sampson, to thank for being alive today.

"How did Damon seem in your classes?" Alex asks. "Was he his usual self? Did he seem concerned or moody, like something was bothering him?"

How many times has he questioned witnesses just like this, seeking answers to some mystery or crime? Including crimes against his own family.

"No, not at all," says Pope. "He seemed fine, joking, answering questions, like always."

"And still nothing from Melissa?"

"I texted her again just before I called you. No response."

Melissa and Damon met as undergrads back at Davidson and have been living together off campus. She's a grad student at UNC like Damon and a busy teaching assistant besides. Melissa is a smart, pretty girl who knows what she wants and where she's going. Alex can't imagine her taking part in some sort of prank or hoax.

He also can't imagine her not calling to let them know Damon is missing.

Did they take off somewhere together? Is Melissa missing too? Are they both off the grid?

"Have you reached out to Melissa's parents?" asks Alex.

"I believe they're traveling in Europe," says Pope. "My assistant is working on contacting them. But I wanted to get in touch with you."

He hears footsteps on the stairs and Bree walks into his office, her face drawn.

"If I find out anything new," says Pope, "I'll let you know."

"Thanks for calling," says Alex. "We'll talk soon."

"Wait!" says Pope. "Let me give you the names and numbers for campus security and the Chapel Hill police."

"I've got them already," says Alex, tapping on his laptop. "But no worries. In a couple hours, I'll be seeing them face to face."

CHAPTER 3

ALEX GETS UP FROM his desk and walks over to Bree. They hug, tight.

Her scent, her touch, everything about her comforts him. Always has.

"I've been calling and texting both Damon and Melissa," says Bree. "Calls go to voicemail, and there're no replies to my texts."

"There has to be a good reason why he's been out of touch." Alex frowns. "I just sent him an email. Let's see if he responds."

Bree breaks the hug. "Alex, I love that boy like he is my own blood. When we find him, I'll give him a big kiss—then a good slap on the butt for scaring the hell out of us."

Alex caresses her cheek. "I'm with you. He might be an adult now, but I'll find a way to ground him if this turns out to be a prank."

They're both just trying to buck each other up. They head down the stairs. Two packed bags sit in the second-floor hallway.

"I called Bluestone's travel people. They've booked us on American," says Bree. "Direct to Raleigh. Leaves from Reagan in ninety minutes. There'll be a Hertz rental for us at RDU. They're also sending an Uber to take us. It should be here any minute."

"Thank God for Bluestone."

Alex calls in a few favors to fast-track approval for getting their weapons on the plane under the TSA's Law Enforcement Officer Flying Armed program.

"Do you really think we'll need our guns?" asks Bree.

"I hope not," says Alex, putting his in a holster.

They each pick up a bag and go downstairs. Nana Mama meets them at the bottom of the stairs, her eyes red and teary. She holds out two Tupperware containers.

"I packed you some food," she says. "I know how you two work. You'll get so focused on asking questions, you'll forget to eat or end up at some greasy-spoon diner."

"You're right as always," says Alex. "You know us too well."

Bree and Alex take the containers of food and tuck them into the pockets of their luggage. When they look up again, Nana Mama seems ready to cry. Without a word, the three of them wrap one another up in a group hug.

Alex kisses one of Nana's wrinkled cheeks. Bree kisses the other. Nana squeezes them both. "I'll be praying for you, every minute, every hour."

"We know you will," says Alex.

Another hard squeeze from his grandmother. "You find that boy."

"We will, Nana Mama," says Bree. "We will."

Nana breaks the embrace and turns toward the front window. "Your ride's here. Get going."

CHAPTER 4

Sampson

LIFE AS A SINGLE parent is not easy. But it has its moments.

One of my most treasured rituals is walking my daughter, Willow, to school, her small hand dwarfed in my own big mitt. I know the time will come when she'll be too grown up to hold Daddy's hand. I'm not looking forward to that day.

But at this moment, I've got something else to worry about.

Our morning ritual was just interrupted by an unexpected phone call from Alex Cross. Damon, he tells me, is apparently missing down in North Carolina.

Willow walks ahead and starts talking and giggling with her friends as I stand outside her school, holding my phone tight to my ear. "Alex, have you talked to the Chapel Hill police or campus security?"

My feet feel rooted to the concrete sidewalk. I'm trying to stay grounded, not to jump to any worst-case scenarios. Bad things have happened to the Cross family before. But I'm hoping this is just some kind of mistake or miscommunication.

"Not yet," he says. "Bree and I will be in Raleigh in just over two hours. We'll get a rental and head to campus. We want to meet with the police in person. You know what it's like—it's hard to ignore somebody who's sitting right in front of you."

"I agree. In person is best. Look, I can be down there later today."

"Can you really?" asks Alex. "I didn't think you had any vacation time left."

"I'll find the time. You get there safe, start your search, and I'll be there as soon as I can."

A brief pause from the other end of the line, then: "I love you, John Sampson."

"I know you do, and I love you too, Alex, and everyone else in your family. If you don't think it would be too taxing on Nana Mama, I'll have Willow stay at your house while I'm down there with you two."

"I'm sure that will be fine. You know Nana Mama just loves your little girl. And Ali...well, he can be a handful, but Willow's like a little sister to him, and she can hold her own," Alex says. "Gotta go, we're pulling up to the airport now."

"Later. You two travel safe."

I disconnect and walk over to Willow. She looks up at me with that 1,000-watt smile and hugs me. My baby is tall—she takes after her daddy—but her head still barely reaches my midriff. I decide not to say anything to her now. *I'll set everything up and tell her about Damon later, when I pick her up this afternoon,* I think. No need to have her spend the day worrying.

"Daddy?"

"Right here," I say.

She laughs. "Remember you said you'd get me a new backpack? This one is still too heavy."

I pat her hair. "Sure. I guess I can do that."

"Yay!" Then her voice gets serious: "Daddy, when are we going to see Rebecca again? Are we still getting married?"

Her question makes me wince a little. I can't help it.

Rebecca is Rebecca Cantrell, the U.S. attorney for Northern Virginia. She's been an important part of my life, and Willow's too. When I'd asked Rebecca to marry me, Willow had cried out, "And me!"

But since then, Rebecca's put things on hold. It's been painful, but she has her reasons, and I have a hard time arguing with them.

"I've seen your scars, John," she told me. "And I know the way you work. You were first to make entry at that hostage situation at Fort Dupont Dwellings. You got shot twice and your vest saved you. I can't go through that again. Please, just give me some time."

So that's what I'm doing.

I look down at Willow. "We're just taking a little break from each other, that's all. I'm sure it'll all work out in the end."

I hope.

"Okaaay," says Willow. The tone of her voice tells me she doesn't quite trust what she's hearing.

I kiss the top of her head and nudge her toward the school entrance. "You run in, now, sugar. Don't be late."

Willow waves and heads through the door, her backpack hanging low.

I'm sure it *is* heavy, but I'm not ready to replace it just yet. Willow doesn't know it, but that backpack has bullet-resistant panels sewn into the fabric. I bought it for her a little while back, when

DC and the country seemed to be trembling on a knife-edge, violence breaking out everywhere for no apparent reason.

I wanted to give my daughter some protection if a shooter ever attacked her school. Sign of the times. A sad one.

Still, it's been peaceful and quiet in DC recently. Maybe I'm just being a paranoid parent. Maybe it's time to replace her tactical backpack with the old-fashioned kind, something fun and appropriate for a little girl, without all the bulletproofing.

My phone rings. What I hear next makes that hopeful thought disappear like a spiderweb caught in a high wind.

"John!" It's my supervisor, Detective Sergeant Moore Taylor. "Get over to N Street and Thirteenth Street Northwest, quick as you can!"

"On my way. What's up?"

Taylor's voice is tight and hard: "Bombing. Multiple victims. Fire and EMTs are en route. I need you to get over there and take charge!"

There goes my peaceful, quiet city.

Up in flames again.

CHAPTER 5

IT TAKES ME THREE minutes to get back to my house and jump in my car. I start up lights and sirens, then run every red light on the way to the scene. Along the way, I call Pam Doolittle, a neighbor who works from home as an IT consultant. Pam's my logistical backup on the home front when duty calls. Her son, Tomas, is a year younger than Willow but goes to the same school.

Pam agrees to pick up Willow after school and take her to the Cross house. I don't even need to call over there. Nana Mama says my daughter is welcome anytime for any reason. No questions asked. A standing invitation.

Even with all the lights flashing and sirens wailing, I hit gridlock about a block away from the bombing scene and get stuck behind a mass of unmoving vehicles, some of them abandoned. I realize that this is as close as I'm going to get.

I pull up on the sidewalk, grab my go bag from the trunk, and run past clumps of civilians, some with hands up to their mouths in shock, others standing on concrete planters or atop stopped cars to see what's going on. A lot of them have their phones raised, taking photos or videos. Two news helicopters and a blue-and-white police helicopter are hovering overhead, the sound of their rotors echoing against the buildings.

The smell hits me like a hard memory of other bombing aftermaths from my years on the police force and my time in the army in Iraq and Afghanistan, that acrid scent of smoke and burning rubber. When I finally reach the scene, two Metro cops are yelling at pedestrians to stay back, to little effect.

"*You!*" I shout, flashing my badge and pointing to the nearest uniform. "Get some barricade tape up! We've got to secure this scene!"

Smoke is still eddying around the intersection. I see two shattered cars plus what's left of a van, flames flickering in the wreckage, and a huge crater in the middle of the street. A broken water main is spraying out water, flooding the whole area.

This is a four-lane road—two lanes southbound and two northbound—with trees lining the sidewalks. The windows in nearby office buildings have been shattered, and the trees nearest the blast have been stripped of their leaves. Branches are bent or snapped off, lying in the road. Up and down the block, car alarms are screeching.

I get closer, and the smells are more intense and more horrific, a choking mixture of spilled gasoline, burned fabric, and scorched flesh.

A woman in a business suit is writhing on the ground about twenty feet away, screaming, her hands squeezing her bloody abdomen. A man is sitting on a concrete planter, his face blackened, shirt torn away, looking down with wide eyes at his left leg, missing from the knee down, while a woman next to him desperately attempts to secure a leather belt around his tattered thigh.

On the asphalt around me, I count at least four lumps of ripped flesh that must have recently belonged to healthy men and women caught in the blast zone. Alive one minute, blown apart the next.

I have a strong impulse to assist the wounded, but well-trained crews from DC's fire and EMS department are already racing past me, carrying bulging shoulder bags and backboards, followed by others pushing gurneys, their wheels rattling as they go by. I need to let them do their jobs. It's time to do mine.

I bring up my handheld radio. "Dispatch, this is Sampson, D-five. We have a mass casualty event at the intersection of Thirteenth Street and N Street Northwest. We need units to block off traffic in a three-block radius. Tell DC Fire to roll as many buses as they can—and get the Metropolitan bomb squad out here!"

"Copy, Detective."

I look down the street and see more survivors, some holding bloody handkerchiefs to their heads as they slowly navigate between the twisted and burning cars and the crater filling with water from the busted water main.

The crater in the road tells the story.

A car bomb.

I pick up my handheld again. "Dispatch, this is Sampson, D-five. Contact the FBI and the ATF. We've got a suspected terrorist attack here."

The dispatcher acknowledges.

It all looks painfully, terribly familiar. I've been at scenes like this from Bogotá to Baghdad to Kabul. As unfortunate as it sounds,

I'd come to expect it in places like that—countries torn by war. Sometimes, sad to say, mass destruction comes with the territory.

But not here. Not in my city. Not in the nation's capital. We used to be safe here.

I start walking through the scene.

Something in a nearby tree looks off. Unnatural. Something colorful is attached to a piece of a branch and lodged between two limbs.

I step closer, looking up. It's a woman's shoe.

I turn away as yellow tape is being strung up by two Metro cops. I try not to think about what I've just seen: a severed leg with a high-heeled shoe still strapped to the foot hanging from the tree, blood dripping down.

CHAPTER 6

Cross

COMPARED TO THE AIRPORTS in DC, Raleigh-Durham International Airport is small and easy to navigate. Barely twenty minutes after disembarking from their flight, Alex and Bree are already in their rented red Camry and speeding west on I-40.

Alex is at the wheel, dodging in and out of traffic. The campus is sixteen miles away. Bree has her laptop open and keeps up a running commentary on what she's learning.

"I've gone back through all the emails and texts Damon sent us as well as his social media for the past three months," she says. "All pretty normal. Classes. Basketball. Tutoring. Dates with Melissa. A few protest activities, complaints about the weather—"

"Tell me more about the protest activities," says Alex, gripping the wheel tight. "What were those about?"

Growing up with an activist great-grandmother and a father in law enforcement, Damon had been warned to be careful when confronting authority. Alex has tried to be realistic but not alarmist in reminding his children that all it takes is one traffic stop with a jittery cop. But he's proud of Damon's activism. Standing up against racism and injustice is a Cross family tradition.

Bree scrolls through the entries, pausing along the way to speed-read. "So far, I see three. Two protests were about the killing of a Black grandmother in Caldwell. A local SWAT team raided her home, thinking it was a meth lab, but they had the wrong address. And, let's see…the other one was a protest against a right-wing extremist group called the YFF."

Alex glances over at his wife. "You think maybe Damon made himself too visible? He's a damn good public speaker, and when he believes in something, he puts it right out there. Maybe he made some noise around the wrong people."

"Watch your speed," says Bree, looking up from her screen. "We don't want to get pulled over."

"I hear you," says Alex, but he presses harder on the pedal. "Anything else?"

"Not that I can see. But you're right that saying the right thing in the wrong place can be dangerous these days." She turns to the window.

Alex looks over. "What? What are you thinking?"

"I'm thinking about Maestro. Wondering if maybe he's coming for our family again."

Alex's gut churns. Maestro was a madman. He'd tried to murder them both and had treated John Sampson brutally after the death of his wife, Billie. Over the years, Maestro had killed scores of people, rationalizing his actions as vigilante justice.

Could he have done something to Damon?

"Last time we spoke," says Alex, "Maestro claimed he was dying. It sure sounded like he was."

"The bastard might've recovered," says Bree. "Or maybe one of his well-trained believers picked up his bloody torch. That sort of thing's been known to happen."

Alex checks the GPS. They're about ten minutes from the building that houses campus security. "Speaking of emails—"

"You're cc'd on all the ones I got from him," says Bree. "Do you have some from Damon that I didn't see?"

"I'm not thinking about Damon's emails," Alex says. "I'm wondering about Melissa." He swerves around a Piggly Wiggly semitruck. "Maybe she was the one who got involved in something that made them both targets?"

"We'd need a warrant to check Melissa's emails," says Bree.

Alex shakes his head. "We don't have the time."

Bree looks at him. "Bluestone, right?"

"Only if you can do it quietly, without a forensics trail and without getting yourself or anyone else in trouble."

"Other times I'd say hell no, but these aren't other times."

"And let's contact Ned Mahoney," says Alex. "You know he'll do whatever he can to help us out."

Mahoney is both a good friend and a trusted contact of theirs at the FBI.

They ride on in silence for a few moments. Bree taps on her laptop, then sits up straight. "Oh, shit!"

Alex glances over. "What is it?"

Bree relays the alert on her screen. "Breaking news from MSNBC. Looks like a car bomb went off this morning in DC, near the intersection of Thirteenth and N Street. Multiple casualties."

Alex flinches. Their hometown, brutally attacked again! If he were here for any other reason than to find Damon, he would throw the Camry into an illegal U-turn, head back to the airport, and jump on the first flight to DC.

But Alex stays the course and says to Bree, "You know what this means."

Bree closes her laptop. "It means we can't bother Ned. He'll be neck-deep. And you know who'll be right by his side."

Alex nods. "John Sampson." He grips the wheel even tighter and glances over at Bree. "We're on our own for this one."

CHAPTER 7

Sampson

THE COPS ON SCENE point me toward a Panera restaurant on Thirteenth Street NW where the FBI has set up a temporary command post. Chairs are piled in one corner, and tables have been pushed together. The aroma of soup and grilled sandwiches still hangs in the air, mingled with the pungent smells from outside.

I walk in and spot my old buddy Ned Mahoney, a supervising special agent with the Bureau. I go over and shake his hand, grimy from soot.

"Glad you're here, John," he says. "This is a terrorist attack for sure, and the FBI is taking charge."

The restaurant is crowded with command staff from DC Fire and EMS, a cluster of men and women in business suits, and DC Metro Police, including my boss, Moore Taylor. No doubt he's pissed that the FBI has once again bigfooted its way into Metro Police territory and taken over.

I know Taylor'll play nice. But he won't like it.

"I'm setting up a task force," says Mahoney, "and we're going to make it lean and mean."

I nod. "The leaner and meaner, the better."

I hate red tape. Always have. It's too easy to get tangled up in it.

Mahoney looks up and calls out, "Homeland Security, you here?"

One of the suits at the next table raises a hand. "Special Agent Tim Smith."

"Did DHS have anything on the threat board? Anything at all?"

"Nothing to report at the moment, but we're doing a deep dive into recent investigations and chatter. We should have an update in a few hours."

"Good," Mahoney says. "Make it as quick as you can." He turns to a pair of police captains. "DC Metro, I want Detective Sampson on the task force. Understood?"

There are pursed lips and slight nods from the brass, including Taylor.

"ATF should be here any minute," Mahoney continues. "Fire, what's the casualty count so far?"

A captain steps up. He's wearing a white bunker jacket and holding his helmet at his side. "Fourteen dead, twice as many injured. A few are critical. We expect the death toll to rise."

Mahoney nods, his expression grim. "We'll look at our own threat assessments, cross-check it against what DHS and other agencies have, see if we can narrow down who might have been responsible and what the target was."

I raise my hand to get Ned's attention; in this setting, he's all professional.

"Detective Sampson?"

"I know we're in the preliminary stages here, but I have an idea of who the target might be, based on an investigation I did on this street nearly a year ago."

All heads turn to me.

"Go on," says Mahoney.

"About half a block away from the bomb crater is the DC office of FIP-PAC."

Mahoney looks stumped. "Sorry. What the hell is FIP-PAC?"

"Friends of Israel and Palestine Political Action Committee. Maybe it's too obvious, but it's something that should be run down."

Mahoney nods. "I agree. The first thing we need is—"

A woman's scream interrupts him.

It's coming from outside.

CHAPTER 8

Cross

ALEX AND BREE PULL into the parking lot of the campus public safety building at the end of a row of blue-and-white cruisers, all marked with the Chapel Hill campus police security logo.

As he shuts off the car, Alex hears a commotion nearby.

"What's happening?" asks Bree, looking around for the source of the noise.

From the driver's-side window, Alex sees that a fight has broken out among a bunch of students, maybe a dozen of them, in front of a wooden kiosk across the street. From what he can tell, it looks like one group is trying to prevent the other group from tearing down some kind of poster. It's getting ugly; lots of grabbing and shoving, even a few punches. Two campus police officers are running toward the fracas.

On any other day, Alex would have hustled over to see what the problem was and try to help calm things down. But this is not any other day. He grabs Bree by the arm as they head for the security building. "Ignore it," he says. "Let's go."

Inside, Bree flashes her old DC Metro Police chief of detectives badge. Alex shows his FBI consultant credentials. A minute later, they're sitting in the office of Chief Rupert Amberson, a handsome man in a tailored gray suit. His office walls are lined with crowded bookshelves and framed photos.

Amberson offers a cordial greeting. "Dr. Cross, Chief Stone, welcome to the University of North Carolina. What can I do for you?"

Bree leans across his desk. "You can help us find our son."

"Find him?" Amberson picks up a pen and pulls over a legal pad. "Sorry, I don't understand. Tell me what's going on."

"My son's name is Damon Cross," says Alex. "He's here doing graduate work in psychology. We've been informed that he's been missing for three days. He's not answering emails or texts, and calls to his cell phone go straight to voicemail. We got a call this morning from one of his professors, and she told us that no one is answering the door at his apartment, and the place looks dark."

Bree adds, "This isn't like Damon at all."

Amberson looks up from his pad. "Grad-student housing is in the Baity Hill apartments. I assume that's where he's living?"

"No," says Alex. "He's renting an apartment on Maxwell Road with his girlfriend. Her name is Melissa Lange. She's a grad student here too."

The chief puts down his pen. "Well, that changes things."

"How so?" asks Bree.

Amberson lifts his shoulders. "Maxwell Road is off campus. Students who live off campus are not under our jurisdiction. Our hands are tied."

Bree shakes her head. "You've got to be kidding."

Alex raises his voice. "Then you need to untie your damn hands!"

"Hold on a sec," says Amberson. He rifles through the contents of an in-basket, pulls out a sheet of paper, and hands it over. "See for yourself."

Alex and Bree lean forward. The paper has a light blue Carolina Housing logo over a black heading: MISSING PERSON PROTOCOL. The rules are underneath.

In accordance with federal, state, and local law, the following protocol has been established to outline the university response procedures in the event university officials receive a report that a person residing in on-campus housing is missing.

Alex barely makes it through the opening paragraph before crumpling the paper in disgust.

"Protocol?" says Bree, her tone icy. "Damon is a student here, isn't he? He's in the PhD program, pays his student fees. And you're telling us you can't do anything?"

The chief's concerned look now seems pasted on. "I'd like to help, but legally, I can't—unless you know that something happened to him while he was on campus."

"We don't," says Bree. "Right now, we don't know anything."

Amberson stands up. Clearly, the meeting is over. "Folks, you need to contact the Chapel Hill Police Department. Talk to Detective Hugh Malone over there. I'll make sure we keep an active interface with him."

"Active interface?" Alex mutters. "What kind of bullshit corporate-speak is that?"

"One more thing," says Amberson. "You might consider printing some flyers to put up around campus. Usually we frown on postings, but I'll make sure they stay up."

Alex feels like reaching over and grabbing this smooth-talking bureaucrat by his necktie. "You mean like the ones across the street?"

"Excuse me?"

"We just saw a brawl near the parking lot over a poster somebody put up."

Amberson shakes his head. "That's a different situation. It still shouldn't happen, but I know what it's about. There's a lot of heat on campus about a speaker who's coming next week. Both sides are riled up."

"Who's the speaker?" asks Bree.

Amberson reaches back to a credenza behind his desk and grabs a small color poster showing a young man at a podium, fist raised, face red with anger. "Michaelson Woods, from Young Freedom Fighters."

"Young Freedom Fighters," Alex repeats. "YFF." He glances at Bree.

Those same initials were in one of Damon's emails.

"It's a right-wing group. Some of our students support Woods's right to be here," says Amberson, "free speech and all, but a lot of people are against what he says." He rolls up the poster and tosses it into his wastebasket. "Between you and me, I'm hoping the little prick cancels his appearance. But that has nothing to do with locating your son. If you put your flyers up, I promise they won't get ripped down."

Amberson takes his pen and scribbles on a small pad. "I'm giving you Hugh Malone's phone number. I'll let him know you'll be calling."

"We won't be calling," says Bree.

"I'm sorry?" says Amberson.

Alex rises from his chair. "We prefer to just show up."

CHAPTER 9

Sampson

THE WOMAN OUTSIDE SCREAMS again, louder. I run out of the Panera and into a street filled with broken vehicles, shattered glass, and injured people. That's when I see her.

She isn't screaming.

She's shouting.

It's a highly agitated woman, about five foot five, wearing jeans and a dark blue windbreaker with the letters ATF on the back, and her shouts are directed at two DC firefighters who are hosing down the burned wreckage of an Audi.

"You idiots, the goddamn fire is out! You expect the thing to spontaneously combust? All you're doing now is wrecking my evidence! For fuck's sake, shut the water off!"

A DC fire chief with a white bunker coat and helmet walks over. "Hey! Hey! What's going on? What's the problem?"

"The problem is these jerks are soaking my crime scene!" the woman says.

The chief looks at the firefighters and makes a quick cut sign across his neck. The firefighters switch off the hoses and the torrent of water shrinks down to a dribble.

Ned Mahoney steps up beside me and points in the woman's direction. "That's the other member of our team. Anna Rizzo. She's an explosives enforcement officer with the ATF."

I'm impressed already. Rizzo obviously knows how to get somebody's attention. Mahoney waves her over. She's an attractive woman—olive skin, brown eyes, black hair bobbed in a short, no-nonsense style.

Mahoney does the honors. "Officer Anna Rizzo, meet Detective John Sampson, DC Metro Police."

We exchange a quick handshake. Then something clicks in my brain. "Hold on, I remember you! *Rizzo*. You're the one who found the guy responsible for that series of bombings out in Iowa. The grain towers."

"That's right," says Rizzo, hands on her hips, looking around at the burned and blackened carnage. "A shitty case. But it wasn't just me, it was my whole team—and the locals who hated seeing their harvests ruined."

"But you were the key. I read the report."

An indifferent shrug from Rizzo. "I got lucky. I was sifting through shards of metal and ceramic and I noticed something on a piece of metal, looked greasy. Turned out to be the bastard's thumbprint. From there, pretty open-and-shut."

"Don't downplay it, Anna," says Mahoney. "I heard you were at that examination table twenty hours straight before you found that piece of metal. That's not luck. That's work."

"Yeah, well," says Rizzo, "that was then, this is now." She looks up at me. "So, Detective Sampson, what's going on at your end?"

Right to the point.

"Our Special Operations Division has officers out gathering footage from security cameras, dashcams, traffic observation posts, and anything else that might have recorded traffic coming into the area. Detectives are interviewing witnesses and survivors to see if anyone saw anything unusual or out of place before it happened."

Mahoney leans in. "Homeland Security didn't get any warnings or threats. Neither did our local field office." He glances at his watch. "One hour since the blast and nobody's claimed responsibility."

"I'll leave that part up to you guys," says Rizzo. "Right now, this entire crime scene is mine, especially everything two hundred feet from the crater." She looks at the ground. The hoses are off, but water from a broken pipe is still flooding the street, eddying around our shoes. "Damn it! Hold on."

Rizzo takes out her phone and taps a number. She turns and walks a few paces away through the rising water. "Hey, is this Paul Baker at the Water and Sewer Authority? Hi, Paul. Anna Rizzo, ATF. Look, I called you folks ten minutes ago to shut off the main on Thirteenth Street Northwest. What's taking so long?" I see her listening, looking impatient, and when she speaks again, her tone is cold. "Tell you what, Paul, either this water stops flowing in two minutes or I'm coming down there and arresting your ass for interfering with a federal investigation. Are you hearing me now? Good."

The call is over. I don't think poor Paul Baker got too many words in.

As Rizzo puts her phone away, I step over and tap her shoulder. "I'll do it if you want."

"Do what?"

"You keep on working the scene, and I'll go down and knock

some people around at Water and Sewer. Starting with Paul Baker."

She gives me a small smile. "Detective Sampson, we're going to work well together, I can just tell."

"Call me John."

"Just get the job done," says Mahoney.

"Oh, we will," says Rizzo. She turns and stares at the crater at the center of the explosion. "FBI profilers say there are two types of bombers, disorganized asocial offenders and organized nonsocial offenders. The disorganized ones make pipe bombs and blow up random people and places because they can, because it gives them a sense of power."

She turns to look back at the rest of the wreckage. "The organized ones are highly intelligent and highly motivated, and they construct very technically proficient devices. They're determined to strike for revenge, for terror, for something that doesn't make sense to most people but makes perfect sense to them."

Her voice gets softer. "In those grain-tower cases, the bomber got sloppy. This is different. It looks sophisticated, well planned. What I'm seeing here shows smarts, experience, and some warped sense of dedication."

I nod. "I agree. And dedicated guys don't tend to get sloppy."

Rizzo looks out over the carnage. "Exactly," she says. "They're fucking fastidious."

CHAPTER 10

Cross

ALEX CROSS STANDS IN front of his son Damon's apartment building on Maxwell Road. It's a one-story extended-ranch brick building that's less than a mile from the center of campus. The lawn is green but thin with a few tall pine trees on one side providing shade.

Alex can make out a steady hum of traffic from U.S. 501, the highway barely visible through the trees. He walks to Damon's front door. Bree is right behind him. She reaches into her purse and digs out the spare key Damon gave them.

She also pulls out two pairs of blue medical gloves and two sets of paper booties.

"Bree..."

Her voice is tight: "You know we have to go in like this. If it's a crime scene, we can't contaminate it."

She's right, and Alex knows it. He just does not like the

implications. *For God's sake, how many times have I entered homes or rooms like this and ended up finding the bloody remains of a homicide victim?*

He takes a pair of the gloves, snaps them on, then slips the booties over his shoes. Bree leans on him as she slides her own booties on. They've both had lots of practice.

Alex steps forward, holding his wife's hand tight. "I love you, Bree."

She squeezes his hand, her eyes wet. "I love you too, Alex."

He slides the key into the lock, turns it gently, then leads the way into the darkness.

CHAPTER 11

Sampson

AFTER THE WATER IN the street subsides, I go to my car and open my kit. I change into a disposable protective jumpsuit, special-ordered for my size, then walk over to where Anna Rizzo is kneeling on the wet, cracked pavement. She's staring down at a huge piece of twisted metal.

Part of a truck axle.

"The bomber's vehicle?" I ask.

"I'd bet on it," she says. "Looks like it was at the center of the blast."

I look around. The initial investigative work is underway. Technicians from the ATF, the DC bomb squad, and other forensics investigators are laying out plastic triangles to mark evidence, taking photos, measuring. The bombing scene looks like a nightmare—broken windows, burned-out vehicles, bare trees. Is this really a street in our nation's capital?

Rizzo stands up and taps my arm. "Let's go for a walk."

"Good idea."

The sound of sirens has finally faded. I've already instructed the FAA to shoo away the news choppers. Sure, they want dramatic footage of the bomb site for their viewers, but the helicopters' rotor blades stir up dust and scatter evidence. As much as possible, we need a clean scene, TV ratings be damned.

As we walk away from the blast zone, Rizzo looks back and forth along the street, then up at the buildings around us. Broken glass and bits of metal crunch under our shoes. Rizzo steps around evidence markers and splintered tree branches. She stops in front of a store and turns to me. "See what I see?"

I do. The windows are intact. "The extent of the blast."

Rizzo slowly turns around. "That's one of the best markers we have—unbroken windows at a certain distance shows you the size and strength of the bomb."

I nod. "Then there's the Erin Woods formula, where you measure the distance human remains have traveled from the epicenter of the blast zone, and that also gives you an idea of the explosive force."

Rizzo smiles. Just a little. "Glad to know you keep on top of these things. Looks like you've got a big brain to go with that big body."

"I'm a fast learner."

Rizzo puts her hands on her hips. "Car bombs, truck bombs, van bombs—they cause incredible damage. But luckily, they also leave a huge reservoir of clues, albeit in bits and pieces. We usually find the source of the vehicle in less than a day, and that's the first big break we get."

"If we find it soon, it means our bomber might actually have made a mistake."

"Right," says Rizzo. "By opting for a big evidence source."

EMTs at the other end of the street are placing the shrouded remains of another victim into a dark blue van marked on the side with yellow letters: OFFICE OF THE CHIEF MEDICAL EXAMINER.

I lean against a pillar in front of the store. "Either that or the bomber's incredibly smart and sophisticated and thinking ten steps ahead of us."

"Possible," says Rizzo.

There's a chime from my phone and I see an incoming text.

Ready for you. Chan.

Dennis Chan is the head of the Technical and Analytical Services Bureau of DC's Special Operations Division and the brainiest guy I know except for my brilliant best friend, Alex Cross.

Shit. *Alex*...

I get a sudden twist in my belly when I remember that Damon is missing, and I'm going to have to stay here instead of going down to North Carolina to help. But Chan wouldn't text if he didn't have something important to show me. That has to be my focus right now.

"What's up?" asks Rizzo, glancing at my phone.

I slip it into my pocket. "Feel like seeing a movie?"

"Depends. Who's in it?"

"Our bomber. Let's see just how organized he is."

CHAPTER 12

Cross

ALEX OPENS THE DOOR and takes a few steps into Damon's apartment, and he feels an immediate rush of relief. The inside of the apartment is musty with a stale aroma of grilled food. But no thick odor like rotting meat and fruit—the smell of decomposing flesh.

Bree is right behind him. "It smells okay, thank God."

Alex finds a wall switch, flicks it up. A ceiling light illuminates a small living room with a couch, coffee table, two chairs, and a large-screen television.

"Hello?" Alex calls out, walking slowly through the room, cluttered with computer equipment and empty take-out cartons. "Damon? Melissa?"

Alex scans the floor and walls. No signs of violence, no overturned furniture. Nothing out of place.

To the right is a small kitchen. The sink is clean. Alex opens the refrigerator. It's lightly stocked with low-fat milk, orange juice, yogurt, and leftovers wrapped in foil.

Bree looks over his shoulder. "If Nana Mama saw this, she'd spend a day cooking just to fill the larder."

Next up is the bedroom on the other side of the apartment.

Two bureaus, a queen-size bed with rumpled sheets, and clothing scattered around the carpeted floor. Alex spots a grouping of framed pictures on one of the bureaus: some photos of the whole Cross clan on various family trips, plus two photos of Damon and Melissa in front of the campus library.

Bree steps up to the bureau and runs a gloved hand over one of the family pictures.

Alex walks into the bathroom, checks the shower stall and sink. He opens the medicine cabinet, looking for any clues, anything out of the ordinary.

But there's nothing.

He joins Bree as she opens the side-by-side bedroom closets. On the right, dresses, blouses, and skirts hang neatly from the rod, with shoes lined up below like a fashion display. Jeans and shorts are stacked on a shelf.

The left-hand closet is clearly Damon's. Sneakers and dress shoes lie in a tumble on the floor along with T-shirts and sweatpants. Half of the hangers are bare; the others hold a few wrinkled dress shirts, a sport coat, and a handful of narrow ties.

Bree sighs. "Just like home."

"Everything looks normal," agrees Alex. "If something happened to Damon, it didn't happen here."

He hears a sound from the living room. He whips around, puts a finger to his lips, and walks slowly back to the bedroom door, which is open just a sliver. Alex looks through the narrow gap; Bree is right behind him.

He sees the front door's knob turn and waits as the door opens slowly.

A man steps in. Mid-thirties. Gray suit, white shirt, blue necktie, carefully combed blond hair. His head swivels around as he checks every angle.

Alex slips a hand under his jacket and pulls out his SIG Sauer P365. Bree reaches into her bag and comes out with a pistol of her own.

Alex looks at Bree and holds up three fingers. Then two. Then one.

He pushes the door all the way open and steps through, pistol raised. *"Freeze!"*

CHAPTER 13

Sampson

I'M IN A CUBICLE in the basement of DC Metro Police headquarters, standing behind Dennis Chan's high-backed office chair in the Technical and Analytical Services Bureau of DC's Special Operations Division. ATF agent Anna Rizzo is right beside me. In front of Chan are two huge computer monitors that look like they belong at NASA's mission control in Houston.

Ned Mahoney is also with us, making the tiny cubicle even more crowded.

I lean down and pat Chan on the shoulder. "Okay, Dennis, what've you got?"

Chan's fingers start tapping on the keyboard as he mutters to nobody in particular, "You know, my uncle worked for the CIA a long time ago, back before it was even called the CIA."

A video pops up on the right monitor showing the intersection of Thirteenth Street and N Street NW.

"Whenever something happened out of the blue," Chan continues, "the agents used a technique they called 'walking back the cat.'"

"Meaning what?" asks Rizzo.

"Meaning you take one piece of evidence and follow it right back to the beginning." Chan leans in toward one of his screens. "Let's walk back that cat."

A time code runs on the upper left side of the image.

It starts at 7:58 a.m. today.

My mouth is getting dry and my chest tight as I watch a typical downtown DC morning: People on the sidewalks, traffic going by. Like any other day.

When the time code reads 7:59 a.m., a white van makes a turn onto the street. Virginia plates.

"No surprise, turns out the plates are stolen," says Chan. "We learned that they came off a contractor's van that was parked overnight at Gallery Place three days ago. We're tracking down surveillance footage from security cameras. Maybe we can ID somebody taking the plates."

"Don't count on it," says Rizzo. She and I exchange a look. We both suspect this guy is sharper than that.

On the video, the van comes to a sudden halt. The hazard lights start blinking.

The driver's door opens. A man jumps out. He's wearing white painter's overalls, a white hat pulled down low on his head, a white face mask, and white gloves. He quickly strolls away and takes a right down an alley.

At the intersection, just a few feet away, a young woman in a blue jacket is pushing a double stroller with two babies. She stops at the curb.

Move, I think, *please move*...

It's too late. A brilliant white-and-orange flash fills the screen. Mahoney grits his teeth.

When the flash fades, there's chaos everywhere—cars overturned, smoke in the air, and carnage on the ground. The woman in blue has fallen into the street. The stroller is a mangled mass of metal and ripped fabric.

"Christ!" says Rizzo.

I ball my hands into fists. Pure instinct. I want to punch somebody.

"Think it was an electronic timer?" Mahoney asks.

"Possible," says Rizzo. "Or the driver could have yanked a sixty-second fuse when he stepped out."

Chan taps a few keys. "All right, let's start backtracking." He explains as he goes.

"Once we had a clear photo of the van, we started the search process that links every traffic camera, store surveillance system, and private doorbell cam."

I nod. All legal since the revision of the Patriot Act. After September 11, we all gave up a bit of our privacy.

It's like watching an experimental film by a high-school student. We see the van approaching the intersection, then follow it back, block by block, street by street, with jump cuts and fadeaways. As the video plays, Chan keeps up a running commentary.

"So he came up Thirteenth Street Northwest, and from Twelfth Street Northwest...bastard was taking the scenic route." Chan taps the screen. "There's the National Museum of Asian Art."

I lean in closer. "I bet the son of a bitch came up the Twelfth Street Expressway—a quick way to downtown."

"I bet you're right," says Rizzo.

"And there he is," says Chan, pointing to the reverse action on the screen. "On I-395 and making good time. Crossing the Potomac on the Williams Memorial Bridge... and now we're in Virginia... and now we're on the George Washington Parkway."

I snap my fingers. "The airport! Reagan! That's where he came from!"

Watching as the van continues backward, I wish that the driver had been pulled over for a broken taillight or an improper lane crossing — anything to disrupt the plan.

"You're right," says Chan. "Reagan National indeed. Parking garage one. That's where he started." He looks up. "The cat has been walked back."

Mahoney picks up Chan's desk phone. "Okay, in about five minutes, that garage is going to be swarming with agents. We're locking it down. And then I'm heading out there." He looks at me. "John, you coming?"

"Absolutely." I turn to Rizzo. "How about you, Anna?"

She shakes her head. "Waste of time for me. I'm off to our ATF lab in Beltsville. While you two work the garage, I'll be sifting through the physical evidence. Maybe we can pull out something useful."

Mahoney nods.

I rub my eyes. "Long day ahead for all of us."

Rizzo claps her hands together like a cheerleader. "Let's get our asses in gear! I want this bastard. I want him bad."

I can't help but smile, just for a second. It's not often that I run across an investigator as gung ho as I am.

I like Anna Rizzo. I like her a lot.

CHAPTER 14

Cross

ALEX CROSS MOVES FORWARD across the living room. "Hands! Get those hands up in the air!" Bree hangs back in the doorway in a shooting stance.

The intruder stops in his tracks and raises his arms. "Wait! Dr. Cross, Chief Stone. Hold on! Everything's fine here."

Alex tightens the grip on his gun. "Who the hell are you?"

"I'm Drake Cannon from the FBI field office in Charlotte. Ned Mahoney told me to connect with you and provide any assistance I can, official or not."

That sounds like Mahoney, all right, Alex thinks. He'd called his friend before hearing about the events in DC. But even with a bombing in his own backyard, Mahoney's the kind of friend who will reach out to help them find Damon.

But Alex needs to be sure. "Mr. Cannon, are you right-handed or left-handed?"

"Right," he says.

"Don't be insulted, but the older I get, the more suspicious I am. I need you to take out your identification with your left hand and drop it on the floor. Don't toss it, just take it out and let it drop."

Cannon reaches into his coat, removes a leather wallet, and drops it to the floor.

"Now," says Alex, "put your hands up again and step back about six feet." He glances at Bree. She lowers her pistol and picks up the wallet. She flips it open, revealing a photo ID and a gold badge. She holds the open wallet up so Alex can see it.

Alex matches the photo with the agent in front of him and nods. Cannon lowers his hands. Bree tosses him his wallet.

"Thanks, Mr. Cannon," says Alex, sliding his pistol back into its holster. "Sorry it had to start like this."

Bree tucks her pistol into her waistband, and the tension in the air dissolves.

"How did you know we'd be here?" asks Alex.

"If my son were missing," says Cannon, "I'd for sure search his apartment. In fact, I'd do that first."

"You're right," says Alex. "The visit with campus security was a waste of time."

"How much did Ned tell you?" asks Bree.

"Not much," says Cannon. "Just that he wanted to make sure the Charlotte office would be at your service. That includes me personally. Whatever you need. He also said that Damon is a very special kid."

Alex looks over at Bree. "Yes," he says, voice cracking. "He definitely is."

CHAPTER 15

Sampson

SPECIAL AGENT NED MAHONEY and I sit in the office of Chief Barbara Lucianne, head of the Metropolitan Washington Airports Authority Police Department.

The Airports Authority provides security at both Dulles International and Reagan National. Lucianne's office is in terminal one, and from the dark look in her eyes and the tone of her voice, I can tell that she's personally offended that one of her facilities was used to help stage a terrorist attack.

Like Mahoney promised, agents are searching every corner of the garage. But I'm hoping the chief can give us some solid leads.

"Here's what I've got," she says, pointing at a monitor on her desk. She taps a keypad to start the footage. "Your van left parking garage one today at about seven thirty a.m. The plates match the numbers you gave me. Sorry, but this is the best shot I have of the driver."

On her screen, we see the van pause at one of the automatic gates as the driver pays the parking fee. She freezes the image. The person behind the wheel is nearly a shapeless form, wearing sunglasses, a plain white baseball cap pulled down low, a surgical mask, hands covered by gloves. I lean forward, wishing I had X-ray vision to see through the bastard's disguise.

"The tricky bastard paid in cash," says Lucianne. "And with the gloves, there's no point in recovering the bills he used for fingerprint analysis."

"He must have known he'd be under surveillance," says Mahoney.

"Why do you think the van was here in the first place?" she asks. "Why not drive directly to the target?"

"Maybe for a handoff," I suggest. "From the bomb maker to the driver. There aren't a lot of people with the balls to transport a van filled with explosives. This guy could have been a hired gun, paid to bring the van into DC and then disappear."

"How long was the van here in the garage?" Mahoney asks.

"Just overnight. Ticket system says it came in at eleven fourteen p.m."

I point at the monitor. "Show us."

Lucianne taps a few keys. The entryway angle is even worse. All I can see is a masked lower face and a gloved hand grabbing the ticket from the toll machine.

"Same guy?" asks Mahoney.

"Looks like it to me. But I don't think there's enough of an image there for biometrics."

"Where did he park?" asks Mahoney.

Lucianne clicks to a view deep inside the garage. The van is parked against a column at the end of a row, at the far end of the camera's range. The time code reads 2:05 a.m.

"Was that camera on all night?" I ask.

Lucianne nods. "I scrolled through the footage at high speed before you got here. Van never moved. And nobody got out."

I look over at Mahoney. "Son of a bitch probably slept in the vehicle. With a bomb inside."

Mahoney nods. "Which makes him either very brave or very dumb."

"Or maybe just very comfortable with explosives."

Lucianne's eyes darken again. "Well, any sorry son of a bitch who drags my airport into this crime better know I'm coming after his ass."

Mahoney's phone rings. He answers it, listens for a few seconds, then says, "On our way." He clicks off and looks at me. "That was Rizzo. She wants us to come over to the ATF lab in Beltsville. She found something."

CHAPTER 16

Cross

AFTER DRAKE CANNON LEAVES, Alex and Bree return to their search of Damon's apartment. Working as a two-person forensics team, they open every drawer, every cupboard, every cabinet. An hour goes by. Then Alex's phone chimes with a text alert. He checks his screen.

Sorry. In library. Phone was off. Will be there soon.

Alex turns the screen toward Bree. "It's Melissa."

"Thank God she's okay. But why hasn't she been in touch?"

Two minutes later, a red Kia pulls into the driveway. Melissa Lange steps out, a tall, slim blonde wearing black jeans and a Tar Heels sweatshirt. She has a backpack slung over her shoulder.

Bree looks out the window. "Here she comes."

"Good," says Alex. "She'd better be ready to answer some questions."

Alex and Bree step out of the apartment onto the sidewalk.

Melissa rushes up and hugs them both. "Oh, Dr. Cross, Chief Stone, I'm so glad you're here. *So* glad. Has Damon called you? Do you know where he is? I've been *so* worried."

Alex tries, and fails, to keep a lid on his frustration. "Melissa, why the hell didn't you call us? We had to find out Damon was missing from one of his professors!"

Melissa lowers her head. "I didn't want to get you concerned," she says softly, looking embarrassed.

As she should, thinks Alex.

"So," says Bree as they all go into the apartment, "when did you see Damon last?"

"Three mornings ago, when he was heading out to his Health Psychology class. I remember him leaving earlier than usual." Melissa puts down her backpack. "I was still half asleep, so I didn't ask too many questions. I think he said something about clearing his head. But then the whole rest of the day, I texted him and phoned him, and he never got back to me."

"Did he ever show up for class?" Bree asks.

"No," says Melissa, pushing her hair back. "By that night, I was getting worried. I texted all our friends, but nobody had seen him since the day before."

"Is Damon in the habit of going off on his own without telling you?" Alex asks next.

Melissa thinks for moment. "Not like this. It's never been more than overnight. But sometimes he does sink his teeth into something and get so focused that he forgets to eat or come home to change clothes. Still, he always texts to let me know that he's okay. And then he'll show up smiling and apologizing and explaining where he's been."

"Like where?" Alex asks. "Give us an example." He points to an armchair. Melissa sits, but stays perched on the edge of the seat. Alex and Bree take the battered sofa across from her.

Melissa begins. "Have you heard about Daisy Grant, that poor grandmother up in Caldwell? The one who was shot to death when a SWAT team went to the wrong address?"

"Yes," says Bree. "Damon mentioned it to us."

"Damon was *obsessed* with that case," says Melissa. "Outraged. The reports said that Daisy didn't have any relatives, but Damon didn't believe it, so he did some digging and found three of her cousins in a little town called Corinth."

"He did all that on his own?" asks Bree.

Melissa nods. "And he set up a GoFundMe site to help with their travel expenses so that when those cops go on trial, Daisy's relatives can be sitting there in the front row."

"Did he tell anybody about it?" asks Bree.

"Just me and a few friends," says Melissa. "He wasn't looking for credit. Just said he wanted to do the right thing."

Alex is proud of his son's actions but worried about whose attention they might've attracted. "What about more recently?" he asks. "Any other social justice projects?"

Melissa shakes her head. "Nothing he told me about."

"For these projects of his," Bree says, "how long would he be gone?"

"One or two days, tops," says Melissa. "And like I said, he always stayed in touch, even if it was just by text. But three days without any contact? That's never happened."

Alex waves his hand around the room. "What about here in the apartment? Is there anything missing that might suggest where he was going?"

"Not that I can tell," says Melissa. "I tried tracking his phone, but he often turns it to DND or puts it in airplane mode to save battery. The last place it showed up was here, but I haven't seen it or his laptop." Suddenly, she stands up. "Hold on! I just thought of something."

Melissa heads toward the kitchen. Alex and Bree hop off the sofa and follow.

"I never go back here," says Melissa over her shoulder as she opens the door to a small mudroom behind the kitchen. It's cluttered with extra furniture, athletic equipment, and storage boxes, so crowded that Melissa has to work her way past a stack of rusted lawn chairs to get in.

"What are you looking for?" asks Bree from the doorway.

"Damon always takes the shuttle bus to campus," says Melissa. "But his bike is missing."

Not much to go on. But it's the first clue they've found.

CHAPTER 17

BACK IN THE LIVING ROOM, Melissa apologizes again. "I am so sorry. I should have called you guys right away. I wasn't thinking straight."

"We wish you had," says Bree. "It might have made a difference."

The first forty-eight hours after a crime are called the "golden hours," the time to process the scene, find witnesses, and secure evidence before it goes cold or gets contaminated. After those first two days go by, it's harder and harder to pick up the threads of a case. And once a case truly goes cold, the odds of getting it solved are only about one in five.

Bad odds.

Melissa glances at her watch. "I'm so sorry, I've got to get to class. But why don't I arrange for us to meet with some of Damon's and my friends tonight? They're grad students too. Maybe together we can shake something out. Somebody might remember something."

"Sounds good to me," says Bree.

"Better than nothing," adds Alex.

Melissa taps her forehead, thinking. "How about the Grotto Tavern on West Franklin?"

Bree nods. "We'll be there."

"Great. See you tonight," says Melissa. And she's out the door.

Alex watches Melissa get in her car and pull away. He turns to Bree. "What do you think?"

Bree doesn't hesitate. "I think she knows more than she's telling us."

CHAPTER 18

THE OFFICE OF THE investigative unit of the Chapel Hill Police Department looks like a hundred other stations Alex Cross has been in over the years: The same shoulder-high cubicles, bulletin boards, filing cabinets, and whiteboards with scribbled notes. The same smell of stale coffee.

Detective Hugh Malone, a sturdy-looking guy in a crisp white shirt and a blue necktie with dark brown hair cut high and short, seems a little surprised when Alex and Bree show up unannounced, badges out. But he's not entirely unprepared, having gotten a heads-up from Chief Amberson about Damon.

"I didn't know when you'd be coming," Malone says, glancing down at some notes. "Are you sure you can't think of any legitimate reason for Damon to be away? Field trip? Research? Graduate students do a lot of projects off campus and in the community."

"He would have told someone," says Alex. "We haven't heard from him for a week, and his last texts and calls to his girlfriend were more than three days ago."

"And there was nothing in those earlier messages that worried you?"

"Nothing," says Bree. "All normal."

Malone checks his notes again. "And what about the girlfriend? Melissa Lange?"

"She says she hasn't heard from him either," says Alex. "No communication at all."

Malone reaches for his office phone. "I'll send a patrol over to his apartment."

Alex stops him. "We've already been there. It's clean."

"You searched his apartment?" says Malone. "By yourselves?"

"It's kind of what we do," says Bree.

Malone sits back in his chair with a deep frown on his face. He looks back and forth from Alex to Bree and taps his pen on his desk. "I have to say that if anybody else had told me that, I would be pretty pissed off right now. Normally, we like to conduct our own searches. But considering your reputations, I'll let it slide."

"You're welcome to go search for yourself," says Bree.

"Be our guest," Alex adds. "But you won't find anything we didn't."

Malone leans forward again. "First, let's address the elephant in the room."

Alex cocks his head. "What elephant?"

Malone lowers his voice: "You, Dr. Cross."

Alex knows exactly what Malone is talking about.

He's been thinking the same thing.

He flashes back to all the serial killers and psychopaths he's helped capture and put behind bars over the years. He thinks again about Maestro, still out there somewhere, still haunting the Cross family. He knows that acolytes and admirers of those twisted criminals are all possible suspects in Damon's disappearance.

Alex nods. "Yes. A revenge kidnapping. Or a copycat. Or somebody with a grudge against me. Of course it's been on my mind."

"Our family's been targeted before," says Bree. "We've made a lot of enemies."

"So you admit it's a possibility," says Malone.

"Of course," says Alex. "But so far, we haven't been contacted. No one's taken credit for Damon's disappearance or sent us a ransom message." Even as he speaks, Alex knows there's a chance that Damon has been kidnapped and the perp is getting off on torturing them with silence. They might get a ransom demand, but they might never hear anything.

"Does Damon have a pattern of wandering away from home? Or of being uncommunicative?"

"No," says Bree. "But according to his girlfriend, Melissa, when he's deep into a project, he can become a bit obsessive, grabbing on to it and not letting go, no matter where it takes him. She told us that sometimes Damon will go off by himself for a day or two."

Alex nods. "But he's never been out of touch completely, and never for three days."

Malone opens a folder on his desk. "Let's do this: We'll alert all shifts and give them Damon's description. We'll check campus surveillance feeds. We'll interview his classmates and professors.

I've got a campus ID photo for Damon, but can you give me something more to work with? A tight head-and-shoulders shot is best."

Bree takes out her phone, retrieves a photo she took of Damon and Alex after a run in their neighborhood a couple of months ago. She expands the photo and crops it, then holds the screen out to Malone. "How's this?"

"Perfect," says Malone. "I'll give you my email—"

"Already have it," says Bree. She taps her phone screen and sends him the photo. "Here's his class schedule, and I'll send you a list of names he's mentioned in emails."

"Good," says Malone. "I'll try to get a court order to get at Damon's phone records. And we'll check any recent ATM withdrawals."

"What about going public?" asks Alex. "Making some kind of announcement?"

"Look, guys," says Malone. "I understand your concern. I truly do. But you're thinking like parents, not detectives. At the moment, we have no proof that Damon is in danger. We typically don't go public as a department unless we have solid information that somebody is at risk. We had a case two years ago where a woman reported that her sister had gone missing. No indication of foul play. A few days later, we learned the sister had left on a hiking trip. It was all a big misunderstanding."

Alex is well aware that his son doesn't fit the typical missing person profile in the National Crime Information Center—Damon is a physically and mentally healthy adult over the age of twenty-one, and despite Alex's fear that someone might be out for revenge, there's no evidence pointing to accident, illness, or foul play. As Alex knows, nothing prevents adults from leaving their homes of their own accord without telling anyone or leaving a note behind to explain where they're going.

But he also knows his son, and Damon wouldn't go silent like this for so long.

"With all due respect," says Alex, "I understand my son."

CHAPTER 19

THE REST OF THE questions from Detective Hugh Malone are rote: Damon's age, height, weight, any tattoos, scars, or other distinguishing marks. As he reels off the answers, Alex feels lost in some kind of waking nightmare. He can't help thinking about all the times *he's* been the one asking these questions.

And all the times his own family has been victimized.

Across the field of cubicles, phones are ringing, officers standing up from their desks. A hum of energy fills the space.

A tall woman with a detective's shield clipped to her belt steps near the entrance of Malone's cubicle. She stands there for a few seconds, clearly trying to get Malone's attention.

"What's up, Gail?" asks Malone.

"Sorry to interrupt. The boss wants a status meeting pronto."

"Tell him I'll be late."

"He says—"

Malone's voice hardens: "Tell him I'll be late, Gail. Thanks."

Gail shrugs. "He won't be happy," Alex hears her mutter as she walks away.

"What's going on?" he asks, craning his neck to look over the cubicle walls. "Seems like your department is gearing up for something."

"The Young Freedom Fighters speech?" asks Bree. "Michaelson Woods?"

Malone sighs. "That's right. It's turning out to be a real shitshow. Some student anarchist organization invited the nutjob to speak. Since then, we've had complaints, suits, countersuits. Students are getting into brawls over it."

"We know," says Alex. "We've seen it."

"Problem is," says Malone, "this is more than just a campus debate. I'm getting crap from all sides and from the top down. The governor, the mayor, and the city council all want peace and order. But everybody's got a different idea of how to manage it. Do we flood the campus with cops in riot gear? Not a good look. Do we stand back and give both sides some space? Nobody wants a repeat of what happened in Charlottesville—one dead, thirty-five injured. But nobody wants an armed camp either."

"Detective Malone," says Alex, "we know our son spoke at a rally protesting Woods's appearance. Could that have exposed him to danger? Drawn the wrong kind of attention?"

"This is a real touchy area," says Malone. "Anything's possible."

CHAPTER 20

AFTER LEAVING THE Chapel Hill Police Department, Alex and Bree check in at the Carolina Inn, a luxurious hotel smack in the middle of campus.

Once in their suite, they flop down on the bed side by side. After a few moments, Bree sits up and opens her laptop. "I ran an under-the-radar Bluestone search on Melissa's phone."

Alex leans over as Bree scrolls through Melissa's outgoing texts to Damon, which take on an increasingly urgent tone as time passes.

Will u b home tonite??

What's going on??

Hey! Take your phone off DND!

Why are u ignoring my texts?! Where are U??

I'm getting rlly worried now! If you're working on something, LMK!

Bree slams the laptop shut. "If she's keeping any dark secrets, they're not here. At least, they're not obvious."

Alex stands up and walks over to the window. "Look. Damon trusts her. Maybe we should too."

"You're right," says Bree. "I'll reserve judgment until we hear what their friends have to say tonight."

Alex realizes that neither of them has eaten since breakfast. His belly is grumbling. "I can't believe I'm saying this, but I'm hungry." He hops off the bed. "Let's see what Nana Mama packed for us."

Alex reaches into the side pockets of their luggage and retrieves the two heavy Tupperware containers.

Bree joins him in the suite's kitchenette as he pulls off the lids and peeks inside.

"Wow, Nana," she says. "You've really outdone yourself."

Each Tupperware container holds several ziplock bags. The largest contains portions of Nana Mana's famed lemon and herb roasted chicken. Another is packed with roasted potatoes. A third has thick slices of homemade cornbread. And a fourth has utensils, cloth napkins, and pats of butter.

Underneath, in another little plastic sealed bag, there's a short note written in Nana Mama's old-school cursive.

I love you both, and I know you'll find Damon soon, safe and sound.

"Bless you, Nana," Alex murmurs. Bree pulls plates from the suite's cupboard and spoons out portions. One after the other, the plates go into the microwave. Alex pulls two bottled waters from the minifridge. In a few minutes, the hotel room starts to smell like their kitchen at home.

When the reheating is done, Alex and Bree sit down at the small table.

"My goodness," says Bree, digging into her chicken. "There's enough food here for three people!"

She stops cold as soon as she says it.

Alex reaches over and puts his hand on hers. "Soon," he says, "we'll all be together again. I promise."

And Alex always keeps his promises.

CHAPTER 21

AFTER THE DISHES ARE cleaned and put away and the extra food carefully placed in the refrigerator, Alex calls home. He puts his phone on speaker. On the second ring, somebody picks up.

"Hello? Dad?"

It's his younger son, Ali.

"Hey there," says Alex, doing his best to sound chipper. "Bree's here too."

"Nana told me what's going on," says Ali. "Is there anything new? Any leads on Damon?" He sounds worried.

"Still gathering information," says Alex. "We've been to Damon's apartment. We've talked to Melissa. It doesn't sound like anyone's been threatening Damon. Nothing looks disturbed or out of place. The Chapel Hill police and the campus police have all the information. That's as far as we've gotten."

"What are the cops doing?" asks Ali.

"Not much," Bree says, chiming in.

"They're being cautious," says Alex, "because there's no solid sign that Damon's in danger. I hate to say it, but right now they're doing just the minimum."

"We're going to talk to some of Melissa and Damon's friends later, see if anybody has any ideas on where he might have gone," Bree adds.

"Where's Nana Mama now?" Alex asks.

"She's taking a nap," says Ali. "Uncle John's neighbor Mrs. Doolittle called and said she's bringing Willow over in a half hour. There's no school tomorrow because of the bombing. Lots of helicopters flying around, and soldiers out in the streets. It's scary out there."

"I'm sure it is," says Bree. "You just stay close to home and listen to your nana, and don't pick fights with Willow."

"I want to come down there and help," says Ali, his voice firm and determined.

"Ali," Bree says. "You can't just—"

Ali interrupts, talking a mile a minute, making his case: "But I wouldn't be missing any school. And I know I can do it. I can ride around on a scooter and ask a few questions, check things out. Like being undercover. Who'd pay any attention to a kid like me?"

"Ali, that's a wonderful gesture," says Alex, "and as soon as we find Damon, we'll let him know how much you wanted to be here."

"If you say so." Ali sounds disappointed.

"Besides, we need you there to help Nana Mama, especially now that Willow will be there too," Bree says.

"Don't worry about Willow," Ali says. "She's gonna be happy."

"Oh, yeah?" says Alex. "Why's that?"

"Because Jannie's coming back from Howard. She says to tell

you and Bree that she'll be here helping out Nana Mama until you guys find Damon and come home."

Alex frowns. "But she has a track meet in Gainesville in two days!"

"She said, 'To hell with the track meet, I need to be home.'"

Alex looks over at Bree. He can tell that she's thinking the same thing he is.

What a blessing to have kids like this.

CHAPTER 22

THAT EVENING, AFTER A shower and a change of clothes, Bree and Alex head down to the Grotto Tavern, one of the oldest bars in Chapel Hill. The walls are covered with posters of past UNC star athletes, and four wide-screen televisions hang from the ceiling.

At the rear of the tavern, Melissa is sitting with a woman and two men, all apparently grad students in their early twenties, just like Damon. A half-empty pitcher of beer sits in the center of the round wooden table.

Alex thinks back to his own student years, first as an undergrad at Georgetown and then at Johns Hopkins, where he earned his PhD in psychology. He remembers knocking back beers in bars like this and trying to solve the problems of the world. But tonight, he and Bree are trying to solve one problem and one problem only.

Melissa makes the introductions as Alex pulls out a chair for Bree. They both sit down.

"Thank you all for coming," says Bree. "We really appreciate it."

"Glad to do it," says Roger Walker, who has an intense academic look and wears wire-rimmed glasses and a blue button-down shirt.

"Anything for Damon," adds Nia Williams, a striking young woman wearing bright red lipstick and a black-and-red BLM jersey.

"How can we help?" asks Carter Harris, a tall guy in a Tar Heels T-shirt. His bald head gleams under the bar lights as he picks up the beer pitcher, fills two glasses, and passes them over to Alex and Bree.

Melissa speaks up first, talking to the grad students. "Everyone is connected to Damon in a different way. I was thinking that maybe one of you remembered some conversation or detail that would give Dr. Cross and Chief Stone a clue about where Damon might be."

Carter shakes his head. "Not me, sorry. I know Damon through volunteer coaching at the YMCA youth basketball camp. I'm sure you know what a great player Damon is. He's also a great coach, always focused on more than just improving the kids' basketball skills. He also wants to show them how important it is to be on time and be helpful."

Carter takes a sip of beer and continues. "I asked him once why he didn't try out for some of the local leagues. He just laughed and said he was taking a break from making basketball the center of his life. But Damon's always first in, last out at practice. He helps scoop up the loose balls and sweeps the gym afterward. I mean, who'd want to hurt a guy like that?"

Across from him, Roger drains his beer. "I feel the same way. I'm one of the leaders at SALE—Student Action in Literacy Equality. We help kids with reading problems. Damon's one of our best tutors. He's always upbeat, never misses a session. He's great with the kids."

"He's always been good at helping out with his little brother, Ali," Alex says.

Under the table, Bree slides her hand into Alex's and squeezes.

"What about you, Nia?" Alex asks. He can tell that she's been holding back something. Nia pushes her napkin around for a few seconds, then looks up.

"Me and Damon, we work together in the Students of Color Movement." Nia offers a shy smile. "I'm sure you two know this, but Damon's a wonderful public speaker. He told me he had no training, he just learned it from growing up around opinionated people."

Well, Alex thinks, *that's one thing you can definitely say about the Cross family: We're opinionated.*

Bree leans in. "Nia, do you think Damon's activism might have attracted attention from the wrong kind of people?"

"The Young Freedom Fighters, for example?" says Alex.

Nia purses her lips. "I don't know. Damon's given some speeches in group meetings and at a couple of equal-rights protests, speaking truth to power. But I wouldn't call him inflammatory or anything."

"Could there have been someone who heard him speak who didn't like what he was saying?" asks Bree.

"I guess," says Nia. "There are a lot of crazies out there these days. We've got a bunch of 'em on campus."

Alex looks around the table, from one face to the next. "So none of you can think of any reason why Damon would disappear for three days?"

Nia is playing with her napkin again. Carter and Roger are looking down at the table.

Finally, Melissa looks around at her friends. "We need to tell them," she says.

"We don't know anything for sure," says Roger curtly.

"Tell us about what?" asks Alex.

"Professor Darius Lucas and Amy Tyne," says Melissa.

"Who are they?" asks Bree.

Melissa leans forward. "Professor Lucas teaches social psychology. We're all in one of his grad seminars. Damon too. Amy Tyne is Professor Lucas's TA for his undergrad classes. She and I were in orientation together."

Nia looks up, ready to add to the story. "A week ago, neither one showed up for class. No warning. No announcement beforehand."

"We went to the department head, Dr. Chase, and he told us that Professor Lucas and Amy were off doing some kind of research project," adds Carter.

"What kind of research?" asks Alex.

"Dr. Chase wouldn't tell us," says Melissa. "He said it was confidential. But one of the other TAs said she heard they were looking into a recently discovered enslaved people's burial site in Tennessee."

"Sounds like a worthwhile effort," says Bree.

"Except that it's not true," says Roger.

Nia speaks up again. "Damon and I made some phone calls, talked to bloggers and history junkies all over Tennessee. The story was fake, debunked six months ago. The site was a cemetery for a white family that was plowed under in the 1800s."

"We think the trip was a cover story," says Carter.

"So where do you think they really went?" asks Alex.

"No clue," says Nia. "They just...disappeared. Like Damon."

Suddenly, the front window shatters. As patrons scream and duck, a brick lands with a thud on the wood floor.

CHAPTER 23

Sampson

NED MAHONEY AND I pull up outside the ATF National Laboratory Center in Beltsville, Maryland. It's already dark out. I'm starting to lose track of the hours as we continue to push the case along, knowing that time is not on our side.

As we head for the forensics lab, Ned gets a text. He gives it a quick read and puts his phone down. "Well," he says, "one theory is out the window." He looks over at me as we walk. "That Middle East political action committee you mentioned?"

"FIP-PAC?"

"That's the one," says Mahoney. "They've been defunct for about a year."

"Damn it!"

"Yeah. So much for peaceful cooperation in the Middle East."

We find Anna Rizzo sitting on a metal stool in one of the evidence-processing rooms. Long white tables stretch out to the far wall, filled with computer monitors, microscopes, and illuminated magnifying glasses.

She greets us with a yawn, then quickly recovers. "Don't worry about me," she says. "I'm still full of piss and vinegar."

Rizzo is wearing a white lab coat and light blue medical gloves. She goes back to examining a small length of what looks like burned string through a magnifying glass. "Anything new on your end?" she asks.

I give her the top line. "We're still canvassing witnesses, trying to determine if anybody saw the driver exit the van before the explosion or saw what happened once he went into that alley. Challenge is, he could have gone one block, ducked into a doorway, stripped off his painter outfit, and hopped into a getaway car."

"Or taken a bus," adds Mahoney. "Or jumped on the nearest Metro."

"Well, lucky for me," says Rizzo, "everything I need is right here and in the warehouse next door. That's where we're reassembling the van, best we can."

"We also met with Chief Lucianne out at Reagan," says Mahoney. "She showed us a video of the van leaving the parking garage. No good views of the driver's face, though. And he paid in cash, with gloves on."

Rizzo nods. "Like I said, fastidious." As she reaches for a notebook, the right sleeve of her lab coat slides up, exposing a tattoo on her wrist. It looks like a stylized bomb surrounded by jagged lines indicating an explosion.

Rizzo quickly pulls her sleeve down and gives me a sidelong glance.

Caught me looking.

"So why are we here?" asks Mahoney.

Rizzo stands up. "I want you guys to take a look at what I've found so far." She walks to the end of the table and points to a collection of curved pieces of broken and burned plastic. "It looks like our guy was inspired by the ghost of Timothy McVeigh. He used a mixture of fuel oil and fertilizer in plastic barrels. Packs one hell of a punch."

"Okay," says Mahoney, "we'll check feed and grain stores to see if anybody made major purchases of fertilizer in the past weeks."

"Good luck with that," says Rizzo. "If he's as smart as I'm betting, our guy would've spread his purchases around several different states so as not to arouse suspicion."

She pokes her finger at a small pile of screws and bolts. "And take a look at this. As if the explosion weren't bad enough, the bomber added this stuff as shrapnel, possibly loaded into plastic bags and duct-taped to the inside of the van. That tells us he didn't just want to destroy buildings and cars—he wanted to kill and maim as many people as he could."

Rizzo returns to her stool. I hang behind for a few seconds, trying to control my rage as I stare at the handiwork of someone who killed and grievously wounded so many innocents less than twenty-four hours ago.

Whoever you are, I'm coming for you.

With a pair of tweezers, Rizzo holds up the bit of burned string that she'd been examining when we walked in.

"Here's your fuse, or what's left of it," she says. "The surveillance video shows the van stopping, its hazard blinkers coming on, and then the bomber stepping out and walking away. About sixty seconds later, the bomb detonates."

I lean forward to look at the string. "So the bomber lit the fuse after he parked the van."

"That's right," says Rizzo. "But come see something else I've found that's giving me the willies. Over here."

Mahoney and I follow her to another wide table. She takes a mounted magnifying glass and moves it over to a small charred object. "Look."

"You first," says Mahoney, nudging me forward.

Peering through the glass, I see a tiny bit of green plastic, no bigger than my pinkie nail, with what looks like a few squiggly gold lines inscribed in it. I step back. "Electronics?"

"No question," says Rizzo. "But nothing that seems to be connected with the van's engine or electronics system. We're still sifting through the debris, but my guess is that we're looking at what's left of a timer. The bomber didn't want to rely only on a burning fuse. He wanted a backup."

Mahoney takes his turn at the magnifying glass. "Maybe it's part of a cell phone apparatus using a command detonation. The bomber walks away and when he feels safe, he enters a preprogrammed number, and *boom*."

Rizzo shakes her head. "Not safe enough. For the bomber, I mean."

"Because of spurious calls?" I suggest.

Rizzo smiles my way. She has a nice smile.

"Bingo," she says. "In an urban environment, there are lots of electronic signals flying through the air on multiple frequencies. It'd be a hell of a thing if some guy was texting his girlfriend and it just happened to match the command detonation frequency. A big *boom* when you didn't want it to explode."

"I think our bomber is too smart to use command denotation in an urban area," I say.

"I found one more thing." Rizzo points to a microscope that has a small piece of jagged green plastic on the specimen stage. Mahoney starts to lean in, but Rizzo tugs him back.

"Save your eyes," she tells him. "What we have here is the fragment of a wrapper for a brick of C-4 explosive."

Interesting. And terrifying. C-4 is a military-grade plastic explosive—very, very hard for a civilian to secure. Available on only the blackest of black markets.

Mahoney gives out a low whistle. "That steps things up, doesn't it? A fertilizer-and-fuel-oil bomb is probably within reach of any competent civilian with an engineering brain. But now we're adding C-4 into the equation. Maybe a backup detonation device?"

"Maybe," says Rizzo, sitting down. "Or maybe a message."

Now I'm lost. "A message? What kind of message? Like a threat?"

"Maybe. C-4 is a great plastic explosive," says Rizzo. "Malleable, easy to use, and safe to handle. You can drop it on the floor or take a baseball bat to it and nothing will happen." She picks up a pair of tweezers and pulls out the wrapper scrap. "But for your terrorist bomber, there's a big disadvantage. Powerful explosives like C-4 and Semtex contain taggants—microscopic markers that identify the manufacturer and the lot number, allowing law enforcement to trace it to the source."

"Sounds sloppy," says Mahoney. "And risky. Why take that chance?"

"What if it's deliberate?" asks Rizzo. "Maybe the bomber wants us to know who he is and where he's from without making TikTok videos or sending out an email blast."

I'm tired and impatient. I feel like Rizzo is teasing us now. I lean down and look her right in the eye. "Anna, can you source this taggant?"

She stares right back. "Usually, yes. But not this sample. It's not in my database."

"Which means what?"

"Which means it came from a classified stash. Probably government. We need someone with clout to break through the bureaucracy and red tape and get to the top security records."

"Look," says Mahoney, "I spoke to the president two hours ago. He wants twice-daily updates. Whatever data you need, I'll get it. Just tell me where to go."

Rizzo gets up from her stool. "Start with Langley, Virginia."

CHAPTER 24

Cross

YELLS AND SCREAMS ECHO inside the Grotto Tavern in the aftermath of the broken window. Alex Cross jumps up so fast, his chair falls over. He takes a quick look to make sure nobody at their table was hurt, then pushes through the mass of dazed bar patrons, some standing, others crouching in puddles of beer beneath tables.

He shoves his way through the wooden doors, steps out onto the sidewalk, and looks left and right.

He can't believe what he sees.

Marching away on the other side of the street are a dozen men, identically dressed in short-sleeved black T-shirts, black pants, black sneakers—and black domino masks on their faces. Their white faces. They're trying to hide their identities, but not their race. That's the one thing they want people to know, Alex realizes.

Each marcher carries a small knapsack and holds a single flickering tiki torch. In sync with their steps, they're loudly chanting,

"Whose streets? Our streets! Whose streets? Our streets!" Over and over. Gruff and aggressive.

A couple of young men burst out of the bar and rush the column, but they're quickly pushed back. The marchers are muscular, determined, and methodical. The beer-buzzed bar patrons have no chance against them. They get thrown aside like rag dolls. And the marchers keep marching.

They're about fifty feet away from the tavern now, approaching a park entrance. In rapid succession, the men thrust their torches into a storm drain, strip off their face masks, throw them into large trash barrels, and pull baseball caps and bright-colored T-shirts out of their knapsacks. The group members put them on and then scatter like droplets from a fallen bead of mercury. Some go into the park, others trot across the street, and a few keep on walking, heads down, merging with college students out for a stroll.

Alex watches them go, breathing hard.

What just happened?

Whatever it was, it was quick and well rehearsed.

Bree comes up next to him. "I called 911."

"Too late," says Alex, looking across the street. "They're gone. And well trained. That was a performance meant to intimidate. It wasn't a bunch of ignorant rednecks out to break windows and pick a fight."

"They just…disappeared?" asks Bree. "In front of all these people?"

"Right," says Alex. "As soon as their message was delivered."

Sirens sound in the distance, and they both head back to the bar, where patrons are murmuring and servers are sweeping up broken glass.

Alex and Bree walk back to the table where they left Melissa and her friends.

But nobody's there.

CHAPTER 25

Sampson

LANGLEY.

As soon as Anna Rizzo says it, there's a stillness in the room.

Ned Mahoney crosses his arms. "Our CIA buds across the river?"

Rizzo nods and sits down again. "Ninety-nine point nine percent of government secrets are to cover up something that got screwed up, something that failed, or something that's just plain embarrassing."

She points to the tiny scrap of green plastic. "My guess is that this falls into category three: embarrassing. If I don't find the taggant in my standard database searches, then I need to go elsewhere. The best place to search is at that certain three-letter agency in a five-sided building. I can make a request, but it'll be kicked around through a dozen different layers. It'll take me a month to get an answer. If I'm lucky."

"File your request," says Mahoney. "I'll push it through."

"Thanks," says Rizzo. "And if they say they can't find it or that whatever they have can't be released due to reasons of national security—"

Mahoney interrupts her. "Anna, I've got a direct line to the Oval Office. I'll get it done."

Rizzo turns to me. "And in the meantime—"

I interrupt her too. "We're doing an info dive into the victims and the injured, who they are and why they were at that intersection at that particular time."

"You think one of them might have been a specific target?" asks Rizzo.

"It's just one angle," says Mahoney. "But we have to look into it."

"Talk about overkill," Rizzo muttered. "Like trying to swat a mosquito with a sledgehammer. A very big sledgehammer." She strips off her gloves. "Hey, I need a caffeine break. You guys care to join me?"

Mahoney checks his watch. "Sorry. I'm already late to brief the director." He raises a hand in goodbye and heads off across the lab and out the door.

Rizzo slides off her stool and looks at me. "How about you, Detective?"

"You buying?"

"Nope. The American taxpayers are, God bless 'em."

CHAPTER 26

ANNA RIZZO AND I walk through the brightly lit corridors of the ATF laboratory, passing other labs and processing rooms. Through the door windows I can see technicians examining and processing evidence. I want to believe that they're all working on our case.

"Hell of a thing," says Rizzo, "a plain old white GMC van spread over downtown DC. Too bad our bomber wasn't still in the damn thing at the time."

Part of me agrees. It would mean one less evildoer to worry about. But the detective in me wants to get the bastard alive so I can find out what twisted his mind and use him to track down whoever else is involved. After that, I'll send him away for good.

Rizzo opens an unmarked door to a break room with couches and chairs, a few round tables, and a refrigerator, a coffee station, and a row of vending machines. She picks up a paper coffee cup from a stack on the counter next to the coffee station. "How do you take it?"

"None for me, actually. But I'll take a water if you have it."

"We can do that." Rizzo opens the refrigerator door, grabs a bottle, and tosses it in my direction. I catch it in one hand.

She grins. "Nice reflexes."

Rizzo gets herself a cup of coffee and leads the way to a small table. We pull up two chairs. She leans toward me conspiratorially even though we're the only people in the break room.

"Okay, John Sampson," she says as she pours a packet of sugar into her cup and stirs, "what's your life story?"

She gets right to the point. I admire that.

I twist the cap off my water bottle. "Born and raised here in DC. Both my parents were drug addicts, in and out of prison. Thankfully, my best bud, Alex Cross, brought me into his family. His grandmother basically raised us together."

"Alex Cross?" says Rizzo. "*The* Alex Cross? The serial-killer expert?"

"The very same. We grew up together. After high school, I joined the army, then went into Metro PD."

"What did you do in the army? Where were you deployed?"

"Iraq. Afghanistan. A few other hot spots. How about you? How long were you downrange?"

I see her eyebrows shoot up. I nod toward her wrist. "Don't be so surprised. I saw your ink earlier. Don't tell me: Explosive Ordnance Disposal?"

"You got it," she says. "EOD team leader, E-six, with the Fifty-Second Ordnance Group out of Fort Campbell. Deployed to Iraq, the 'stan, some other lousy places."

"And before that? You don't strike me as a local."

Rizzo shakes her head. "My mom's originally from around here, but I grew up in Nebraska. Bit of a wild child, I guess. Loved firecrackers and cherry bombs, blowing stuff up. Always in trouble. I was working for a fireworks company when I ran into an army recruiter at a county fair who convinced me to join up."

"And use your skills for good, not evil."

"Yep," says Rizzo. "That was the pitch." She blows on her coffee. "So. Married?"

"Widowed. Few years back. But I'm a dad to a wonderful young daughter, Willow, who sometimes acts twice her age."

"Tell me about it. I've got a nine-year-old daughter *and* a ten-year-old son," Rizzo says. "Tina and Juan."

I take a sip of my water. "So how about you? Married?"

"Divorced. My husband couldn't handle me — or my hours."

"Must get complicated as a single parent with your job, raising two kids on your own."

Rizzo lifts a shoulder. "I'm sure you know how it is. This life makes it hard — but I do my best. Luckily, I can rely on my abuela Marina. She's in line for sainthood. Great cook and always there to help. God bless all abuelas, wherever they are."

"I'll drink to that." I'd put Nana Mama in the sainthood category too.

Rizzo looks across the table and catches me rubbing my eyes. "Long day," she says.

"Yeah. For a lot of people."

She drains her coffee and pushes her cup aside. "We've got some rooms upstairs if you want to bunk here. It's nothing fancy, but I hear the cots aren't bad."

I shake my head. "Thanks for the offer. But my daughter's

staying over at the Cross house and there's a room there for me too. I promised to stay there with her."

"You sound like a good dad, John Sampson," Rizzo says, standing up. "We'll talk tomorrow, then."

"Count on it."

CHAPTER 27

Cross

ALEX WAKES TO THE ringing of his phone. He rolls over in bed as Bree stirs beside him.

"Is that yours?" she mumbles.

"Yes," he says, picking the phone up. NO CALLER ID. It's 6:01 a.m. A call at this hour usually means either very good or very bad news.

Alex answers, feeling a surge of adrenaline race through his body. "Hello?"

"Dr. Cross? This is Drake Cannon, from the FBI field office in Charlotte."

Alex sits straight up in bed and puts the call on speaker. Bree turns on a lamp and moves closer.

"What do you have, Drake?" asks Alex.

"I'm sorry to call so early, but I wanted to update you as soon as I could. I just got an advance on a report from the Chapel Hill PD.

We've been able to establish that there's been no activity on your son's phone for the past four days," says Cannon, "but before it was shut off, cell tower pings determined where he was. Or at least where his phone was."

"And?" Alex asks as Bree squeezes his arm. "Where was it?"

"About five miles south of his apartment," says Cannon, "at a place called the Mason Farm Biological Reserve. A few hundred acres of protected forest, wetlands, and bogs. The last distinct location we've been able to fix is just off of Barbee Chapel Hill Road, near the Pearson Trailhead."

Bree grabs her own phone off the nightstand and enters the location in Google Maps. A second later she calls, "Got it!"

"Drake," says Alex. "We can't thank you enough."

"I promise you, I'm doing everything I can on my end. I'll call you the minute we learn anything else."

Alex thanks him again, then disconnects and throws back the covers. He looks across the room.

Bree is already dressed.

CHAPTER 28

Sampson

THE TINY GUEST BEDROOM at the Cross house is as cozy as I remember it, even if my feet now stick out over the end of the bed. I spent a lot of nights in this room as a kid, taking refuge from my broken family. Whenever I visit, it still feels like home.

Willow was asleep when I arrived last night, but she's wide-awake now. I was hoping to sleep in, but my daughter has other ideas.

"Daddy! Wake up! Nana Mama made breakfast!"

I let Willow nearly drag me out of bed and down to the kitchen, where the aromas from Nana Mama's cooking instantly make my mouth water and my stomach rumble.

I sit down at the round kitchen table. Willow sits right next to me, elbow to elbow. Nana Mama comes over with two large plates and sets them down.

Sitting in front of me is a stack of blueberry pancakes, thick and fluffy, with six bacon slices cooked crisp, just the way I like it.

There's also a bowl of sliced melon and a big tumbler of fresh-squeezed orange juice.

Nana Mama hugs me around my shoulders. "I'm counting on you to be a hungry man, John Sampson, so don't disappoint me and leave anything behind."

I take a sip of juice and put my napkin on my lap. "Thanks, Nana. This looks great."

"I promise to clean my plate!" says Willow, digging into her slightly smaller portions.

Nana Mama walks to the counter and returns with a steaming cup of coffee. "Your favorite," she says. "Jamaican Blue."

"You're spoiling me," I tell her, covering my pancakes with maple syrup—the real stuff from a farm in Vermont.

"When have I *not* spoiled you?" Nana asks. "It's my job. Among other things."

Willow looks up. "Nana, may I have another glass of orange juice?"

"Yes, you may."

I focus on my breakfast, trying not to let yesterday's tragedy cloud my thoughts. But there's something else on my mind. Something just as important.

I turn to Nana Mama. "Any news from Alex or Bree?"

"Not a word," she says. "But that doesn't worry me. It means they're working hard to find our boy. When they have good news, they'll let us know."

I hear voices from the living room. I'm expecting to hear Ali, Alex's youngest, but I'm surprised when I hear another familiar voice.

Then Jannie and Ali, the two younger Cross kids, burst into the kitchen.

"What are you doing here, Jannie?" I ask my goddaughter as she comes over for a hug.

Usually, I'd get a bright smile, but not today. "I left campus to be here with the family," she says. "Any news about Damon?"

I shake my head. "Not yet. But it's early. What are you two up to this morning?"

"Thought I'd take Ali with me on a loop," she says. "He can bike while I run. We need to get out of the house. Can't stand being cooped up."

"Running?" asks Nana. "Where?" I can hear the concern in her voice.

"Nowhere special," Jannie says. "We'll maybe go up to the Mall and back."

I put down my fork. "Nope. No way."

My tone is so forceful that Ali scrunches his face and Jannie rocks back a bit. "Why not?"

"I want you to stay off the streets. I'd rather you work out at the King-Greenleaf Center." I pump my hands into the air. "Use the machines. Make it an arms day."

"Is this because of what happened yesterday?"

"Yes. It is."

Nana Mama says, "You two listen to John. He knows what he's talking about."

I turn to her. "Thanks. I appreciate the backup."

Nana smiles. "These two know better than to defy me." She stares at her great-grandchildren with her hands on her hips. "Isn't that right?"

Ali and Jannie respond in unison, "Yes, Nana." They both know the discussion is over.

Jannie walks over and opens the refrigerator, leans in, and pulls out a couple bottles of water.

My phone rings. I pick up. "Sampson here."

"John, it's Anna Rizzo." She sounds tense.

"Morning. What's up?"

"There's been another bombing."

Damn it!

I ask Rizzo to hold on, then I stand up and look around the kitchen. "Change of plans. Nobody's going anywhere today. Except me."

CHAPTER 29

Cross

ALEX DRIVES THE RED Camry up Pearson Trail Road as fast as the rugged terrain allows, Bree holding tight to the handgrip. They turn off onto Barbee Chapel Hill Road, a two-lane country road with thick trees and brush on both sides, no homes or buildings in sight.

The dirt road widens and comes to an end at the trailhead. Bree is out the door before Alex comes to a full stop. He gets out and joins her.

For a moment, they stand side by side in the empty parking area. It's cool and quiet. The early morning mist is still rising from the woods surrounding them. No other vehicles are at the trailhead. No sounds except for birds.

"What was he doing out here?" Bree asks.

"Clearing his head?" Alex suggests. "At least, that's what he told Melissa."

"Right," says Bree. "But remember, he was on his bike. Wouldn't he have told Melissa if he was going on a trail ride?"

She points to where two dirt trails lead into the woods. Even with the sun coming up, the trails look dark and foreboding.

"I have a lot to ask that young lady," says Alex, "including why she and her friends disappeared so fast last night."

"She still hasn't answered your texts?" asks Bree.

"Nope."

"Mine either. I left a voicemail too."

Alex and Bree walk to the spot where the two trails begin. "You go left," says Alex. "I'll go right." He reaches over to squeeze his wife's hand, then heads down the steep incline.

After Alex takes just a few steps, the parking lot and the Camry are out of sight. Alex can feel his heart racing. He's picturing Damon somewhere down the slope, maybe with a concussion or a broken leg, but at least alive.

"Damon!" he yells. "Damon Cross! Are you out here?"

From the other trail, he can hear Bree shouting too, her voice growing fainter as the trails diverge. When Alex looks down, he sees plenty of bike tracks in the dirt—far too many to hope that they'd find a match for Damon's treads.

That's assuming he was even on his bicycle when he got here.

Alex plunges on, ducking through brush and nearly tripping over exposed rocks. He's nearly fifty yards from the trailhead, with no end in sight.

"Damon!" he calls out again. *"Damon Cross!"*

His phone vibrates in his pocket. He pulls it out, a little surprised that there's even reception out here.

It's Bree.

"Hey," he says. "You okay?"

"Get over here fast," says Bree. Her voice sounds tight. "I found it."

CHAPTER 30

Sampson

WE'RE SPEEDING WEST ON U.S. 50; Anna Rizzo's in her government-issued Ford Taurus, siren wailing, emergency lights flashing, and I'm following in my black Grand Cherokee, trying to keep up as she dodges in and out of traffic like a football player making a ninety-nine-yard run to the end zone.

I pick up my handheld Motorola radio. "Dispatch, this is Sampson, D-five. Where's ground zero?"

This dispatcher responds, "Henry Bacon Drive off Constitution Avenue Northwest. Near the Vietnam Veterans Memorial."

I sit back in shock. "Dispatch, Sampson, D-five. To clarify, was the memorial targeted?"

"Negative. Roadway and entrance."

Rizzo boosts her speed from eighty miles an hour to ninety. I'm just a few yards behind her. Closer than I should be, but we both want to get to the scene as fast as possible.

By the time we get to the District via Route 50, Metro Police have set up detours, leaving Constitution Avenue NW relatively open as we get closer to the bombing site.

We roll past the National Museum of African American History and Culture and the Ellipse grounds.

Straight ahead, I can see a hazy cloud of smoke and reflections from flashing emergency lights. Rizzo slows down, and I match her pace. We make our way through two Metro Police checkpoints manned by grim-faced cops in ballistic helmets and body armor carrying M4 automatic rifles. Yellow police tape flutters in the breeze, and the street is cluttered with abandoned vehicles, police cruisers, and fire trucks.

Rizzo pulls onto a sidewalk near the intersection with Henry Bacon Drive. I pull up right behind her. We jump out of our vehicles, pop our trunks, and grab our go bags. As we trot down the sidewalk, I hear the grumble of parked emergency vehicles and sirens sounding in the distance.

"How bad is it?" I ask.

"Bad," Rizzo replies.

"Of all places to attack..."

We both break into a run down the drive leading to the entrance to the Vietnam Veterans Memorial. My fury builds with every stride. This is sacred ground to me. Six names on that wall belong to boys from my neighborhood who were shipped off to Vietnam—and never came back. Over the years, Alex and I have made rubbings of their names, left flowers, and said prayers to make sure they're never forgotten.

It's like yesterday's scene—all around us I see shattered, charred cars, their windows broken and doors torn off. The smell of explosives and burned rubber is strong in the air. Trees are bent, broken, or blasted out by the roots.

I see first responders around a body nearby. He's in jogging gear, arms spread out, his left leg gone below the knee. There's a zigzag blood trail behind him. I put the scene together quickly.

Shit. Lost his leg in the blast, then died trying to crawl for help.

Along the entrance to the path leading to the memorial, food stands and souvenir kiosks have been blasted into splinters. Fire trucks and ambulances crowd the area. Firefighters are watering down a few vehicles still burning. I see yellow blankets scattered on the ground, presumably covering more bodies. EMTs are hard at work on the survivors. A woman sits on the edge of the sidewalk as two EMTs bandage her bloody head. She rocks back and forth, wailing at the top of her voice, "Jenny! Where are you? Mommy's right here! Jenny!"

Rizzo puts her go bag down and squats beside it. "Jesus."

I take a knee beside her. "Something here is different, Anna. See what's missing?"

Rizzo scans the road, filled with broken glass and twisted metal. "No, John, I don't."

"Think about it. There are no buildings here. He wasn't going after structures or offices. He didn't even damage the wall itself. He was aiming for regular people, tourists and locals going about their morning routines."

I see Rizzo's jaw tighten. "What kind of monster does that?"

"I wish to hell I knew."

The bleeding woman on the sidewalk is still calling out, "Jenny! Where are you, baby? Mommy's right here!"

CHAPTER 31

Cross

ALEX CROSS LOOKS DOWN at the abandoned bicycle half covered by underbrush that Bree found. Then he picks up a stick and uses it to part the branches.

"It's all in one piece," he says. "Nothing looks bent or broken." He stands up. "We need to be sure it's Damon's."

"I think he sent some pictures of it a while back," says Bree. She starts flicking through photos on her phone.

"We'll also need fingerprints," Alex continues. "What's the weather been like? I don't think it's been rainy here, so nothing should've washed away." He looks over at Bree, who's still searching her photos. "Check with Melissa. She'll know if it's Damon's bike."

Bree nods, clicks out of the photo app, and opens her contacts. She dials Melissa's number and leaves yet another message.

"Hi, Melissa. This is Bree Stone. Again. Damon's dad and I are at the Pearson Trailhead, off Barbee Chapel Hill Road. We need you here. *Now.* If we don't hear from you, we're calling the police."

Bree stabs the End Call button. Alex puts his hand on his wife's shoulder. He can see the frustration on her face. "We can just take a photo of the bike and send it to Melissa," he says.

"No," says Bree. "I want her out here. She needs to be a part of this. And we need to be sure." She puts her phone away and sighs, then looks down the trail. "Let's explore a little farther. Maybe Damon got hurt falling off the bike and went down the trail for help."

"Why down, not up?" says Alex. "That wouldn't make any sense."

Bree shoots him a look. A little desperate. They're both grasping at straws. What does it mean that they've found Damon's bike abandoned halfway down the trail? Where did he go from here? Was he alone?

Alex nods toward the trail. "Let's stick together this time."

He leads the way past the abandoned bike, wanting answers but more nervous than ever about what they might find.

CHAPTER 32

Sampson

I'M BACK IN THE basement of DC Metro headquarters. Dennis Chan is at his usual station, slumped in his chair, exhausted. After leaving the bombing site, Anna Rizzo and I parted ways. I took Chan, and Rizzo went back to her lab to see what she could dig up with her forensics team.

I lean over Chan's shoulder. "What've you got on this one?"

"Not as much," he says, sitting up straighter. "I know that's not what you want to hear."

Chan taps a few keys and his monitors light up. We're looking at surveillance footage from early this morning on Henry Bacon Drive. Not much traffic, just a few pedestrians and joggers.

"What time?" I ask.

"Six thirty-one a.m. Coming right up. See, here we go."

We're looking at a black Ford pickup with a blue tarpaulin over the truck bed. The truck pulls over to the side, near a bunch of shuttered vendor booths and souvenir stands. The truck's hazard lights start flashing.

Like an apparition, the driver steps out.

White painter overalls.

Gloves.

Face mask.

White baseball cap pulled down low.

He walks around the front of the truck heading toward the wall—and disappears.

Chan freezes the image and turns to me. "You ready?"

"Let it roll."

Even though I know what's coming, it still feels like a punch to the gut.

As soon as Chan restarts the video, a bright white-orange flash fills the screen. When it recedes, billowing smoke obscures everything.

When the smoke dissipates, the pickup truck is gone. Completely destroyed. Two cars parked nearby are shattered.

I stare at the screen, where there's chaos: injured people stumbling around, a few people helping the victims using handkerchiefs or neckties as temporary bandages.

One man is moving. Dressed in jogging gear.

Leg gone below the knee.

He falls and thrashes on the ground as blood gushes out.

Chan turns in his chair. "John, whatever we've got here, it's not some hermit like Ted Kaczynski. He's bold and he's not afraid to be out there in public, and he delivers the bomb right where he wants it. But why?"

"The purpose of terror is terror."

"But we still have no one claiming responsibility and no leads."

"Right. And no clue about what he plans to blow up next."

My phone vibrates with a text alert.

It's from Rizzo.

See me soonest.

CHAPTER 33

Cross

AFTER AN HOUR OF searching the trail with no further results, Alex and Bree sit in their Camry back at the trailhead. Bree taps furiously on her laptop.

Still no reply from Melissa.

The sun has fully risen now, and the temperature with it. They're both sweaty and covered with bug bites and scratches. Alex gets a news alert on his phone.

"Christ! Another bombing in DC."

"Where?" asks Bree.

"Vietnam Veterans Memorial."

"Casualties?"

Alex nods. "No final count yet, but it's not good."

Bree shakes her head. "I'm sure John is on it. Ned too. We need to stay focused."

"What are you doing?" Alex asks.

"I'm borrowing some Bluestone software to check emails from the kids we met at the bar. I want to see if there's anything else they're not telling us. Deep dive this time."

Alex leans over to look at her screen. All he sees is a mishmash of lists and codes. This is way beyond everyday Gmail.

"They all have encrypted accounts," says Bree. "Nia, Carter, Roger…" She taps a few more keys. "Damon and Melissa too." Bree freezes on an exchange and enlarges it. "Wait. Look at this."

At that moment, a car pulls up behind them. A Red Kia. It's Melissa.

"Hold that thought," says Alex.

Bree snaps her laptop closed and steps out of the car. "About time!" She sounds annoyed, and Alex doesn't blame her.

He exits the driver's side and meets Melissa as she opens her car door. "Where did you disappear to last night? We were worried about you!"

"I'm so sorry," says Melissa. "We were pretty shaken up and we all just took off. I stayed at Nia's last night. I didn't realize my phone was on Do Not Disturb until this morning."

"Come this way. We found a bike."

"Is it Damon's?"

"You tell us."

Alex leads the way down the trail. Melissa follows, with Bree bringing up the rear, clutching her laptop. About thirty yards in, Alex stops and points. "There it is."

Melissa ducks down and reaches for the bike. Alex grabs her hand. "Don't touch it. It could be evidence."

Melissa gets down on all fours and crawls under the branches that cover half the bike. She stretches forward, brushing her hair back from her face. Then she turns around. "It is Damon's! There's a scrape on the front end of the frame."

"Are you sure?" asks Bree.

Melissa nods. "Damon was riding one afternoon when he went by a parked car. Idiot driver opened his door without checking. Damon was okay, but the bike got scraped. He was really pissed off about it. He showed me the mark when he came home."

Progress, Alex thinks. *Now we just need to get the bike to a police lab.*

"Thanks, Melissa," he says. "This helps."

Melissa sits back and brushes the dirt from her hands and knees. "Is there anything else I can do?"

Bree opens her laptop and holds the screen in front of Melissa's face. "Yes. You can explain *this.*"

CHAPTER 34

Sampson

WHEN I WALK INTO Anna Rizzo's office at the ATF facility, she's busy typing on her keyboard.

"Sit," she says, nodding toward a chair without even looking up from her screen.

Unlike the lab, Rizzo's office is cluttered with bookcases, filing cabinets, and bomb diagrams. There are also some photos. One is her in full army battle rattle standing with her bomb disposal crew next to an up-armored Humvee. The landscape behind her looks to be from the same part of the world where I spent many miserable months.

In another photo, I see a young boy and girl smiling at a birthday party.

I point to the kids. "Juan and Tina?"

Rizzo looks up from her screen and smiles. "Impressive, Detective. You remembered their names."

"What can I say? I'm a good listener."

Behind Rizzo is a frame holding a small piece of an American flag, torn and burned on one edge.

"What's that about?" I ask.

"A reminder," she says in a tone that doesn't invite further conversation.

I move on. "So you have something?" I ask.

"Yeah. I've been thinking back on things."

"Back on what things?"

"Back to guys like Timothy McVeigh." She clicks on her screen and pulls up a photo from April 19, 1995, showing the wreckage at the front of the Murrah Federal Building in Oklahoma City. "A hundred and sixty-eight dead on that day."

"Right. Men, women, and children."

Rizzo clicks on a close-up of McVeigh's face. Short hair. Round jaw. Cold eyes.

"I remembered that Oklahoma City wasn't his first bomb," she says. "Two years earlier, he was doing practice runs, making explosive devices on a farm in the middle of nowhere."

"You think our guy practiced too?"

"I know he did."

Rizzo clicks to a Google image of a small rural town.

"Kansas? Texas?" *Could be anywhere,* I think.

Rizzo shakes her head. "Palmer, Georgia, near the Alabama line. Population nine hundred fifty. About a year ago, a farmer thought he heard an explosion in a sandpit. When the cops came out, they found remnants of a van. And a very big hole. There wasn't much of an investigation, but they did the best they could."

"What else did they find?"

"Remains of a fertilizer bomb in the wreckage of the van. And this…"

She clicks a link and a photo pops up on the screen. Spread out on a white evidence table are a bunch of charred bolts and nuts.

"Look familiar?" asks Rizzo.

"It sure does. Same kind of shrapnel we've seen here. Twice."

"That's right. Same contents. Same proportions." Rizzo swivels her chair around to face me. "I think you know what this means for us."

"Us? You and me?"

"Right."

"Road trip?"

She nods. "There's an air force transport leaving Andrews for Lawson Army Airfield at Fort Benning this afternoon. I called in a favor. We're on it."

CHAPTER 35

Cross

MELISSA'S FACE IS FLUSHED. Alex Cross can see how nervous she is.

Bree is staring straight at her, holding up the laptop screen. "Okay, Melissa—tell me all about breaking into Professor Lucas's house."

"How do you know about that?" Melissa asks, her voice shaking.

"I work for a very technologically advanced investigation firm. You'd be surprised what we can dig up. You and your friends all talked about the break-in—in encrypted emails."

"Okay," says Melissa. "Yes. When we couldn't get a straight answer from the school, we went to Professor Lucas's house and checked it out. We figured out how to hack the alarm code and we all went in together."

"You know that's unlawful entry, right?" asks Alex.

"That's why we didn't tell anybody."

Alex scowls. "Including us."

Melissa nods. "With you being cops."

Alex is furious. "We're not cops, Melissa! We're investigators! We're on your side!"

"So what did you find?" asks Bree.

Melissa takes a deep breath. "The place was empty. But Professor Lucas's cat, Otis, was there, no food or water, litter box stinking. He was so excited to see us, and he'd clearly been alone for a while. Lucas talks about Otis all the time. He *loves* that cat. No way he would have just left him like that."

"Where's the cat now?" asks Bree.

"Otis? Nia took him. She's taking care of him at her apartment. Wait—is that stealing?"

"Never mind that," says Alex. "What about Amy Tyne's place?"

"We checked there too. Her neighbor hadn't seen her in a week."

"Did you report all this to the department head?" Alex asks.

"Damon said it was no use," says Melissa. "He said we'd have to investigate ourselves. Then a few days later, he disappeared too."

"I'm calling Malone," Alex says. He puts the call on speaker when Detective Hugh Malone picks up.

"Hello? Dr. Cross?"

"We found my son's bicycle," says Alex.

"Where?"

"On a trail in the Mason Farm Biological Reserve."

"Anything else there? Clothing? Phone? Laptop?"

"No."

"Any signs of violence? Disturbed vegetation? Scuff marks on the ground? Blood?"

"None of the above," says Alex. "How long before you can get somebody out here?"

"I'll do my best, but we've got a lot on our plate here. I'll send someone to retrieve the bike and photograph the scene. Make sure you don't touch anything."

"I know how to handle evidence."

"No disrespect meant," says Malone. "I'm sure you do."

"Detective, I think we need to set up a search party. The sooner the better."

"I'll tell you what — let's get the bike back to the station, dust it for prints, and see where that takes us."

"Fine. You do that," says Alex, his voice hard and cold. "In the meantime, we'll look for Damon ourselves."

Alex hangs up and turns to Melissa. "Ready to go to work?"

She nods eagerly. "Anything."

"If we're going to conduct a proper search, we need volunteers. I want you to contact everybody you and Damon know around campus, including your friends from the Grotto. Tell them to meet us out here at two o'clock, in hiking gear." He hands her a credit card. "Then I want you to go to the nearest supermarket and buy plenty of water and snacks. As much as you think we'll need."

Melissa tucks the card into her pocket. "I'll do it, Dr. Cross. Don't worry. And again, I'm sorry about not telling you guys everything."

"One more thing," says Bree. "I want you to go to Staples and print up a few hundred missing person flyers with Damon's photo on them, the same photo that the police are using. I'll text you the number I want at the bottom."

"Sure, Chief Stone. No problem." Melissa heads up the trail to where the cars are parked.

"Think we can trust her?" Bree asks Alex as Melissa disappears from view.

Alex looks at his watch. "Guess we'll find out at two o'clock."

CHAPTER 36

ALEX PULLS OUT HIS PHONE.

"Who are you calling?" asks Bree.

"I need a touch of home."

He puts the call on speaker. A few seconds later, Jannie's voice comes through. "Dad! What have you found out? Do you know where Damon is?"

"Not yet," says Bree. "We just found his bike, left on a trail in a nature reserve. We're putting up flyers around campus and setting up a search party for later today."

"What do the police say?" asks Jannie.

Alex speaks up. "They say there's no evidence that Damon's been harmed or in danger. They're following their own policies and procedures. As far as they're concerned, Damon is an adult and if he wants to go somewhere on his own without telling anyone, that's his right."

"Those by-the-book fools!" Nana Mama's reedy voice crackles all the way from DC. "You can bet if it was a white boy, maybe the son of the mayor or something, they'd be following some different... *procedures*." She spits the last word like it's an obscenity.

"Anything we can do to help?" Ali pipes up.

"Just stay home and take care of one another," says Bree. "Don't be wandering around outdoors. Knowing you're safe will make our job easier."

"Nana," says Alex, "we heard about the bomb at the Vietnam memorial this morning. How are things in the city?"

"Crazy," says Nana. "I'm keeping the children inside today. John left from here to check things out. Haven't heard back from him yet."

A girl's voice comes through, sweet and high-pitched: "I know my daddy will find this guy and stop him. He promised!"

"Willow!" says Bree. "It's good to hear your voice, baby. You stay there with Jannie and Ali and Nana, okay?"

"I will. I promise. No bomber is gonna get me!"

CHAPTER 37

Sampson

ANNA RIZZO AND I are standing in a sandpit with Wilma Grace, the police chief from Palmer, Georgia. The chief sounded a little surprised by our call, but when we told her we were on our way down, she agreed to meet us at the site, a few miles outside town.

The pit takes up about half an acre. It's clearly been used for plenty of parties and target shooting over the years. I see shot-up paper targets propped up against the pit's sandy walls and rusty fifty-five-gallon drums riddled with bullet holes. Firepits are scattered across the sandy ground, as are crushed beer cans and empty wine bottles.

"Looks like a popular hangout," says Rizzo.

Chief Grace nods. "Not much else to do around here."

The chief is in her mid-fifties, tall, with a tan and weathered face. She wears khaki trousers, a blue uniform shirt, and a dark blue baseball cap with a badge insignia on it.

"On weekends," she tells us, "high-school kids come out here to drink and raise hell. During the week, good ol' boys come out to exercise their Second Amendment rights. Once in a while, we get a call to break up a fight here, but otherwise, we pretty much leave the place alone. It's like a no-man's-land."

"Were you around last year when the bomb went off out here?" I ask.

"I was," she says. "A farmer down the road called 911 and said he heard something explode. At first, we thought it might be somebody shooting off a shotgun or blowing up a tree stump, but when we got out here, we saw it was a lot bigger than that."

"You found the van?" asks Rizzo.

"What was left of it," says Grace. "You could hardly recognize it as a vehicle except for an axle and what was left of the engine block."

I can see that Rizzo is only half listening. She's walking around, head down, moving in expanding circles. "Excuse me, Chief," she calls out. "Do you remember where the van was located?" She kicks the sand with her boot. "Was it right about here?"

"It was. How did you know?" asks Grace.

Rizzo digs into the sand with the toe of her boot as the chief and I walk over. "Look. Even now, a year later, this spot is more depressed than the surrounding area. And some of the sand is fused from the heat of the explosion."

I turn to Grace. "What happened to the remains of the van?"

She frowns. "We took a lot of photos and kept some of the nuts and bolts. But nobody in our department is a forensics expert. We knew we were in over our heads. So we called in the GBI. They rolled up one day, collected all the evidence, and that was that."

"They never told you where the van came from?" asks Rizzo. "Or the explosives?"

Grace chuckles. "The GBI isn't big on returning calls from little old Palmer."

Rizzo stares at something in the distance. "John, in my go bag, there's a measuring tape. Grab it for me, will you?"

I unzip the bag and fumble around inside until I find it. It's a three-hundred-foot reel on a big plastic spool, the kind builders and surveyors use. I hand it to Rizzo.

"Hold this end," she says.

I grab the reel and stand in the small depression. Rizzo starts walking, unspooling the tape as she goes, farther and farther across the pit, then up a slope lined with small trees and bushes.

She stops and calls back to me. "What's the distance?"

I look down at the tape. "One hundred seventy-four feet!" I yell.

"Why did she stop?" the chief asks me.

"She's measuring the blast zone. You can see where the explosion took out branches and scarred tree trunks. See where she's standing? That's where the damage stopped."

Rizzo walks back over to us as I roll up the tape.

"The first DC blast zone was one hundred and seventy feet," she says. "The blast zone at the Vietnam memorial was one hundred seventy-seven feet."

I hand her the tape measure and she drops it into her bag. She looks across the pit.

"He knew exactly the blast range he wanted," says Rizzo. "The son of a bitch started right here. This was his practice field."

CHAPTER 38

Cross

ALEX AND BREE ARE leaning on the rear fender of their Camry when they hear a car coming up the park road.

"She's back," says Bree, her voice rising.

Sure enough, a few seconds later, Melissa's car pulls up beside them and stops. Melissa hops out and lifts the back hatch. The cargo area is filled with cases of bottled water and plastic shopping bags.

Melissa hands Alex his credit card. "Hope I got enough stuff," she says. She reaches into the bags and pulls out carton after carton of Clif Bars. Then she picks up a white cardboard box. "I went by Staples like you said, then I stopped by campus on my way here and put a few dozen of these up."

Alex's breath catches in his throat when he sees the flyer. He's seen hundreds of them in his career, but he never expected to see one with his own son's face on it.

Bree picks up one of the flyers and checks the boldfaced phone number at the bottom to make sure it's correct.

Alex runs his hand over Damon's picture. "I hope Bluestone is ready for the calls."

"Don't worry. They are," says Bree. "Former police dispatchers will be answering the phones. They'll know which calls are bullshit, which ones to follow up on. If there are any good leads, they'll pass them along to us — and the Chapel Hill PD."

"Bluestone?" asks Melissa. "Who are they?"

"The company I work for these days," says Bree. "Trust me, they're people who know how to get things done."

"Were you able to recruit some volunteers?" Alex asks Melissa.

"I texted everybody I know. I think we'll have a pretty good turnout. At least I hope so."

Alex reaches into the back seat of the Camry and pulls out a topographical map. Using the edge of one of the flyers as a ruler, he starts drawing boxes on the area of the map showing the nature reserve.

Melissa leans over his shoulder. "What are you doing?"

"Making search grids," says Alex. "We can't have people just wandering aimlessly through the woods. There needs to be a plan, a process."

"You've done this before?"

Alex looks up. "Too many times."

The sound of vehicles grinding their way up the dirt road reaches them.

"They're here!" Melissa shouts, running toward the crest of the hill.

First one, then two, then three cars pull in. Then two more. Doors fly open, and more than a dozen young men and women in all sizes and shapes and shades pile out. A few look like they're out for an afternoon stroll, but most are carrying small knapsacks and wearing heavy walking shoes or hiking boots.

Nia, Carter, and Roger, the trio from the Grotto, emerge from a battered Volvo.

In a low whisper, Bree does a head count. Fifteen.

Fifteen searchers to cover more than three hundred acres.

Not a lot, but better than nothing.

Melissa runs over to greet the group, then leads them back to Alex and Bree. "Everybody, this is Dr. Alex Cross and Chief Bree Stone. They're Damon's parents."

Awkward hellos and handshakes, then Alex gathers them all around the trunk of the rental car. "Thanks for coming. I've got a map here that we can—"

Everybody turns at the sound of gears grinding up the road.

Bree turns to Melissa. "You expecting anyone else?"

Melissa shakes her head.

A black Ford Police Interceptor pulls up, followed by a bus marked TRAINING ACADEMY.

A tall woman in jeans and a black polo shirt steps out of the Interceptor. Alex has a good memory for faces. He recognizes her as soon as she walks over.

"You're Gail, right?" says Alex. "From the Chapel Hill PD. You're the one who stopped by Hugh Malone's office when we were there."

"That's right, Dr. Cross. I'm Detective Gail Bailey. I wanted to introduce myself to you and Chief Stone then, but it didn't feel like the right time. I'm a big fan of yours—of both of you. I've studied your cases. Taught a few in my lectures at the academy."

"Appreciate it," says Bree. "What's with the bus?"

"Malone sent me to pick up Damon's bike," says Bailey. "And I figured you might need some extra help with the search."

"But it seemed from Detective Malone that... well..."

"That he didn't want to help?" says Bailey. "Don't blame Malone. He's doing the best he can. He's getting a lot of pressure from a lot of people about this speaker coming up. He's worried about outside agitators and violence. He's worried it could spill over from the campus to the town."

"I'm worried about my son," says Alex.

"I am too," says Bailey. The front door of the bus opens and the passengers step out—about a dozen strapping men and women around the same age as the grad students, all dressed in gray sweats with PD TRAINEE across the chest.

"Police cadets?" asks Bree.

"Yes," says Bailey. "I thought an unscheduled training exercise would be good for everybody." The cadets line up behind her at parade rest. "This bunch is yours for the afternoon."

"That's very generous of the department," says Alex.

"Nothing to do with the department," says Bailey. "My call."

She stares into the woods for a few moments. "Years ago, my older sister Laurel left home and never came back. This was up in Pennsylvania. She was twenty-two. No note, nothing. She just... disappeared. Back then, they wouldn't let us file a missing person report for two days. Most people assumed that she'd just run off with a guy. But I knew that wasn't what happened. The case went cold. We never saw her again."

"I'm sorry," says Alex.

"I'm not letting you guys go through that," says Bailey. "One way or another, we'll find your son."

CHAPTER 39

GAIL BAILEY FOLLOWS BREE down the trail and comes back holding Damon's bicycle in her gloved hands. She places it carefully on a sheet of plastic in the trunk of her Interceptor as Alex and the others stand by.

"It looks clean to me," says Bailey. "I don't see any blood. But we'll have the lab take a look and I'll let you know what they find."

"We owe you, Gail," says Alex.

She lowers the trunk gently until it latches, then nods toward to the waiting crowd of searchers. "Go find your boy."

As she drives off, Alex calls to the crowd of students and cadets, "If I can have your attention please!" Everybody turns in his direction. "Bree and I can't thank you enough for coming out here today."

"Damon thanks you too," adds Melissa. She holds up a flyer and points to his picture. "For those who don't know, this is what he looks like. And I love him very much."

Alex's throat tightens. He coughs to clear it. "Okay, let's get started." He surveys the crowd. "Does anyone here have experience reading topographical maps or orienteering?"

Four hands go up—two cadets, two civilians.

"Great. Step forward. You four are team leaders."

He brings the four over to the Camry and unfolds his topo map. They all lean over and study the trails and natural formations.

"Sorry I don't have maps for everybody," says Alex. "You'll have to orient yourselves with your phone compasses and landmarks. Chief Stone and I have already checked both of the main trails. I'd like you guys to concentrate on the woods."

"No problem, sir," says one of the cadets, running his finger over the map. "I'll take grid one." He looks over and points to the other three team leaders, left to right. "You guys take grids two, three, and four in that order. Everybody clear?"

The others nod.

Bree addresses the rest of the volunteers. She points to the open hatch of Melissa's car. "There's plenty of water and snacks over here. Stock up, stay hydrated, and, above all, be careful. Look out for snares, gullies, exposed tree roots, snakes, and anything else that can hurt you. We don't want to have any injuries while we're out here."

The searchers crowd around the Kia, stuffing supplies into their pockets and backpacks. After some milling around, four separate groups of searchers stand at the edge of the parking area, ready to go. Alex gives them his cell phone number and waits for the searchers to enter it into their contacts. Then he offers some final advice.

"The best way to proceed is to line up not much more than an arm's length from the person to your left and to your right. Move slowly, stay in a straight line as best you can. If you see anything out of the ordinary — drops of blood, a torn piece of clothing, broken branches — don't touch it! Just stay put, take pictures, and call me."

The searchers shuffle into rows and get into position.

Alex checks his watch. "It's two o'clock. Head out and search until four p.m., then turn around and come back." The four groups are at the edge of the parking area now.

He can tell they're eager to get going. But he's not done.

"Listen! This is important! The way you return is not the way you went out. I need the farthest searcher on the left and the right to stand still and turn around in place. Then half of the searchers will rotate on him or her, keeping the same distance. Then you'll have two wings of searchers on the way back, covering new ground. Any questions?"

Silence.

"Be safe, be careful," says Alex. "And don't ignore anything you find, no matter how small it may seem."

"Godspeed, all of you!" adds Bree.

Godspeed to us all, Alex thinks. *Where are you, Damon?*

CHAPTER 40

Sampson

THE U.S. AIR FORCE generously flew us down to Georgia, but Rizzo and I are on our own getting back, so we're flying commercial out of Atlanta. Chief Grace said she'd look through her department's files on the bombing, but she's pretty sure they turned everything over to the GBI.

I'm sitting next to Rizzo in our rented Corolla, seat belt tight, as she speeds along I-85 toward the Atlanta airport. We flipped a coin for who got to drive, and she won the toss. Occasionally my right foot thumps down on an imaginary brake pedal. Can't help myself.

Rizzo glances over the third time I do it. "You don't like my driving?"

"I love your driving. It's arriving in one piece I'm worried about."

"Former army guy afraid of a little ground speed?" She smiles.

"I guess I'm just used to being the one risking my own life behind the wheel."

"So do something to distract yourself. Get on the phone with the Georgia Bureau of Investigation and see what you can pull out of them about the Palmer site."

I look down at my phone. "Good idea. That way if we crash, maybe I won't see it coming."

Rizzo presses harder on the accelerator.

I get through to the main GBI number with no problem. But after that, it's a bureaucratic rabbit hole, and I'm handed off from one office to another.

Finally, I reach a guy who seems like he's about ten minutes from retirement and unwilling to exert himself in the meantime. He refuses to answer any of my questions until I give him my badge number and the name of my DC Metro Police supervisor. This seems to have an effect, but not much of one.

"Once I get you verified, son, I'll call you back."

"I'm not your goddamn son!" I shout into the phone. But the guy's already disconnected.

Twenty minutes later, we're starting to see signs for the airport when my phone rings.

It's the lazy guy.

"Having some trouble finding any record of that investigation, son. What was the name of that town again?"

"Palmer!" I say. "As in Arnold, the golfer."

"Got it. Look, I'm just about on my way out. This'll have to wait."

This time, I hang up first. Then I bang my phone repeatedly against the dashboard.

Rizzo slows down as we approach the car-rental drop-off.

"Once upon a time," she says, "if somebody from DC contacted an outside police agency, those folks sat up and took notice, eager to help. Not anymore. Everybody's protecting their own turf, doing their own thing—like that rogue FBI office up in Boston, cooperating for years with that murdering drug dealer."

"You mean Whitey Bulger?"

"Yeah. Him."

I start looking for the Enterprise sign where we'll drop off the rental. "You're right. There's too much distrust. Everybody's worried that DC will come in and either take all the credit or screw things up and throw the locals under the bus."

"Not that it hasn't happened," says Rizzo.

As she pulls into the drop-off lane, my phone pings with a text.

GBI? Could it be lazy guy coming through after all?

Nope. It's Dennis Chan.

See me.

CHAPTER 41

Cross

IT'S 4:15 P.M.

Crunching sounds and mumbling rise from the underbrush near the trailhead.

Alex and Bree watch as the search teams emerge from the woods, moving like a defeated army. Their clothes are soaked with sweat, and their faces are drawn and grimy. Most of the searchers are scratched up and probably dotted with bug bites.

Nia comes out limping, grimacing from pain, helped along by a sturdy police cadet. Bree grabs a first aid kit from her go bag. "Over here, Nia. Sit down."

"Twisted ankle," says the cadet. "Nothing broken." He eases Nia down onto the lip of the Camry's open trunk.

Bree shakes an instant ice pack. She applies the plastic bag gently as tears run down Nia's cheeks.

"I wanted to find Damon. I didn't want to give up. I know he wouldn't quit. Not ever."

Other searchers move past Alex, overheated and exhausted. A few of them reach for fresh bottles of water and pour them directly over their heads. The water spills onto the dirt in small dark puddles.

Melissa is in the last team to emerge. She walks up to Alex, her hair matted across her forehead, and collapses against him, sobbing. "Dr. Cross, I'm so sorry. We didn't find him. We didn't find a damn thing!"

Alex hugs her. "Don't get discouraged, Melissa, you did your best. You came through with a solid bunch of volunteers. That's a big deal. We've only just started."

As he comforts Melissa, Alex realizes that he's giving himself the same pep talk. It's not the first time he's supervised a field search. Nor is it the first time he's had to search for members of his own family. It's too soon to admit defeat.

Alex turns around as Gail Bailey's black Ford Interceptor powers up the dirt road and stops in front of the bus from the academy. Two of the police cadets walk over when Bailey steps out. She stands straight, hands on her hips, as she listens to their report. Then she walks over to Alex, glancing around at the exhausted searchers. "Sorry it didn't pan out," she says.

Bree grimaces. "Yeah. So are we."

"We'll search again," says Alex. "And we'll come up with something else."

Bailey nods. "I put a rush on Damon's bike. We had his fingerprints on file."

"From where?" asks Bree.

"YMCA," says Bailey. "They do a background check on volunteers who work with minors."

Bree takes a deep breath. "And?"

"Damon's prints are all over the bike," says Bailey. "But nobody else's."

CHAPTER 42

Sampson

ANNA RIZZO AND I are once again with Dennis Chan in the basement of the DC Metro Police headquarters, hovering over his shoulder as his fingers fly over the keyboard.

As Chan works, his eyes never move from the two large monitors on his desk. "When John asked me to go back to the old style of catching arsonists, I have to say, I was skeptical," he says. His voice sounds weary.

Rizzo turns to me. "Why arsonists?"

"Something I remembered from working with Alex Cross," I tell her. "It has to do with their psychology. Some arsonists get off on seeing the results of their work and watching the emergency response. That's why when police photographers show up at the scene of a suspected arson, they take pictures of the spectators in addition to the fire damage."

"But arsonists and terrorists are two different animals. Seems like a stretch to me," says Rizzo.

"I thought so too," says Chan. "But John asked me to give it a shot."

"What did you do, exactly?" Rizzo asks. I can tell she's intrigued.

"What I did," says Chan, "was load every frame of surveillance footage, raw media footage, and personal photos we could find from anywhere near the bombing sites. Then I processed them all through a facial-recognition program that doesn't officially exist and that I'm not supposed to have access to."

On Chan's side-by-side monitors, still images are whizzing by in a blur.

"The program is called Flash Talbot. It uses AI and a borrowed quantum computer system from Fort Meade."

"What's going on in here? Movie night?"

It's Ned Mahoney. He steps into the cubicle next to me. He reeks of McDonald's, and he could use a shower.

I point to the screens, where the image flurry is slowing down. "Dennis says he might have something."

"Any luck with Langley and my C-4 taggants?" asks Rizzo, her eyes glued to the screens.

"Progress is supposedly being made," says Mahoney. "But nothing yet."

"I thought you were best buds with the president," says Rizzo.

Mahoney nods. "Langley wasn't overly impressed. Presidents come and go."

On both monitors the images have slowed to a crawl.

Then they freeze.

One image on the right. One image on the left.

We all lean in.

I hold my breath.

The frozen image on the left screen shows a white male in a tan jacket and black baseball cap, hands in his pockets. He's standing in a crowd, looking straight ahead.

The other image shows a white male in a dull yellow jacket and black baseball cap, hands in his pockets, also looking straight ahead. Same kind of setting. Same outfit. Same posture.

The images are fuzzy, but in both photos, the man has a strong chin, prominent cheekbones, heavy eyebrows.

"It's the same guy," says Rizzo softly.

"Can you sharpen the pictures?" asks Mahoney.

"They *are* sharpened," says Chan. "I'm limited by the quality of the raw material and the degree of enlargement. This is military-grade software, but it's not military-grade footage. We can't count nose hairs."

I look back and forth between the two screens, squinting and angling my head as if that will help. "Do we know who he is?"

"Not yet," says Chan. "That's the next step, crunching through a ton of visual data from Homeland Security, Bureau of Prisons, all the military branches, the DMVs, private security companies—and any foreign assets we can tap into."

Rizzo smiles. "You mean *hack* into?"

"Only if they refuse to play nice," says Chan.

I reach out and tap the frozen images with my fingertip, one after the other.

"Whoever he is—that's our guy."

CHAPTER 43

Cross

AFTER LONG SHOWERS AND a change of clothes, Alex and Bree are sitting in the Crossroads Restaurant on the main floor of their hotel. Alex is just two sips into his wine when Melissa appears in the entryway.

"She's here," says Bree, waving the young woman over.

Melissa walks across the crowded dining room to their table. She's wearing a floral dress and low heels. Her hair is pulled back into a neat ponytail. Alex realizes that it's the first time he's seen his son's girlfriend dressed in something other than jeans.

When Melissa sits down, Alex notices scratches on her hands from the afternoon's search.

"Did you get some rest?" Bree asks.

Melissa shakes her head, her expression somber. "I tried to take a nap, but I couldn't close my eyes. Just knowing that Damon is out there…" Her lower lip starts to quiver and her eyes glisten.

Bree reaches over and squeezes her hand.

"How about some wine?" asks Alex.

Melissa nods and wipes her eyes. Alex picks up the bottle and pours her a glass.

"Thank you, Dr. Cross." She takes a sip, then lets out a long breath.

A cheery server appears at the table. "Good evening, folks. Can I start you off with one of our appetizers?"

Alex gives him a tight smile. "We need a few minutes."

The server nods. "Of course. Whenever you're ready." He walks off.

Melissa takes another sip. She looks across the table at Alex, then at Bree.

"Dr. Cross, Chief Stone, again, I'm so sorry I wasn't up front with you from the start. I should have called you right away."

"Yes," says Bree. "And you should have told us about the professor and his student."

"She's his TA, not his student," says Melissa. "Teaching assistant. Most of us grad students are also TAs in undergrad classes. So Amy helps out in Professor Lucas's undergrad class, collecting assignments, grading exams. That kind of stuff."

Alex leans forward, hands folded on the table. "What's Lucas like? Do you guys think he's a good teacher?"

Melissa nods. "Yes, definitely. He's inspiring, makes you think. And he's active in the same causes Damon and I support. Voters' rights. Literacy. Anti-poverty programs. We see him all the time at rallies and meetings. He's been like a mentor to a lot of us."

"What about Amy?" asks Bree.

"I don't know her that well, honestly. We've talked at a few TA meetups. She's nice. Smart. Quiet. Doesn't say much. I've seen her with Professor Lucas at events and speeches. I think they have the same philosophy about things. Makes sense. I mean, he hired her, right?"

"What about Michaelson Woods?" asks Alex. "The Young Freedom Fighters guy. Did Darius Lucas have an opinion about him coming to campus to speak?"

"Oh, yeah," says Melissa. "Out of all the faculty, I'd say Lucas was the most outspoken against it. He thinks Woods promotes hate speech." Melissa lowers her eyes. "One time, I remember some white dude shouting at Lucas and Amy at a rally after Lucas spoke up."

"Shouting what?" asks Bree.

"Well…Professor Lucas is Black. And Amy is white. And the guy yelled something about how Lucas should watch his mouth around true Americans. And that…" Melissa hesitates. She clears her throat. Her face flushes.

"And that what?" asks Alex.

Melissa says in a nervous whisper, "He said that Professor Lucas needed to leave 'our women' alone. And he used the N-word." She grabs her wineglass and takes a big gulp.

Alex leans back. "I've heard the word before." He looks at his wife. "So has Bree. We've heard it all our lives."

Bree turns to Melissa. "Okay. As long as we're being blunt, is there any chance Lucas and Amy were a couple?"

"No way," Melissa says flatly.

"What makes you so sure?" Alex asks.

"Because Amy Tyne is gay."

Bree's phone rings inside her purse. She pulls it out and glances at Alex. "I should take this. It's Elena."

Bree gets up and heads for an alcove on the other side of the room. Alex looks over at Melissa. "Elena's her boss," he explains.

After an awkward silence, Melissa asks, "So what do we do now, Dr. Cross? About finding Damon?"

"I'm hoping Bree is getting some information right now. The toll-free number she had you put on the flyers goes directly to her company."

"You mean the company that spied on my phone records?"

Alex smiles. "That's the one."

"No! Absolutely not!" Bree says. Alex can hear her from across the restaurant.

He gets up from the table and glances at Melissa. "Excuse me for a moment."

He walks over to Bree, who has the phone pressed against her ear. She's not talking anymore, just listening.

And her expression is getting angrier with every second.

CHAPTER 44

THIRTY MINUTES LATER, ALEX is behind the wheel of the rental car. Raleigh-Durham International Airport is five minutes away.

Bree is huddled in the passenger seat, arms folded, staring out the window.

"Bluestone is asking too much this time," she mutters. "I should quit."

"Quitting is always an option," says Alex.

"But you don't think it's a good one. I can hear it in your voice."

Alex takes the airport exit. "Bree, I love you to the moon and back. You've saved my life and sanity more times than I can count. You're the best wife and partner any man could wish for and a rock for our family."

"Mm-hmm," says Bree, turning toward her husband. "I'm waiting for the *but*."

"Well, then, here it is," says Alex. "You know I'll support you in anything you do, Bree, but Bluestone is calling you in because the feds are all-hands-on-deck with these bombings. They know you have contacts. You have skills. You have experience."

"But Damon—"

"I know, I know," says Alex. "But if you quit Bluestone, how do you know they'll keep on answering that number on the flyer? Maybe they'd back-burner it or turn it over to a B-team."

"They wouldn't dare."

"Bluestone has other priorities—especially now."

Bree sighs. "Damn it. I know you're right, but I hate to leave before we have Damon home safely."

Alex nods, feeling his throat constrict. He understands the conflict Bree is feeling and her anger at being torn away from the search for Damon. But he also knows that she's a patriot. And it's their home city under attack.

Is he nudging her to go back? Sure. But it's still her choice.

He pulls up to the curb at the departure terminal and puts the car in park.

Bree unbuckles her seat belt and opens her door. Alex jumps out his side, grabs Bree's bag from the trunk, and wheels it onto the walkway.

Then he reaches for her and gives her a long, hard, loving squeeze.

"I feel like I'm abandoning you," Bree says into his shoulder. "I feel like I'm abandoning Damon!"

Alex kisses the top of her head. "No, you're not. You're helping the country. And while you're doing that, you'll also be able to ride herd on that tip line. And you know I'll be here looking for Damon twenty-four seven."

Bree draws back, tears welling in her eyes. "I can't stand this."

Alex hugs her again. "You can do it. We can do it. We *have* to do it."

She wipes her eyes and grabs the handle of her luggage. "I know, I know."

She steps forward for one more kiss and leaves him with a final, fierce whisper. "Go find our boy."

CHAPTER 45

Sampson

I'M SITTING IN Anna Rizzo's office. Dennis Chan's cubicle was getting a little crowded, and I could tell he was ready for us all to get lost. He made Ned Mahoney promise to go home and bathe.

I stare at the two images that are now on Rizzo's desktop screen. Same guy. Two different crime scenes. I'm wishing I had the power to reach in and grab this guy by the throat.

"What if it's a coincidence?" asks Rizzo. "I mean, he could live and work somewhere nearby. He might just be a fire-truck chaser."

"No way. DC is full of fire-truck chasers, but he was the only person we found at both scenes. I'm telling you—"

Our phones chime at exactly the same time. Group text message. I look down at my screen. "From Chief Grace."

Got you the promised info. Sorry for the brief delay, mayor had to chew on me about budgets first.

Here's three locals we considered suspects from previous records or suspicions. All three names were passed along to the GBI. Probably ignored.

Good luck to you both.

Attached are three files.

Three names.

Leroy Foster

Andrew Goss

Aiden Phillips

We look at Foster's mug shots first. He's a fleshy guy with long black hair and a full beard.

"Doubtful it's this guy," says Rizzo. "Unless he started taking Ozempic recently."

"Wrong head shape anyway. Looks like a bearded bowling ball."

Next up is Andrew Goss. He's skinny and bald, and his upper neck, chin, and forehead are covered with tattoos.

"Hard to disguise all that ink," says Rizzo. "It would have shown up."

One more to go. I'm actually crossing my fingers.

Hello, Aiden Phillips.

Rizzo sucks in her breath.

Phillips is staring defiantly into the camera.

Strong chin, prominent cheekbones, heavy eyebrows.

"What did the Palmer police bring him in for?" I ask.

Rizzo pulls up the local reports. "Let's see…one misdemeanor assault. Looks like a bar fight. One DWI. And look! They questioned him after the explosion in the sandpit."

"I don't suppose they found any fertilizer in his trunk?"

Rizzo shakes her head. "I'm shooting this picture over to Dennis Chan. See if he can match it." She attaches the image to a text and clicks Send.

About thirty seconds later, Rizzo's phone rings. She answers. "Well?"

She slams her hand down on her desk. "Thank you!" She hangs up and turns to me. "He says it's a match. That's our guy."

"Great! Now we need to find out—"

Before I can finish my sentence, Rizzo starts receiving file after file.

"Damn," Rizzo says. "Dennis is fast!" I lean in over her shoulder as she starts reading off details from her screen. Everything you'd ever want to know about one Aiden Evan Phillips.

"Thirty-four years old. Separated, two kids. Ex-military, spent nine years with Third Special Forces Group Airborne at Fort Bragg in North Carolina." Rizzo scrolls down. "Overseas deployments...one tour in Iraq, three in Afghanistan. Other military records redacted."

"Black ops?"

"Who knows?" says Rizzo. "Maybe something sensitive with the State Department." She looks up from the screen and turns to me. "Get this—spent six months as an instructor at the army EOD school at Fort Gregg-Adams in Virginia."

I know that school. Their mission is to train explosives technicians. "He's a bomb expert!" My heart is pounding. I can feel my palms starting to sweat.

"What about other criminal activity post-army?"

Rizzo scrolls again. "Aiden is a naughty boy. Assault, assault with a deadly weapon, and...holy shit!"

I pull a chair over and plop down next to her. "What?"

"Look! He was arrested for criminal trespass at the U.S. Capitol Building but later released for lack of evidence."

"What else?"

"He was a patient at a VA hospital in Richmond."

"Combat injury?"

Rizzo clicks through the records. "Nope. Mental-health issues."

"Not a surprise. Him and a few million other vets." I scroll down the contacts on my phone and tap.

"Who are you calling?" asks Rizzo.

I put the phone on speaker and lay it on Rizzo's desk. On the second ring, the line connects. "Chief Grace, Palmer Police."

"Wilma! It's John Sampson and Anna Rizzo in DC. We got your files."

"Good. Hope to hell you can do something with 'em."

"We already did," says Rizzo.

I lean toward the phone. "We're looking at the guy named Aiden Phillips. Do you remember anything about him?"

"Phillips? Let's see…well, I remember that he was a real anti-government type. Told people he served in Afghanistan and was pissed off when the Taliban took over."

"What about the bomb in the sandpit?"

"We picked him up the day after based on his record. He had an alibi and we couldn't place him at the scene. Had to let him go. Never saw him again."

Rizzo chimes in. "Did you test his hands and clothes for explosive residue?"

"Guys, this is Palmer, Georgia, not DC. Like I said, we sent all our evidence and suspect files to GBI." She pauses for a second. "Hang on! You guys like Phillips for the bombings up there?"

I pick up the phone and hold it close. "We do, Chief. We like him a lot."

CHAPTER 46

Cross

ALEX CROSS PULLS THE rented Camry into the Carolina Inn parking lot. He's feeling tired and empty. It's been only twenty minutes since he dropped Bree off at the airport, and already he misses her like crazy.

Alex walks into the lobby and sees a cluster of reporters and TV cameras. It takes only a second for him to realize why they're there.

They're waiting for him.

As soon as they spot him, the reporters surge forward, holding up mini-recorders and iPhones.

"Dr. Cross!"

"How long has your son been missing?"

"Where was Damon last seen?"

"Have you received a ransom note, Dr. Cross?"

Alex sets his jaw. Obviously, with the flyer out, the news has broken. And now, like it or not, he's about to hold a presser. Right here in the hotel lobby.

He's dealt with the press for decades on dozens of cases. Sometimes they're a help. Sometimes they're a hindrance. But one thing he's learned: The media is a hungry animal, and it demands to be fed. Better to control the story than let it control you.

Alex stops in front of a small seating area in the lobby. He holds up his hands. "I'll answer your questions," he calls out, "but first I have a statement to give."

A polished-looking woman with a cameraman at her side takes charge. "Everybody, hush up!" she demands. "Let the man speak!"

Alex nods to her in appreciation as the group settles down.

"Thank you," he says. He looks from face to face, then stares directly into one of the TV cameras. "I'm Dr. Alex Cross. My son Damon Cross is a grad student at the university here in Chapel Hill. And right now, he's missing."

Alex stands his ground as the reporters and cameras push in closer.

"Damon was last seen when he left his apartment a few days ago. Nobody's heard from him since then."

The polished-looking woman pushes forward. "Dr. Cross! Do you suspect foul play?"

"There's no evidence of that so far. But obviously, I'm worried."

Another reporter calls out, "Dr. Cross, do you think your son's disappearance could be connected to one of your previous cases with the FBI?"

Once again, Alex flashes to the long line of killers he's encountered over the years. Of course he's concerned that there could be a connection. His family has been targeted before.

"There's no evidence of that at the moment," he says.

"Dr. Cross, are campus security and the Chapel Hill police involved in searching for your son?"

Just barely, Alex thinks. "The local authorities have been very cooperative."

Another reporter: "Dr. Cross! We heard there was a search conducted earlier today in the Mason Farm Biological Reserve. Was anything found?"

For now, Alex decides to keep the discovery of Damon's bicycle to himself. "We did not locate my son," he says. "The search will continue."

Alex notices one of the reporters holding the missing person flyer with Damon's picture. He leans forward and gestures for it, then holds the flyer up in front of the TV cameras. "This is my son Damon Cross. And this is the number to call if you have any information. Thank you."

The reporters press forward with more questions.

"Was Damon having trouble at the university?"

"Do you think drugs could have been involved?"

"Are your contacts at the FBI working on the case?"

Enough. Alex is done. He puts the flyer in his pocket and pushes through the scrum to the elevator.

He manages to press the Up button. The door opens. Two reporters try to jam themselves into the elevator with him. Alex plants his feet and shoves them both out but not before one of them shouts directly into his ear:

"Dr. Cross, do you think your son is still alive?"

Alex flinches as the doors slide shut.

CHAPTER 47

Sampson

I'M IN A FORMER army Black Hawk helicopter belonging to the Virginia State Police, watching the rural landscape of Virginia slide under me as we race toward a dot on the map—a small town in western Virginia.

Riding with me is Anna Rizzo and six heavily armed officers from the Virginia State Police tactical team, all wearing black tactical gear, gloves, and ballistic helmets.

Rides like this stir mixed memories in me. Flying into hot LZs in the mountains. Escaping under fire. High fives in the back after a successful mission. Sitting quietly, heads down, after a failure or after losing brothers in a firefight. Too many times, I flew back to base with body bags on the floor and bloody dog tags in my hand.

The chopper I'm in now is one of three flying to the same site. The lead bird in the assault force is carrying Ned Mahoney and members of the FBI Hostage Rescue Team—a misnomer if ever there was one. Most of the hostage rescue team's missions don't involve rescuing hostages but rather breaking into buildings and arresting bad guys. Or, if push comes to shove, killing them.

I hear Rizzo's voice crackle through my headphones. "Five minutes out."

"Hope it's not a clusterfuck when we get there."

"I'll make sure that doesn't happen."

"How?"

"By the force of my charming personality."

Our Black Hawk swoops down and hovers a few feet above the middle of an empty parking lot next to a gymnasium. I feel the slap on my shoulder that tells me it's time to jump out. Rizzo is right behind me. We duck low. The tactical team fans out around us. I feel the blast from the rotors as the helicopter climbs back into the air.

We're at the staging area. Our target is a motel about four miles away.

The motel where intel says Aiden Phillips is presently residing.

Mahoney's helicopter dropped him off just before we came in. He's already heading for a door in the side of a large windowless building with aluminum sides. The HRT guys move in a pack, some carrying long guns slung over their backs.

Rizzo and I follow the crowd. The door opens to a hardwood basketball court with a set of bleachers along the far wall. A large whiteboard is set up at center court, with folding tables and chairs clustered around. Rizzo and I take our seats with the tactical teams as Mahoney walks up to the head of the class.

Taped around the edges of the whiteboard are printed photographs of Aiden Phillips. Mug shots. Military ID. Driver's license photo.

In the center of the board is a detailed diagram of the target building, the Sunset Shores Motel. It's a small building, only a dozen rooms, with an office at one end and a wooded area at the rear.

All around us, agents are checking equipment and muttering in low voices.

"Okay!" Ned Mahoney calls out. "Let's settle down."

He uses his pen to tap one of the photos on the whiteboard. "This is our target. Aiden Phillips. Considered armed and dangerous. He is the prime suspect in two recent DC bombings. Dozens injured and killed. Phillips is ex–Special Forces and a former patient at the VA hospital in Richmond, where he was treated for a variety of mental-health issues."

Mahoney next taps the schematic. "Recon tells us he's in the end unit, number fourteen. For the past few months, he's been working as a security guard at a construction site up the road. Two weeks ago, he was fired."

"For cause?" one of the troopers calls out.

"Yep. Got in a fistfight with his shift supervisor," says Mahoney. He opens a folder and plucks out a slip of paper. He says, "Supervisor reports that Phillips said, quote, 'I smoked a lot of assholes like you in Afghanistan, and it'd be easy to do you too.' Unquote."

The room gets very quiet.

Mahoney continues, "The supervisor says Phillips drives a 2018 Ford F-150 pickup. Latest drive-by shows the truck is parked near his unit."

He turns back to the whiteboard. "Under normal circumstances, we'd have done some run-throughs with a mock-up of the motel." He looks out at the group. "But we don't have the time. And this isn't normal."

All around me, I see folks shifting in their chairs. Nervous, but itching for action. I know the feeling.

Mahoney points to the schematic of the motel. "The Virginia State Police tactical team will set up blocking units here in the wooded area behind the motel as well as in the wooded area to the south of the parking lot and in this abandoned gas station and convenience store on the north side."

He then points to an area in front of room 14. "HRT Alpha will be the breaching force. Once they gain entry, other HRTs will sweep in and provide support."

Mahoney checks his watch. "We execute at eleven hundred hours. Keep in mind, this guy is former Special Forces. He knows how to fight and how to resist. He's got the tactical skills to pull off two urban bombings and evade detection. But his head might be scrambled."

Mahoney puts down his pen and steps forward. "Let me make this clear: I want this guy alive. Wounded, bruised, bleeding, I don't care. But alive. It's very possible that he did not act alone, and we need to learn from him who his coconspirators are. Understood?"

Murmurs of assent from the team. Here and there a shouted "Yes, sir!" and "Roger that!"

Mahoney wraps it up. "Let me say again, as tempting as it might be, do *not* smoke the son of a bitch."

I'm glad to hear the point emphasized. Because I want Aiden Phillips to survive long enough to be questioned, and when he is, I intend to be the first in line.

CHAPTER 48

TOM PETTY GOT IT right. The waiting is the hardest part.

Rizzo and I are crammed together with Mahoney and two FBI technicians in the rear of a van kitted out with communications gear, computers, and video screens. Behind the wheel in front is an FBI agent with a beard and long hair. He's wearing a tattered baseball cap, dirty jeans, and a sweatshirt.

From the outside, the van isn't much to look at. Faded blue paint, rusted body, bald tires, tinted windows. Stick-on letters say STEVE'S LANDSCAPING with a fake local phone number. We're parked on the side of Route 40 about half a mile from the Sunset Shores Motel.

Inside, we sit on metal stools staring at two of the video screens. One screen displays the feed from a video camera hidden in the woods on the south end of the parking lot, giving us a good view of the building and room 14. Aiden Phillips's room.

The second feed is coming from a stealth drone overhead; it shows an external view of the motel and an infrared image of the room's interior.

"He's there," mutters Rizzo, pointing at the screen on the left.

I nod. "Sure looks like it."

The infra shows a glowing red image right where the motel bed likely is.

The Ford pickup is still sitting in front of the unit. Unlike every other vehicle in the parking lot, it's backed in, facing the highway.

I tap the screen. "See that? He's positioned for a quick escape."

Mahoney picks up a handheld radio. "All teams, this is Alpha. Maintain radio silence. Drone is showing a heat source coming from the room's interior, left side. No motion. Target could be sleeping."

A digital clock over the screens counts down.

Three minutes to go.

I'm suddenly feeling very claustrophobic. I don't like being safe and secure in the rear of a van. I want to be with the entry team.

But that's not my job today.

My job is to observe and investigate. Doesn't mean I have to like it.

Two minutes to go.

Rizzo looks at me. "You're not used to sitting on your ass, are you?"

"No. I'm not. I'd rather be the first one through the door."

"Me too," she says. "With a fire team right behind me."

We have a lot in common, me and Rizzo.

One minute to go.

The clock hits 11:00.

Mahoney puts the radio to his mouth. "This is Alpha. All units, execute!"

I lean forward, my face just inches from the video screen on the right. I watch as a brown UPS truck rolls into the parking lot and stops near room 14, blocking the Ford pickup. An FBI agent in UPS brown steps out with a package and an electronic keypad.

As he starts walking casually toward the motel's office at the other end of the building, the UPS truck's side door slides open and four heavily armed HRT special agents jump out. One is carrying a metal battering ram. Another holds a small sledgehammer. The other two have ballistic shields on their backs.

The agent with the ram smashes Aiden Phillips's door in as the guy with the sledgehammer breaks the small side window and tosses in an M84 stun grenade—a flash-bang.

I see the flash and a burst of smoke. Anybody in that room is now blinded by the light and deafened by the 170-decibel blast.

The door is hanging loose on its hinges. The two agents with ballistic shields lead the way into the room.

Mahoney slaps the van driver on the shoulder. "Now! Go!"

CHAPTER 49

THE SECOND OUR VAN comes to a full stop in the motel parking lot, Rizzo opens the rear door and jumps out.

"Anna! Wait!" I'm right behind her.

Ned Mahoney is right behind me.

A dark green Lenco BearCat armored vehicle roars into the lot and brakes to a halt. The rear doors fly open and ten members of the Virginia State Police tactical team swarm out. Even more emerge from the woods, all converging on the broken door of room 14.

A few other doors in the motel pop open. Troopers wave the gawkers back inside. Mahoney and I move in front of Rizzo. I have my Glock at the ready. As we get closer, I can smell the smoke from the flash-bang.

One of the entry-team officers comes out and takes off his helmet. He looks at Mahoney and shakes his head.

Mahoney kicks the bottom of the doorjamb with his boot. "Damn it!"

When I lean in through the open door, another agent stops me.

"Careful," he says. "The bomb disposal tech is taking care of business."

Rizzo is right behind me. "What's in there? Explosives?"

"Slowly," the agent says. "Don't crowd around."

Inside, I see an FBI tech on his knees closely examining a curved gray-green plastic case that's sitting on short legs a few inches off the floor.

My gut flutters. I've seen hundreds of these things.

It's a Claymore mine.

Embossed across the plastic in bold letters are three words: FRONT TOWARD ENEMY.

Meaning us.

"Impressive," says Rizzo. "He didn't just pick that up at an army surplus store." She's right. The Claymore is one of the deadliest antipersonnel weapons ever devised. The curved plastic case contains shaped C-4 explosive and about seven hundred steel balls, each about an eighth of an inch in diameter. A perfect close-range killing device.

If the Claymore had gone off, the entry team and anybody within about fifty yards of the front of the device would have been shredded.

But it hadn't gone off.

"Why didn't it detonate?" asks Rizzo.

The tech picks up a nearly invisible length of fishing line. "It should have," he says. "One end is tied to a triggering device. The other end was tied to that eye hook in the door. Either he didn't have time to tie it off or the knot didn't hold."

I walk over to the bed, where two agents are standing.

Twisted under the covers are two electric blankets, radiating heat.

"Smart little bastard," says Rizzo from behind me.

I holster my gun. "Right now, he's smarter than us."

CHAPTER 50

I STEP OUTSIDE THE room for some fresh air. FBI forensics techs are swarming over the pickup truck. I hear a roar from overhead. Another Black Hawk? Nope. It's a news helicopter.

Somebody must have reported the bang or spotted all the black uniforms and called a tip line. I'm sure the news crew above us was expecting to see carnage. If it bleeds, it leads.

I step back into the motel room. Rizzo is talking shop with the bomb squad. I notice that the room's walls are bare except for a white sheet tacked up behind the bed.

Mahoney nudges my elbow. "What's that about?" he asks. "Movie screen?"

"Don't touch it until the techs clear it," says Rizzo. "It might be booby-trapped."

"Sir?" an agent says from behind us. I turn around. Standing beside the agent is a stout middle-aged woman in black stretch pants and an Epcot sweatshirt.

"Who's this?" asks Mahoney.

"Margie Coffey," the agent says. "She owns the motel."

Mahoney holds up his ID. "Ned Mahoney, FBI."

Coffey isn't impressed. "What the hell just happened here?" she asks. From the sound of her voice, she's a longtime smoker. "And who the hell is gonna pay for it?"

"Sorry, Ms. Coffey," says Mahoney. "I apologize for the mess. This was an FBI and state police raid."

"You couldn't give me a heads-up, at least?"

"That's not how we work. We're searching for a criminal suspect and we couldn't afford any tip-offs." Mahoney pulls a folded printout from a side pocket. "Do you recognize this man?"

Coffey pulls a pair of glasses from her pocket and puts them on. She leans in toward the picture. "Sure," she says. "That's Aiden. Good guy. What did he do?"

"That's what we're trying to find out," says Mahoney.

I step up and introduce myself. "Ms. Coffey, I'm John Sampson, DC Metro Police. You said Phillips was a good guy? What do you mean by that? Good how?"

"Paid his bill every week," says Coffey. "None of the usual bullshit about waiting for a paycheck to come in. He even paid me extra to leave him alone. Didn't want anybody coming in and cleaning his room. He'd pick up clean towels and sheets at the office and bring the dirties back in a sack, nice and neat."

"Any visitors while he was here?" Mahoney asks. "Deliveries? Dates?"

"Not that I saw," says Coffey. "Like I said, he kept to himself, paid his bills, gave me extra every week." She looks around the room and shakes her head. "Now, tell me again, who's gonna pay for all this?"

"There's a claims process with the government," says Mahoney. "We'll get you the forms."

"The government? And how long will that take? A year? Ten years? Forever?" Margie Coffey waves her hand in disgust and turns to leave.

I step in front of her. "How did he sleep?" I ask.

Coffey stops. Takes off her glasses. "To tell you the truth, terrible. I live right above the office, and some nights I could hear him yelling from his room—awful screams. A couple of times, he woke up the guests in the next room. When I knocked on his door, he came out wrapped in a sheet, so apologetic. Told me he had nightmares. Other nights, I'd come home late and see him sitting in a lawn chair outside his room, covered in a blanket, smoking a cigarette and drinking a beer, looking out into the distance but like he wasn't really seeing anything."

"You mean like a thousand-yard stare?" I ask.

"That's exactly right," says Coffey. "A thousand-yard stare. How did you know?"

"Because I've seen it a thousand times."

CHAPTER 51

I SLIP MARGIE COFFEY my business card. "Please call me if you remember anything else about Aiden Phillips."

She looks around. "Only if you promise to pay for the room damage."

"You file the forms, and I'll make it happen. I promise."

From her expression, I don't think she believes me.

On her way out, Coffey steps around Rizzo, who's on her hands and knees on the worn orange carpet, staring at the bottom of the door.

"Interesting," Rizzo says. She dangles the trip wire with the eye hook at the end. "The knot was secure. The line was intact. But the bottom of the door has dry rot. Looks like when the entry team hit the trip wire, the eye hook popped out of the wood."

I reach down to pick up the tiny piece of hardware. "I guess we should thank Margie for letting the place go to hell."

"Detective Sampson!" one of the techs calls from the bathroom.

Rizzo gets to her feet and we walk over together. Mahoney is already in there.

Inside the tiny room, a forensics tech is dusting a broken mirror over a cracked porcelain sink.

The center of the mirror is smashed. When I lean in, I can see dried brownish bloodstains in the cracks. "Looks like a fist punched into it. Guess something set him off. But what?"

"Who knows?" says Mahoney with a surly attitude. "Maybe the death count for the bombings wasn't high enough for him. Maybe he was having a flashback to Kandahar. Maybe his internet got glitchy. I think we've established that the guy is a head case."

Rizzo, Mahoney, and I leave the bathroom, and I hear a tech on a stepladder next to the sheet on the wall say, "All clear. No wires. No timers. No fuses. We're good to take this down."

He gets off the ladder as we all move closer.

"Can I do it?" asks Rizzo.

"Be my guest," says Mahoney.

Rizzo steps onto the ladder and yanks out the pushpin that's holding up the top left corner of the sheet. The sheet falls away, exposing the wall behind it.

Everybody in the room looks up and stops working. The place goes quiet.

One of the techs is the first to speak. "Holy shit" is all she says.

A guy on the forensics team picks up his camera and starts snapping pictures.

"Nobody touch anything," cautions Mahoney. "Just document it."

I step forward until I'm only a few feet away. *Jesus!*

The wall is filled with taped-up clippings from *USA Today*, the

Washington Post, the *New York Times,* and the *Richmond Times-Dispatch,* all fitted together like a madman's mosaic.

The stories and pictures are on a single topic: the DC bombings. In some spots, there are circles in red marker. A circle around the word *dead* in a headline. Another around a picture of a blackened baby stroller. Another around a close-up of a bloody shoe.

Rizzo steps back from the ladder and looks at me. "John, what the hell is this? Some kind of sick scrapbook?"

"Not quite. I've seen displays like this before. It's his trophy wall."

CHAPTER 52

Cross

ALEX CROSS'S RINGING PHONE wakes him from a bad dream. He grabs it from the hotel nightstand and slides to answer. His eyes are so blurry from sleep that he doesn't even see the caller ID.

"Hello, this is Alex Cross."

"Hello, love."

"Bree, it warms me just to hear your voice." He settles back against the pillow in the dark room and checks the time on his phone. It's just after midnight. "How are things in DC?"

Bree sighs. "I just got home. Things are crazy at Bluestone. We're coordinating with the FBI, Homeland Security, and everybody else about the bombings. But at least Nana Mama left a plate for me. How's it going down there?"

Alex lets out a long breath. "I wish I could say we've had a breakthrough. I feel like we're just plodding on."

"I heard you showed yourself on TV. Did you plan that?"

"No. I just happened into an ambush," says Alex. "I was stupid. I should have used the rear entrance. But once the media found me, I figured I might as well make use of the platform."

"What's the plan for tomorrow? Are you going to go search in the reserve again?"

"I think Melissa is trying to rally the troops for another pass, but I doubt we'll get the cadets again. I'm heading to campus to talk to the head of the psychology department. Cold call. I want to find out why he's not concerned about Lucas and Tyne disappearing. There's got to be more there."

"Agreed," says Bree. "Those two go missing, then Damon? I don't believe in coincidences like that."

"Is Bluestone getting anything on Damon's tip line?"

"Nothing useful so far," says Bree. "Just some reported sightings of Damon at various shops or bars around campus. All before he disappeared. Plus a few cranks leaving nasty hate messages or asking why valuable police resources are being wasted on looking for a grad student who's probably out somewhere drunk or high. Oh, and we've also had a few psychics who say he's near water or trees."

"That's a big help," says Alex, rubbing his eyes. "What about ransom demands?"

"A few," says Bree. "All flaky."

"Like what?"

"One demanding a million dollars in Bitcoin sent to an encrypted account on Tor. Another wants two million in cash in a lunch box. That kind of thing. But no proof that there's any connection to Damon."

"People watch too many movies."

"Everyone thinks they know how to game the system. Most of the ransom calls are coming from burner phones, guys thinking they'll stay anonymous," says Bree. "But they won't. Sooner or later, we'll track down every one of these bastards and charge them with extortion."

"Small satisfaction," says Alex. "That won't bring Damon home."

"I'm working on another angle," says Bree. "It's tied to the DC bombings."

"The bombings? How?"

"It's not out yet, but they've identified a suspect. Ex–Special Forces, anti-government, experience with explosives, spent time in the psychiatric ward of a VA hospital."

"What does that have to do with Damon?"

"Bluestone is using a proprietary software program to help track the bomber's associations and movements over the years. It uses AI and algorithmic programs to find word patterns and key words in communications systems, from open email to internal intranet systems."

Alex is getting impatient. "Bree, spare me the details. How does this help?"

"I'm tight with one of the techs on the team," says Bree. "I talked to him an hour ago. I convinced him to help with our search for Damon and insert a line of code in the system to see if we can track his latest movements or find anyone talking about him. I told the tech I'd take full responsibility."

"Is that legal?" asks Alex.

"Absolutely not. It violates a couple of domestic intelligence surveillance laws and a few of my NDAs. If somebody finds it, I could be fired. Or called in front of a congressional committee."

Alex has always admired Bree's passion and ingenuity. And her willingness to take risks for the right reasons.

"I'm sure you thought long and hard about this," he says.

"I did," says Bree. "For about two seconds."

CHAPTER 53

Sampson

THIS MORNING, I'M RUNNING solo. Feels good for a change. I just hope I can accomplish my mission.

After the raid on Aiden Phillips's motel room yesterday, Ned Mahoney headed back to DC and Anna Rizzo to her lab in Maryland. A little while later, Mahoney sent me a text with a link to an address outside Richmond, Virginia—and the name of my target for today.

Lisa Phillips, wife of Aiden Phillips.

I follow the GPS south on I-95 to Trent Avenue, located in a pleasant-looking suburban neighborhood. The homes are two-story brick or wooden Colonial-type houses with front porches and nicely trimmed lawns.

"Your destination is on the right," says the upbeat GPS voice.

Sure enough, there's a mailbox at the end of the driveway with the name PHILLIPS.

I turn into the driveway and shut off the engine. I get out of the car, walk up the flagstone path, and ring the doorbell.

After a few seconds, the door opens. A girl about Willow's age is standing there. Plaid skirt, white blouse, and a blazer with a patch that says NOAH RIVER ACADEMY.

"Boy, you're tall!" the girl says. Big smile.

I smile back. "So I hear. Is your mom home?"

"Hold on, I'll get her." She turns around and calls, "Mom! There's a tall man at the door!"

A few seconds later, a woman comes to the door. She's wearing black pants, a white blouse, and a string of pearls around her neck. Blond, late thirties. Pleasant face. Cautious expression.

She rests one hand protectively on her daughter's shoulder. "Yes?" she asks. "Can I help you?"

"Are you Lisa Phillips?"

"I'm sorry, who are you?"

I hold my badge and ID in my right hand and lift it so she can look at them. "My name is John Sampson. I'm a detective with the DC Metro Police. I'm here about your husband, Aiden Phillips."

I watch the woman's reaction. She flinches like she's been stung by a hornet, then leans down and speaks softly to the girl. "Mary, honey, go upstairs now, and tell your brother I'll be up soon to check on him."

Mary stands her ground. "Why does the man want to talk about Daddy?"

"I'll tell you all about it later, hon. I promise."

The girl frowns but turns and heads up the staircase, stamping a little harder than necessary. Lisa Phillips opens the door a bit wider. She waits for her daughter to disappear upstairs. Then she leans in close to me. I can see the agony on her face.

"Is he dead?" she asks in a low voice.

I step inside. "No. I believe he's alive."

Her shoulders drop slightly as she whispers, "Thank God."

She leads me into a wide, luxurious living room with bookshelves, matching couches, and nicely upholstered chairs. On the near wall are a series of framed photos. I recognize Aiden Phillips in his dress military uniform, looking young, eager, supremely confident. *Like we all were.*

In the civilian photos, he's posing cheerfully with his wife and young children.

"Lovely house," I say.

Lisa ignores the compliment. She sits down on one of the sofas. "Where is he?" she asks. "Where's my husband?"

"I was hoping you could tell me, ma'am. Has he been home recently?"

Lisa lowers her head. "No. I haven't seen him for a long time."

"Not even to drop in on the kids?"

She shakes her head.

I point to a chair across from her. "Okay if I sit?"

She nods. I plant myself at the edge of the cushion.

"Ma'am, I know this won't be easy to hear, but your husband is being sought in connection with two bombings in Washington, DC. We know they weren't suicide bombings. And your husband was identified at both scenes. He's a definite suspect."

Lisa hunches forward and wraps her arms around her knees. I can see her trembling. "No, not Aiden. I heard about those terrible bombings. Just awful. There's no way he would do something so violent."

I lean forward, folding myself down so that my eyes are level with hers. "What makes you so sure? I assume you know that your husband has a criminal record."

"I know my husband," she says. Her voice is firm now. She sounds defiant. Or defensive. "I know he's made mistakes. He has a temper. But not this. No way."

"Lisa, your husband was photographed near the scenes of both explosions. After the fact."

"I don't believe that."

I take out my phone and click to the surveillance photos. Lisa leans in. I point to the first photo. "This was taken near the intersection of Thirteenth Street and N Street Northwest. The site of bomb number one."

Lisa's expression is blank.

I slide my finger and show her the next photo. "And this one was taken by the Vietnam Veterans Memorial. The site of bomb number two."

"The pictures are blurry," says Lisa. "You can't really tell if it's him."

I pull up another photo. "Is this your husband's military ID photo?"

She glances at it. "From the army. Yes."

"Ma'am, the Technical and Analytical Services Bureau of DC's Special Operations Division ran this picture through a photo identification program and compared it with the other two photos I showed you. Without getting too technical, they found multiple matching points in the facial measurements and proportions. All three of those pictures show the same man."

"What if it's one of those photo tricks?" asks Lisa. "AI. A deepfake."

"Not possible. That's your husband in those pictures. There is no doubt about it. None."

Lisa seems to melt. She rocks back on the couch and puts her hands over her mouth. Her eyes well with tears.

I can see that the truth has just hit her — like a freight train.

CHAPTER 54

I LET THE SILENCE hang between us for a few moments.

I can see how destroyed she is. How much she wants me to leave. But I think she knows I'm not going anywhere.

I fold my hands and wait.

She'll talk when she's ready.

Finally, Lisa Phillips shifts forward on the sofa. She wipes her eyes with the back of her hand, smearing her mascara. When she starts speaking again, her voice is quiet, but firm.

"Aiden is a patriot, a good soldier, a good husband, a great dad. He did his duty. Multiple deployments. But when he came back, he would never talk about it. He said what he did over there was better left alone."

"I understand. Sometimes that's the best way to handle it."

"Were you there too?" asks Lisa.

I nod. "Same place. Different time."

She sighs. "The kids just loved having him home. They were so proud of him. When they jumped all over him and hugged him, it was like this hard armor shell he had just faded away. But there were problems underneath that shell."

"What kind of problems?"

"I noticed small stuff at first. His having three beers with dinner instead of one. Nightmares that made his arms and legs shake. Small annoyances got outsize responses. Like if we were stuck in traffic, he'd get jumpy and angry. But we worked through it."

"You and Aiden are separated now, is that right?"

"His idea, not mine," says Lisa.

"Something must have happened to get you to that point."

"He was here at home when Afghanistan fell. After that, things just started cracking. He let his hair grow. His drinking got worse. He spent a lot of time watching cable news and just mumbling at the screen. 'A waste,' he kept saying. 'A goddamn waste. All those friends of mine, killed and crippled—for nothing.'"

"A lot of us felt that way. What happened next? Did things get worse?"

Lisa nods. "His dreams became more violent. Lots of yelling and flailing around. Aiden knew he was starting to scare me and the kids, so he checked himself into the VA hospital here in Richmond. He promised he'd come back better than before, but—"

She's interrupted by the thump of footsteps on stairs. I look over. It's Mary and her little brother peeking through the banister halfway down the staircase.

"Upstairs!" Lisa shouts. "Both of you!"

The kids retreat with startled expressions.

Lisa lowers her voice and leans closer: "One day he checked himself out of the facility against medical advice, and that was it.

We haven't seen him since. I've gotten a few phone calls from him, but he never says where he is. When I call back, the call never goes through." She dissolves into sobs again.

I grab a box of tissues from the coffee table and hand it to her. "Ma'am, if you have any idea where your husband is, it might save a lot of lives. It might save his."

She shakes her head. "I don't. I would tell you if I did, honest, but I have no idea."

I believe her.

"I gave my husband to the army, and they sent me back a haunted, broken man," she says sourly. "How is that fair? Tell me!"

"I can't. Because it's *not* fair. It's a goddamn disgrace."

CHAPTER 55

NOT LONG AFTER LEAVING Lisa Phillips, I'm in the parking lot of the sprawling VA hospital on Broad Rock Boulevard in Richmond. The main brick building of the hospital campus is directly in front of me.

I'm close enough to get a good look at the entrance. I watch patients come and go, some in wheelchairs or hobbling on crutches. Visitors walk in with flowers or balloons. Medical workers pass one another on their way in and out. Some are in a rush. Others stop and chat under the entrance canopy.

I glance down at my phone and check out the photo of the RN I'm looking for. Gina Maine. Lisa Phillips remembered the name. She told me that Aiden had liked her, that Gina treated him kindly. After a quick LinkedIn search, I came up with her profile picture. Round, friendly face. Pleasant smile.

I have 20/12 vision and a knack for remembering faces. Comes in handy as a detective for perps. Suspects. Witnesses. When I'm this close, it's not hard at all.

I spot Gina walking briskly toward the hospital entrance, looking both ways as she crosses the driveway. She's in white sneakers and light blue scrubs, has a bag over her left shoulder, and is carrying a Starbucks cup in her right hand. Her brown hair is in a short bob and she's wearing old-fashioned black-rimmed eyeglasses.

I get out of my rental car and walk at an angle to intercept her about ten feet from the door. "Excuse me. Gina Maine?"

Gina stops and turns around. I can tell she's scoping me out to see if she recognizes me.

She doesn't. "Yes?" she says warily. "Who are you?"

I pull out my ID and badge. "I'm John Sampson, a detective with Washington, DC, Metro Police. I just need a few minutes of your time."

She starts backing toward the door. "Sorry. I don't have any time to spare. I'm almost late for my shift." She turns and walks off. I follow her.

"Ma'am, please. Just one minute. I'm conducting an investigation that involves one of your former patients."

Gina stops and turns. She shakes her head. "Sorry, can't talk to you about that. HIPAA regs. You should know that. You need to file the paperwork, get my supervisor's approval, maybe talk to the hospital lawyers."

I put my badge away and try a softer touch.

"I understand. It's just that the patient's wife said you were his favorite nurse, that you paid attention to him, listened to him when others didn't."

Flattery. But also the truth.

Gina looks around. Her eyes narrow a bit. She takes a step

closer. I can tell she's curious. She lowers her voice: "What's the patient's name?"

"Aiden Phillips."

Her eyebrows shoot up. "Shit! Why didn't you say that in the first place?"

CHAPTER 56

GINA MAINE PULLS OUT her cell phone. She calls up to her floor and asks somebody to cover her patients for ten minutes.

"Follow me," she says, leading the way to a bench near a green stretch of grass. "Is Aiden in trouble?"

I take a seat alongside her on the bench and wait for a group in scrubs to pass by.

"I'm sorry to say we're looking for him in connection with the DC bombings."

I see Gina's face fall. She stares down at the ground. "You mean another vet going psycho? I hate those stories."

"I do too. Because they're mostly lies. But not this time, I'm afraid."

"What makes you say that?"

"We have evidence. Photos of him at the scenes."

Gina looks up. "No way. Aiden was troubled, but he wasn't

crazy." She turns to me, looks closely at me for the first time. "Did you serve, Detective?"

"I did. Iraq, Afghanistan. Other places."

"Afghanistan? That's where Aiden was too," she says.

"Different units. And I don't think our deployments overlapped."

"Would've been pretty ironic if you had run into each other there, I guess."

"What can you tell me about him?"

"This is off the record?"

"Just between us."

"You're not recording this?"

"Nope." I raise my palms. "I'm just listening."

Gina looks around, then slides a little closer to me on the bench. "Aiden was part of a recent patient surge we've had. The Kabul Kids, we call them. A lot of them got shook up after Kabul fell."

"And after what happened with the evacuation, right?"

"*Evacuation?* How about *utter disaster?* Aiden says it was like passengers on a sinking ship running for the last lifeboats, kicking and screaming to get the last spot."

"That's how it looked to me too. Not our finest hour."

Gina stares out over the grass. "Some of those patients had done two or three tours over there. They lost friends. Lost limbs or parts of their skulls. And then, after twenty years of promising the Afghans a better life, we just let the Taliban walk in and take over. In *days!* We had a lot of PTSD patients who were consumed with guilt, shame, a sense of loss."

"And Aiden? What was his issue?"

"Rage, pure and simple," says Gina. "And I don't blame him. He was furious at the way things got swept under the rug, with no one held responsible. After all the hearings and investigations, how many Defense or State Department officials were fired? How many generals were disciplined or forced to retire?"

Simple answer. "Not one."

"Right," says Gina. "He told me that he could have been brought up on charges if he lost a piece of equipment in the field, but then seven billion dollars' worth of military gear gets left behind for the Taliban, and no one says anything. He talked about the double standard all the time."

I turn the topic back to Aiden's hospital stay. "How long was Aiden a patient here?"

"About two months. He self-admitted, without a doctor's referral."

"What was he like?"

"Kept to himself, mostly," says Gina. "He told me he checked himself in because he didn't want to scare his wife and kids. He said he'd put them through enough already."

"You said Aiden's issue was rage. Did you ever see him get angry or violent?"

"Hold on," says Gina, suddenly nervous again. "Should I be telling you this stuff?"

"I could get a warrant for the hospital records, but that would take time I don't have. Besides, I'd rather hear it from somebody who knew Aiden Phillips. Somebody who understood what he was going through."

Gina checks her watch. "They'll be looking for me upstairs…" She starts to stand.

I put my hand on her shoulder. "Just tell me what you saw. What you heard."

She takes a deep breath and settles back down. "Okay. We had a new doctor on our wing. Dr. Tosi. Army captain. Full of himself. The kind of guy who thought he pissed golden honey."

"Yeah. I know the type. I served with a few."

"So I heard that Tosi was leading a group discussion and one of the vets had had a moment. He was shaking. Didn't want to join the conversation. Tosi started pushing him and pushing him. And finally, Aiden spoke up and told Tosi to leave the guy alone."

"Then what happened?"

Gina rubs her face. "I guess it escalated from there. Tosi kept saying it was his session, his patients, his rules. Aiden told him to back off. Tosi told Aiden to sit down and shut up. That's when Aiden jumped up and punched him out. Absolutely *flattened* him. Everybody just sat there, stunned. Aiden said something like 'Session's over.' Then he went back to his room, packed up his stuff, and took off. That was the last time I saw him."

Interesting. I suppose that explained the checking himself out of the facility against medical advice. "Did the VA or the doctor press charges?" I ask.

Gina shakes her head and cracks a small smile. "Dr. Tosi filed a complaint, but it went nowhere. They couldn't find any witnesses. All the other patients said they were taking a bathroom break when it happened. Within a week, Tosi was gone. Transferred to Fort Hood."

My phone buzzes. It's a text from Rizzo.

Call me.

Gina stands up. "Listen, Detective, Aiden's the kind of guy who'll punch out a senior officer to protect one of his own. But bombings? Innocent people? I can't see it. I just can't. I don't think his heart is that dark."

I wish I could agree.

CHAPTER 57

Cross

ALEX CROSS SITS IN the office of Dr. Reuben Chase, head of UNC's department of psychology. The space is luxuriously decorated with fine furniture and bookcases filled with leather volumes. Chase is a slim man, wearing a crisp dark gray suit, white shirt, red tie. He has a spare white beard and the kind of expression that gives nothing away.

"How can I help you, Mr. Cross?"

Alex smiles. "*Dr.* Cross."

"Of course, my apologies. *Dr.* Cross."

"I assume you know that my son Damon is missing."

"Of course. The faculty is sick about it. Any new information?"

"Nothing that I can share right now."

"Is there anything I can do?"

Alex leans forward. "Yes. You can help me figure out why nobody here seems concerned that Professor Darius Lucas and one of his grad students, Amy Tyne, have also disappeared."

Chase rocks back in his chair and folds his hands over his vest. "The two of them aren't missing, Dr. Cross. They're undertaking important research in their field of study."

"Private research?"

"*Sensitive* research."

"Then they should have been more careful with their cover story."

"I beg your pardon?"

"One of the other teaching assistants told my son and some other students that Lucas and Tyne were investigating an abandoned cemetery for enslaved people in Tennessee."

"And?"

"That story is bogus, Dr. Chase. You know it's not true. That's not where they are."

Cross can see that he's making the professor uncomfortable. Which is exactly his intent.

Chase clears his throat. "Dr. Cross, you're a man of science. You've been in the academic world. Surely you understand that there are times when promising new avenues of research need to be kept confidential so that there is no undue pressure or outside influence."

"Meaning you don't want to risk alerting your big donors until you know what the research is going to reveal."

"The research at this point is exploratory. Professor Lucas and his assistant are unavailable but totally safe."

"You're in touch with them?"

"All I will say is that they're overseas. We agreed that this project would be handled confidentially."

"I get it," says Alex. "No phone calls. No emails. You could at least have done a better job of pretending they were in Tennessee. That's basic spy craft."

Chase stands up. "We're not spies, Dr. Cross. We're educators. Is there anything else?"

Alex gets up from his chair. "You're telling me that there's absolutely no connection between whatever Lucas and Tyne are engaged in and my son's disappearance?"

"Yes. That's what I'm telling you. Trust me."

"Sorry," says Alex. "I'm running low on trust right now."

CHAPTER 58

Sampson

I FIND ANNA RIZZO in front of her computer screen, as usual. She sits up and brightens a bit when I walk in. I have to admit I brighten a bit too. She has that effect on me.

"Where have you been, stranger?" she asks.

"On a trip down memory lane."

"Meaning what?"

I quickly brief Rizzo on my talks with Lisa Phillips and Gina Maine, the two women who seem to know our suspect Aiden Phillips best. "They both say he couldn't have done it."

"Well, I say let's follow the evidence."

"So what's going on here?" I ask. "Why did you text me?"

Rizzo picks up a sheaf of papers and shakes it in my direction. "Initial reports from the FBI and ATF forensics teams. Other than the newspaper clippings and the Claymore, the place was totally clean."

"What do you mean? Didn't we get a blood match on the broken mirror?"

"Yes, but that just proves Phillips was there, which we already knew. According to the reports, there were no traces of C-4. No traces of fuel or fertilizer. No wires, no fuses, no electronics, nothing. No bomb-making material at all."

"Are we surprised? That was his crib, not his workshop."

"I know, I know. But there should have been *something* there."

"You mean trace evidence."

"Exactly. If he'd been working with C-4 or ammonium nitrate, he should have transferred it to the sheets and towels. We took apart the toilet, the sink trap, the shower. But there was nothing."

"So maybe he wore PPE while he worked. Or showered someplace else."

Rizzo tosses down the reports. "All we know for sure is that Aiden Phillips was in the room and that he was obsessed with the bombings."

"*And* that he planted a Claymore mine in his hideout. It could have taken out the assault team. It could have ended you and me both."

"I've been thinking about that too," says Rizzo. "What if that loose trip wire wasn't a mistake? I mean, would a master bomb maker be that careless? What if the Claymore was never meant to go off?"

"That's a pretty dangerous kind of mind game."

"I don't think we're dealing with a totally rational mind."

I roll a chair over next to Rizzo's. "From what Lisa and Gina told me, Aiden Phillips is a very angry man."

Rizzo nods. "Combat vet with anger issues. Hostile toward authority. Definitely fits the profile. At least, that's what the experts would say."

"But you're not convinced." I can read it in her face.

Rizzo turns in her chair. She points to the framed bit of charred American flag, the one I'd noticed on my first visit. She clears her throat. "At one point in my deployment, my unit was responsible for a stretch of highway outside Jalalabad. Our job was to locate IEDs and dig them up or detonate them every morning before the convoys passed through."

I was on that road myself many times. Pros like Anna Rizzo kept me from being killed more than once. "You were doing God's work," I tell her.

"One day," Rizzo continues, "I just had a feeling. We'd already done one sweep that morning, but I wanted to go out again. The CO said no. The experts had told him that they'd just reached a truce with a local tribal leader and that the road was safe. He told me that going back would disrespect the elder, show that we didn't trust him. So I shut up and stood down. The next convoy that went out got hit. Multiple KIAs."

Rizzo taps the frame over the charred scrap of flag. "That came from the lead Humvee. About all that was left. It's my little reminder: Never trust the experts."

CHAPTER 59

Bree

BREE STONE LOOKS OUT through the glass wall of her office onto Bluestone's main floor. At midnight, the place is still humming.

She'd spoken with John Sampson earlier; he wanted to know if there'd been any progress in North Carolina.

"Alex has a few leads he's chasing down, but nothing solid," Bree told him. "The locals aren't really exerting themselves to help."

"I should be down there with him," Sampson lamented.

"You and me both," said Bree. "But we've got our work cut out for us here. Alex knows that."

Bree glances at her coworkers, hunkered in cubicles over laptops or tapping on their phones. A lot of them aren't much older than Damon. Bree is the most old-school investigator in Bluestone's cyberworld. Day to day, she relies on her experience and judgment.

But right now, she's questioning that judgment. She's taking a risk that could put her whole career in jeopardy.

Bree rolls her chair close to her desk and pulls out a slip of paper with the proprietary passcode an associate gave her, the eight-number key to a software patch that will let her isolate information about Damon from the official searches related to the DC bombings. The passcode will grant access to the private data tranche from her terminal and nobody else's.

Bree angles her screen away from the glass wall. Elena, her boss, is still in a late meeting with DC Metro. She hopes nobody will pop into her office unannounced.

She types in the code and waits.

It takes only a few seconds for Damon's entire digital life to download in front of her. Page after page. Image after image. Site after site.

Bree sets a timeline limit for two weeks back and starts scrolling. The code is a crude edit to the main program, so the results are scattered and unorganized — a hodgepodge of GPS locators, credit card charges, Venmo payments, online searches, text messages, and emails, including his most recent ones to her and Alex days ago. But nothing after the morning he rode away on his bike. No communication or activity at all after that time.

Digitally speaking, Damon has simply disappeared.

Bree whips through a mosaic of images scraped from Damon's iPhone library. She blinks and goes quickly past a series of Melissa posing playfully in the bedroom of the Maxwell Road apartment. She sees selfies of Damon with friends, with his bike, with his YMCA youth basketball team. She sees photos from a free-speech workshop, a voter-registration rally, and an anti-discrimination march. Bree freezes on a few of the frames and zooms in. Could whoever took Damon be lurking in one of those crowds?

She scrolls back and isolates an online-forum discussion from a few days before Damon was last seen. She finds conversations about Michaelson Woods, arrangements for protests, links to human-rights blogs.

Bree clicks through the conversations, looking for locations, meeting times, travel plans. She checks for bus tickets or plane or hotel reservations.

Nothing.

As she sifts through Damon's online forums, Bree lands on a platform with an odd-looking interface. She's familiar with Discord and Slack, but this is different. Totally encrypted with crude graphics like a throwback to the early days of AOL or Prodigy.

At the top of one forum, Bree spots the username Stonewall. A gay-rights discussion? Then she notices the other handles on the scroll: Lee. Davis. Longstreet. All icons of the Confederacy.

The snippets of exchanges here hit her like a gut punch.

> White makes right, am I right?
> MLK. No big loss.
> Clean up America! Bring back White-Only bathrooms!
> Black Crimes Matter!

Bree blinks hard at the casual cruelty of the hatred on display. What the hell was Damon doing in alt-right forums like this? Had he been spying? Trying to track these haters?

Then Bree has a horrible thought. What if it's the other way around?

What if they've been tracking *Damon*?

CHAPTER 60

Sampson

THE LAST THING I remember before falling asleep last night is passing Willow's empty bedroom, seeing a framed photo of the two of us on her bureau, and thinking how grateful I was that she was at the Cross house, safe and secure with people who love her as much as I do.

The next thing I know, my doorbell is ringing. Damn. Is it morning already?

I roll out of bed, still in my clothes, feeling achy and fuzzy-headed. And a little bit paranoid.

I reach into my nightstand and push my thumb against an ID pad. A small gun safe pops up. I pull out my service weapon and head downstairs.

The doorbell rings again, followed by a few hard knocks.

I check the simple camera setup that lets me see who's on the doorstep. I could have gotten a fancier electronic surveillance system, but those can easily be hacked. Sometimes old-school is best.

I see two men in dark suits looking around. Feds or law enforcement. Or Mormons.

I slip my gun into my rear waistband and open the door.

"Good morning, gentlemen. Can I help you?"

The guy on the left has short brown hair and rimless eyeglasses. Slight and slim. Looks like an accountant. His companion is bald with dense black eyebrows. He's got a thick build and wears an ill-fitting wrinkled jacket.

The accountant-looking guy steps up. "Detective John Sampson?"

"Who's asking?"

In perfect sync, they both hold up small leather wallets with government IDs.

"Roland Perkins, CIA," says the accountant. "This is my associate Tom Walsh. Can we have a few moments?"

"You already woke me up, so you might as well come in." I step aside as they both pass through the doorway. I nod toward the kitchen. "Coffee?"

My visitors both turn me down, so I make a cup just for myself in my WORLD'S GREATEST DAD mug. A Father's Day gift from Willow.

I sit down and stretch out my long legs. "You're here about the bombings, right?"

Walsh, the heavyset one, adjusts himself in his seat. "Who says?" His tone is a little snappish.

I sip my coffee and check my watch. "Because it's the only case I'm working on. Also, it's the only kind of case that merits a visit from federal officers this early in the morning."

Perkins speaks up. "Detective, we're here to offer our help. I apologize for Officer Walsh. He's just got in from overseas. Bad case of jet lag."

I lean in. "Apology accepted. Which section you with?"

"I'm with the Office of the Inspector General. Officer Walsh is in the field."

I look at Walsh. "So CIA paramilitary." That explains the bad suit. He probably hasn't bought a new one in years.

Walsh stares at me with steely eyes. I glance down at his hands. They're scarred and lumpy with a few patches of healed burns. Definitely not a desk jockey.

I look back at Perkins. "You say you're here to help?"

"That's correct. We want Aiden Phillips as much as you do."

Walsh speaks up again. "A few years ago, Phillips was temporarily detached from army Special Forces and brought into the Special Activities Center. He was skilled, focused, and good at his job. We offered him a permanent transfer, but he declined. Said he loved the army too damn much."

"Sounds like a stand-up American. And a loyal soldier."

"Not anymore, obviously," says Perkins. "We know that Metro Police, the FBI, the ATF, and the Virginia State Police had a little gathering in his motel room yesterday."

"Glad to hear you're up on the latest. But you still haven't said what you want from me."

"We've talked to your bosses at DC Metro," says Perkins. "You're now a contract consultant with CIA."

"Meaning what? Do I get a raise?"

Walsh doesn't appreciate my joke. "It means we'll pass along information to you if you agree to pass along information to us."

"Okay. What've you got that we don't?"

"For starters," says Walsh, "some names you'd never find on your own."

"Look," says Perkins, "we're on the same team. We want to stop the bombings."

It can't be that simple. With CIA, it never is. "What's the connection? Did Phillips come back to work for you?"

"That's right," says Perkins. "After Kabul fell, he had a change of heart. He contacted us and we put him back into our Special Activities Center."

"Where'd you send him?"

"Back to Afghanistan. Under our wing."

"How many missions?"

"Just one," says Perkins.

"What was the mission?"

"Classified," says Walsh.

I take a sip of my coffee and look back and forth between them. "Let me guess. He went rogue."

CHAPTER 61

I CAN ALWAYS TELL when I've hit a nerve.

The two CIA agents look at each other. Walsh fiddles with his wrinkled lapel.

"What did Phillips do when he stepped out on you?" I ask.

Perkins breaks the silence. "Broke a bunch of laws and regulations. He joined up with other Special Forces members out there, freelancing, conducting confidential missions against orders. He self-deployed for about six months before coming back stateside. We also know he later spent some time in a VA hospital in Virginia, then checked himself out after some trouble there."

"A month after that," says Walsh, "is when the first bomb went off."

"You guys think there's a link between those bombings and what Phillips was up to overseas?"

"We *know* there's a link," says Perkins.

I sit quietly for a minute, running through the case in my mind. Every conversation. Every interview. Every detail.

Then it hits me.

"The C-4! That's it, right? When ATF asked Langley for the taggants we found, somebody got spooked. Because the taggants matched the supply Phillips brought back from his mission in Afghanistan."

Perkins and Walsh look at me but say nothing. Which means I'm on the right track.

I decide to keep going. "Whatever he was doing over there needs to stay buried. So you guys need to get to Phillips before he decides to go public with something that will compromise the Company."

"We think Phillips was deep in-country, trying to rescue some interpreters and informants who worked for us before the fall," admits Perkins. "He failed in that mission, but he brought out some of the C-4 that we left behind. Stuff that had been in the hands of the Taliban."

"Why would he take it?" I ask.

"Maybe he was planning the bombings already," Perkins says. "Maybe he figured there'd be no way to trace it."

I can see Walsh getting itchy in his ill-fitting suit. "So are you with us or not?" he asks bluntly.

"Tell you what. Add Anna Rizzo from ATF to the team. Make her a consultant too," I say. I don't know how much leverage I have with these guys, but why not push it? "Give her the taggant data and anything else she asks for. We need to know how much C-4 Phillips had access to and how much he brought back with him. And how much he might have left in his stash."

"Okay," says Walsh. "We'll get Rizzo cleared."

Perkins stands up and pulls a card from his wallet. He puts it down on my counter. "We'll stay in touch. You do the same."

I pick up the card. "In other words, you keep my secrets and I keep yours."

"Something like that," says Walsh.

CHAPTER 62

Phillips

Forty-eight hours earlier...

NEAR THE PEAK OF a wooded hill overlooking the Sunset Shores Motel, Aiden Phillips lies flat on his belly, using his Zeiss monocular to observe activity at the motel.

He's got a radio receiver with a single earpiece, which allows him to listen in on the law enforcement frequencies while keeping one ear open for threats behind him.

But he doubts that anybody will bother him.

From the way the assault went down, it looks like the operation was quickly staged and executed. No blocking units on the road. No recon patrols in the woods. No hunt for a second getaway vehicle. Too much focus on searching the motel room and impounding his pickup truck. Probably assuming the former occupant is miles away.

Overhead, Phillips hears the hum of a surveillance drone, but he's not worried. His ghillie suit has a built-in barrier to deflect thermal imaging. From above, he looks like just another leafy lump in the woods.

Even from ten feet away, nobody could spot him. He's that well camouflaged.

Phillips watches the FBI agent in charge speaking with the motel owner, Margie Coffey. Nice lady. Always concerned about him. He feels bad about breaking the mirror. But the rage came on so fast, he couldn't stop himself.

That was weak.

He can't afford to be weak.

Phillips recognizes the tall Black man talking to the FBI supervisor: Detective John Sampson. This is serious business, bringing in a heavy hitter like him. From what Phillips knows, Sampson is tight with Dr. Alex Cross, the famous forensic psychologist.

But Cross has his own problems, Phillips has learned. A missing son down in North Carolina. Good. Maybe that'll keep him out of this case.

A stern-looking Hispanic woman with ATF on her blue windbreaker comes into view. That must be Anna Rizzo — a sharp investigator, according to Phillips's research. And a former EOD specialist with the U.S. Army.

Another Afghanistan vet. Like Sampson.

Like him.

In a fair fight, Phillips knows Rizzo and Sampson would beat him in no time.

Unfortunately for them, he doesn't play fair.

Phillips keeps watching until the sun sets, then slips away to the Dodge Charger he hid deep in the woods under a camo tarp.

The vehicle they never found.

The one they never even looked for.

CHAPTER 63

IT WAS HARDER TO locate a good vantage point today, but Aiden Phillips lucks out in finding an abandoned house about half a block away from his target.

All signs scream *empty house*. It takes him only a few minutes to check for surveillance cameras and determine there are none. No lights. No sounds. No movement from inside. The lawn is unmowed. Looks like nobody's been here for quite a while.

Phillips enters through an unlocked cellar window, then scouts the second floor until locating the perfect spot for a nest. He drags a worn mattress over to a bay window, draws the shade down so that just a crack of daylight shines through, then settles in to wait.

The most important part of surveillance training—the part they never show in the movies—is learning how to be perfectly still. Ninety-nine percent of this work is waiting and waiting and then waiting some more—without losing focus.

Phillips saw what happened when a spotter on a two-man sniper team got twitchy after a few hours. What happened was the spotter got a bullet through his brain. So did his partner. That's one reason Phillips prefers to work alone.

In his gloved hands he again holds a Zeiss monocular. He scans the street, then settles the lens on a plain yellow Cape Cod–style house down the block.

The one belonging to Detective John Sampson.

The garage door is closed. There's a black sedan in the driveway. Government vehicle. Virginia plates.

As Phillips watches, the front door opens and two men in dark suits walk out. One thin, one thickset. Behind them, Sampson looks tired and annoyed.

The chunkier guy looks up and down the street. For a split second, he looks right into Phillips's lens.

Phillips recognizes him instantly, even in the business suit.

It's Tom Walsh from the CIA's Special Activities Center. He was Phillips's former contact in-country. And now, clearly, Walsh and his partner have connected with Sampson.

Phillips expected it to happen. And it didn't take long.

He's starting to wish he had his long rifle with him.

Blowing off Tom Walsh's head would be a gift to the world. And a deep source of personal satisfaction.

But there's other work to do this morning. As soon as Walsh and his buddy leave, Phillips disappears too.

Leaving no trace that he was ever there.

CHAPTER 64

Sampson

I PARK ABOUT TWO blocks away from the Cross house, still thinking about my meeting with the two CIA spooks. I'm looking forward to another classic Nana Mama breakfast and, even more than that, to seeing Willow. I miss my daughter's sweet little face.

I turn the corner and get a signal on my police radio.

Shit. What now? Can't I get one minute of peace?

I pull the radio up from my waistband. "Sampson, D-five, go."

"Dispatch, D-five, respond to fourteen forty Montgomery Northeast."

"Dispatch, Sampson, D-five, what's the situation?"

"Another bombing."

I turn around, run back to my car, and start driving—in the opposite direction from the Cross house. Away from Willow and my second family.

When I get a half a block from the site, patrol cars are blocking the street. I climb out of my car and hang the lanyard with my badge around my neck. I see broken glass and chunks of brick on the pavement. A whitish-gray cloud still hangs in the air.

This is a quiet DC neighborhood with mixed-use zoning, mostly three- and four-story brick apartment buildings and small offices.

But there's something different here.

I don't see any bodies in the street. No amputated limbs in the trees. No victims screaming on the curb.

The action is centered on a corner building just ahead. Two fire engines are already on scene, with firefighters hooking up hoses to hydrants. I see a team with axes and Halligan tools rushing into the entrance.

It looks like the whole side of the second floor facing the street has been blown out. Window frames are twisted; flames are licking around the edges. The brick siding is broken and blackened. On the street below, parked cars have huge dents and gashes from blast debris.

But there's no crater in the street. No burning cars.

The bomber has changed tactics.

This time, the blast came from the inside.

CHAPTER 65

IT DOESN'T TAKE LONG for DCFD to knock out the fire. Water pours down the side of the building and goes out through the door onto the street in a filthy, frothy stream.

"*John!*"

I turn to see Anna Rizzo running toward me, her go bag in her hand.

"What've we got?" she asks, short of breath.

I point to the second story. "It looks like the bastard decided to change tactics. He blew up an office floor."

Rizzo looks up at the torn hole in the brick, the shattered windows, and the scattered debris below.

Fire chief Pat Campbell heads over, his fire suit dripping wet and covered with soot. He gives me a nod as he walks up. We've been at dozens of scenes together over the years. "Hey, John. You got here fast."

"Yeah. Bombings are kind of my hobby these days." I pull Rizzo over. "Pat Campbell, DCFD, meet Anna Rizzo, ATF. She and I are working the case together."

Rizzo nods. "How many casualties, Chief?"

"Two dead upstairs with positive IDs from the office supervisor: Jean Baptiste, the overnight maintenance guy, who was getting ready to go home after his night shift, and Abigail Grant, a student at GW. She was an intern in the office. Her second day. Got in early. That's all off the record until they notify the families."

I look up at the blackened building. "Whose office was it?"

"Interfaith Coalition for War Refugees," says Campbell. "It's an umbrella organization for small charities assisting refugees from war zones." He looks up at the building too. "I guess these days, no good deed goes unpunished, right?"

"What in holy hell was the purpose of this one?" asks Rizzo.

I shake my head. "Doesn't make sense. The first two bombings were terror for the sake of terror. Public spaces. Mass casualties. Big statements. But this seems more—"

"Intimate?" says Rizzo.

"Yeah," says Campbell. "If you can call a fatal semi-contained explosion intimate." He turns to walk back into the thick of the scene. "Good luck with this one."

Behind a police barricade, a woman is pointing at the building and screaming. She tries to crawl over the barrier, but two burly cops hold her back. "Damn you all!" she wails in a French accent as she drops to her knees on the wet pavement. "Is my man in there? Is he? Jean! Are you there?"

I think back to the trophy wall in the motel room.

Is Aiden Phillips starting a new wall someplace else?

Is this his latest addition?

What does he have against charities?

CHAPTER 66

Phillips

AIDEN PHILLIPS IS STRETCHED out on an apartment building's roof a block and a half away from the bombed-out office. No ghillie suit today, just a military-grade camo tarpaulin that blends in with the smooth asphalt surface. He looks like part of the roof.

Through his spotting scope, he takes in the scene—smoke, flashing lights, first responders moving with discipline and purpose.

The bomb did a fair job tearing off a chunk of a corner office of the bland-looking building, but Phillips has seen only two body bags so far.

He shifts under the tarp, picks up his M42 sniper rifle, and slides forward.

He rests on his elbows and peers through the scope.

He gets the blasted building in view, then brings the crosshairs down, down, down until he locks on two people standing in the middle of the water-soaked street.

John Sampson and Anna Rizzo.

One about six foot nine. The other five feet and change.

It would be difficult, but not impossible, to drop them both with one round.

If that was what he wanted to do.

He tightens his grip and flicks on his laser sight.

Time for a little motivational exercise.

CHAPTER 67

Sampson

I TAP ANNA RIZZO on the arm. "Let's go inside and see what we can find."

"We should wait for the bomb squad," she says.

"I thought you *were* the bomb squad."

"I guess we could sneak a peek before the rest of the team gets here."

As soon as she says it, a red laser dot appears on her forehead.

"Down!" I drop my go bag and tackle her to the sidewalk.

"What the hell?" she shouts. I cover her with my body and drag her behind a dented BMW.

"Sniper! Stay low! He had you zeroed in!" I lift my head and shout as loud as I can: *"Everybody down! We've got a shooter!"*

There's a lot of noise, so I don't know if any of the cops or firefighters heard me.

I pull out my service weapon, raise myself up slightly, and peer around the front bumper. Rizzo grabs my shoulder and yanks me back. "He's got *you* zeroed now!"

We both flatten ourselves on the soaking-wet pavement. When I turn my head, I can see the dot dancing on the side panel of the car, inches from my skull.

"My radio!" I turn my head in the other direction. There it is. Lying on the sidewalk about six feet away.

Feels like sixty.

I look at Rizzo and push her head down. "Hold still. Don't go anywhere."

I get on my knees, then lunge forward and grab my Motorola. I see the red dot on the back of my hand as I pull the radio in and start talking. "Dispatch! Dispatch, this is Sampson, D-five, Sampson, D-five. I'm at the corner of Montgomery Northeast and Trenton."

"Sampson, D-five, go."

"We've got a sniper, elevated position, somewhere along Montgomery Northeast fourteen hundred block."

"Sampson, D-five, acknowledged. Shots fired?"

"Negative. But we need to search and secure the area. Subject is armed and dangerous. Sampson, D-five, out!"

Rizzo is curled up against the side of the BMW. The red dot is gone.

"What the hell was he doing?" she says. "Taunting us?"

"I don't know," I say, thinking it over. "If it was the bomber, why wouldn't he put a couple of rounds through us? He definitely had the range."

A DC Metro Police chopper roars overhead, then seems to brake in midair, hovering over a row of buildings down the street.

"Think they'll catch him?" asks Rizzo.

"I wouldn't bet on it. He's too damn good."

CHAPTER 68

TWENTY MINUTES LATER, Anna Rizzo and I get the okay to move from behind the BMW. The bomb squad has cleared the building. The cops searched every rooftop on Montgomery.

No suspects. No evidence.

No surprise.

Rizzo scrambles to her feet. "Let's get back to work."

We retrieve our go bags, put on paper booties and medical gloves, and make our way to the entrance of the building. I keep looking back over my shoulder. Being tagged by a sniper will do that to you.

We get to the second floor, and CSI is already there, marking the scene. The tile floor in the foyer is smeared with water, soot, and blood. I can see blast damage on both sides of the wall. All the doors and windows are broken. Most of the window glass is blown out onto the street, but our feet crunch over shards from the inside door panels.

The floor and walls are soaked from the fire hoses. Desks and chairs are blackened and upended. Computers are smashed. There are wet papers and file folders everywhere. The suspended ceiling is mostly gone, exposing pipes, wires, and insulation.

A firefighter emerges from a wrecked office with his pike pole. "Watch your step," he says. "Not sure about the floor joists."

There's a breeze coming in from the opening blasted in the exterior wall; it's surrounded by cracked wallboard, splintered wood, and crushed brick.

Rizzo points to one yellow plastic triangle near the door entrance and a second one about a yard away. Each triangle sits next to a splotchy pattern of blood. "That's where the maintenance guy and intern must've been standing when it went off," she says.

I take a few seconds to say a silent prayer. Two innocent lives, snuffed out in a split second. Why?

"What are you thinking?" asks Rizzo.

Focus, Sampson, focus!

"I'm thinking that the first two bombings had a certain terrible logic. Car and truck bombs designed to cause mass casualties, spread terror, make people afraid to live their lives."

"Right," says Rizzo, looking around the wreckage. "This was a serious bomb, but it doesn't look like the plan was to kill a lot of people. Especially at this time of the morning."

"I agree. If you were targeting the Interfaith Coalition, wouldn't you wait until there were a lot more people here in their offices or together in a conference room? Tactically speaking, this seems like a wasted opportunity."

Another ATF tech comes in behind us, taking photographs. I nudge Rizzo. "Let's get out of her way."

As we head down the stairs, we pass a few other techs coming up. Rizzo's phone buzzes. She checks the screen just as we get out onto the sidewalk.

"Holy shit!"

"What's that?" I ask, sneaking a peek at her screen.

"I just got the taggant codes for the C-4!"

"You're welcome."

She narrows her eyes at me. "What do you mean? What did you do?"

"I had a visit this morning from two CIA operatives. It turns out that Aiden Phillips was one of theirs — at least temporarily."

"Huh. Do they know where the C-4 came from?"

"He stole it from the Taliban."

Rizzo checks her screen again. "But these are American codes. This is our stuff."

"Correct. Part of the huge pile we left behind in August of '21. I'm thinking Phillips brought it back. Maybe he thought nobody would be able to trace it."

"I'm thinking the other way. Maybe he knew we *would*. Maybe — just maybe — he wanted us to find out."

If so, I think with a shiver, *that's a whole different kind of message.*

CHAPTER 69

Cross

ALEX CROSS IS IN his hotel room at the Carolina Inn, hanging up a few shirts that have just been delivered from the laundry service downstairs.

His phone rings. NO CALLER ID. It's FBI agent Cannon, from the Charlotte field office.

Alex answers and starts pacing. "Drake! What's going on?"

"To be clear, Dr. Cross," says the agent, "I'm not officially calling you."

"Got it."

"Here's the deal. We've got a wiretapping operation underway targeting a local chapter of the Dixie Mafia. Drugs, weapons smuggling. Nothing solid yet for our case, but in one of the meetings we recorded, I think your son might have come up. Not sure. One of the agents on the surveillance team tipped me off. I listened to the recording myself."

Alex grips his phone tighter. "Damon came up? Came up how?"

"Not by name. And it could just be a coincidence. It was hard to make out, with all the crosstalk, but it sounded like a couple guys were laughing about some 'uppity kid' getting what he deserved."

Alex feels his heart racing but keeps his voice level and calm. "Go on."

"It wasn't part of the main conversation, but they said something like 'Why didn't you take the bike when you were done with him? Could have gotten a few Benjamins for it.'"

Done with him?

Alex says, "Drake, can you bring these guys in for questioning?"

"Sorry," says Cannon. "Like I said, we're in the middle of an investigation. It's been six months. We can't compromise it now. Can't give away the wire. I could get in big trouble for even telling you this."

"I get it," says Alex. "Where's the bug?"

"I can't tell you that. But they have another meeting spot, one we don't have wired yet. You didn't hear it from me, but if you go to the Bracken Motel near the old Horace Williams Airport around ten o'clock tonight, you might get lucky. Room one oh five. You're looking for two guys, Larry and Brett. They're the ones I heard on the wire."

"Larry and Brett," Alex repeats. "Thanks, Drake. I owe you."

"Be careful, Alex. These good ol' boys don't fool around."

Alex reaches into the nightstand drawer and grabs his gun. "Understood," he says. "Neither do I."

CHAPTER 70

Nana Mama

NANA MAMA SITS ON the sofa in the dimly lit living room. Her great-grandkids Jannie and Ali are asleep upstairs. So is Willow Sampson. A few hours earlier, Nana had filled them up with a supper of pork chops and garlicky greens, plus apple pie and ice cream for dessert. Comfort food at its finest.

God knows they all need comforting.

When Ali said, "This is one of Damon's favorite meals," Nana had had to turn away from the table. Couldn't let the young ones see her crumble. She had to stay strong. For them. And especially for Damon.

Wherever he is.

Nana reaches up to a shelf over the sofa and pulls down a thick photo album. It's been a long time since she looked at it. The edges are worn and some of the pages are loose. When she flips the book open, a snapshot falls onto her lap.

It's a picture of her grandson and John Sampson back when they were young boys, sitting on the front steps of the house. John was such a regular visitor, he practically moved in. He and Alex were thick as thieves. Still are.

Nana runs her hands over the acetate sleeves, looking back through time. She sees Christina Parks, Alex's mom, in a photo taken just a year before her death. And a smiling portrait of Alex's father, Nana's son Jason, long before he disappeared from their lives.

After he was gone, Nana Mama stepped up. She'd taken Alex and his brothers in, but the older boys moved on quickly. Alex was the youngest, not even ten years old when he moved in with her in Washington, DC. She'd raised Alex—and pretty much raised John Sampson too—then opened her home to Alex again later, this time to help the single father raise his children while chasing down killers and trying to figure out what made them tick. Even now that Alex had Bree, Nana finds that from time to time, she still has to remind him that family comes first.

With her, it always does.

Nana Mama has suffered plenty of tragedy and loss in her nine decades. But she cannot lose her eldest great-grandchild now. Not Damon. Simply *cannot*.

She flips to one of the last pages in the album and finds a picture of Damon at his high-school graduation. Smiling, beaming, so handsome.

She presses her palm to his picture and says a silent prayer—the same prayer she's said for Damon's father, Alex Cross, many, many times.

"Keep him safe, dear Lord, and in Thy mercy, bring him home."

CHAPTER 71

Cross

ALEX CROSS DRIVES SLOWLY past a row of fast-food restaurants and laundromats. Not a great neighborhood. The Horace Williams Airport has been closed for years, but some of the run-down stores and shops still have aviation themes: Cockpit Lounge. SkyView Cleaners. Pilot Diner.

From what he can see, none of them are doing much business.

He passes a small oval park with a statue of a grim-looking Confederate soldier, musket on his shoulder. By coincidence, the stony Southerner is staring directly at the Bracken Motel.

Alex slows down and pulls his rental car to the curb across the street. This place was probably bustling when the airport was in operation. Not anymore. The overhead sign announcing BRACKEN MOTEL has a few holes in it, from either bullets or rocks. A placard on the end of the building says DAILY, WEEKLY, MONTHLY RATES AVAILABLE. The parking lot's asphalt is cracked and sprouting weeds. Two Jeeps and two pickup trucks are the only vehicles in the lot. The building is shabby and worn, with peeling paint.

Alex counts ten rooms. Room 105 should be the one right in the middle.

He continues driving until he spots a warehouse with a utility road leading behind it. He pulls in to the back of the building, parks facing out, and gets out of the car.

It's hot outside—and quiet.

Alex walks toward the motel, his hand gently patting his right hip, where his holstered Glock is nestled under his jacket. He knows how reckless this is—confronting a criminal gang based on nothing but what Drake Cannon *thought* he heard. The conversation might not have been about Damon at all.

Alex had thought about calling Detective Gail Bailey in Chapel Hill but doesn't want to get in trouble if this turns out to be a wild-goose chase. He's wishing he had John Sampson along for some extra muscle, but John has his hands full in DC, especially with that third bomb going off this morning.

Alex feels for his gun through his jacket again, then slips along the row of rooms to 105, hoping to hell two guys named Larry and Brett are inside.

Time to find my son.

CHAPTER 72

ALEX PRESSES HIS LEFT ear against the cracked wooden motel door. The numerals *1* and *0* are still there, but the *5* is missing, leaving only its impression in the weathered paint.

This is the place.

From inside, he can hear music and loud male voices with Southern accents. Most of it is unintelligible. Music from a radio obscures a lot of the conversation, but it doesn't sound like an organized-crime meeting; it sounds like a frat party.

Alex listens to the laughter and the conversation laced with colorful obscenities. Then from just inside the door, somebody says, "Damn it, Brett, I told you before—"

That's all he needs to hear.

Alex pulls out his gun, then steps back and centers himself in front of the door. He leans back, lifts his stronger leg—the right one—and kicks the door just above the doorknob, hitting hard with his heel as he balances on his other leg. The flimsy door gives way.

"Hands!" Alex shouts as he pushes through, Glock pointed into the room. "I want to see everybody's hands! *Now!*"

One guy jumps up from the bed. "What the fuck?"

"Sit!" Alex shouts. "Hands up!"

The man complies, hands in the air.

Alex quickly scans the room. Ratty green carpet. Two single beds. Two men on each. The men all look about thirty to forty years old. A witness would probably describe them all the same way: big white guys with thick dark beards.

He also spots two duffel bags and a case of Corona on the floor. Two guns on the nightstand.

"Who the hell are you?" one of the other guys snarls. Huge belly. NRA T-shirt.

"Shut up!" Alex orders. He nods toward the guns. "You. NRA. Take both guns by the barrels and put them on the floor."

The guy does it.

"Now kick them over toward me."

The guy does that too.

Alex picks up both guns and sticks them in his waistband. Keeping his own gun pointed at them, he moves farther into the room. He notices a bunch of clear plastic bags packed with white powder peeking out of the duffels.

One of the guys sees him looking. "You a narc?"

Alex ignores him. "Which one of you is Brett?"

All four men try to keep their expressions blank, but Alex sees two pairs of eyes flicker involuntarily toward the guy with the NRA shirt. Positive ID.

"And who's Larry?"

This time one of the other guys wiggles the fingers on his hands. "Right here, asshole."

"Good. Go sit with Brett."

Larry switches places with one of the other guys. Now he and Brett are side by side on the same bed.

Alex points the gun at the men on the other bed. "My business here is with Larry and Brett. If either of you two speak or move, I'll shoot you in the knee."

He turns to Larry and Brett. "A few days ago, you two had an encounter with a young Black man."

"Not us," says Larry with a sneer. "We don't hang with young Black men."

"Somebody saw you. Described you. Right down to the beards. Heard you call each other by name."

Alex is bluffing. He can't reveal what the FBI has on tape, but he's hoping that his lie will flush out the truth.

"You think we're the only Larry and Brett with beards in this country?"

"The young man was riding a bike. Does that refresh your memory?"

Larry spits on the floor. "I got nothing to say to you."

Alex turns to Brett. "So, what happened? You and your buddy see a Black kid on a nice bike. You stop, tune him up a little?"

"If it was a nice bike," says Brett, "the kid probably stole it. But we're not supposed to say that stuff anymore, right? That would be profiling."

Larry stares up at Alex. "Who are you, anyway?" he asks defiantly. "The kid's parole officer?"

Alex moves closer. The barrel of the Glock is millimeters away from Larry's forehead. "No, you mouth-breathing bigot. I'm his father."

Alex hears a sound behind him. Starts to turn.

Too late.

"Freeze right there, boy, or I'll take your damn head off!"

CHAPTER 73

ALEX DOESN'T MOVE. He sees the men on the bed grinning.

"'Bout time, Danny," says Brett.

Behind him, Alex hears a man with a syrupy Southern accent say, "I got a call from my front-office lady. Told me she saw a suspicious-looking Black sneakin' around my motel. I ride on over here and see a door busted in and find this man of color threatening y'all."

Alex lowers his gun. "I'm with the FBI."

"Drop your gun."

Alex stoops and lays his Glock on the floor.

"He's got two of ours, Danny!" Brett calls.

"Put those down too."

Alex feels his neck tingling. He reaches into his waistband and puts down the other two pistols. Larry and Brett scramble to pick them up along with Alex's Glock.

"Now turn around," says the voice from behind. "Do it slow."

Alex carefully rotates one foot, then the other.

A thickset man in a white tank top is aiming a .45 at his midsection. The man's face is flushed and sweaty, covered with white beard stubble.

"Mind telling me what the hell you're doing here, boy? Threatening these fine citizens and damaging my place of business?"

"I'm Dr. Alex Cross. I'm a contract employee with the FBI." His eyes narrow. "And I haven't been a boy for a long time."

Danny wiggles his gun. "You got any identification there, Doc?"

Alex fishes out his ID and holds it in front of Danny's face.

"Goddamn!" says Danny. "This is impressive. Says Alex here is a forensic psychologist. I think that means he's a headshrinker."

Now all the men gather around Alex. Larry and Brett have their guns raised. One of the other men is holding Alex's weapon.

Five men. Four guns.

Not good.

Suddenly, a look of recognition comes over Danny's face. "Wait a minute! Alex Cross! I saw you! I saw you on the news! You were bellyachin' about your missing kid. He's been kidnapped or some damn thing."

"That's right," says Alex. "And I have information that Brett and Larry here know something about it."

"The hell we do," says Larry.

Danny shakes his head. "I know these gentlemen. All four of 'em. None finer. If they say they had nothing to do with your missing boy, then that's God's truth."

Alex's heart is thudding hard and cold in his chest. "Let's just call the local sheriff and let him sort this out."

"I guess this is your lucky day," says Danny. He pulls a badge out of his pocket and holds it up. "You're talkin' to him." He points around the motel room. "Hospitality is just my side gig."

Alex checks the badge. Looks authentic. "Okay, then, Sheriff," he says. "You might want to check those duffels on the floor. I observed bags of white powder when I entered the room."

"That so?" says Danny. "Brett, what've you got in there?"

Brett grins, exposing thick yellowed teeth. "I bought a box of cornstarch this morning at the Piggly Wiggly over in Dalton. Damn box fell and split open here. Me and the guys scooped as much as we could into those little plastic bags. Didn't want anything to go to waste."

"Sounds very prudent," says Danny. He lifts the .45 toward Alex's head. "Now, Dr. Cross, you wouldn't happen to have your concealed-weapons permit on your person, would you?"

"That's ridiculous," says Alex. "Why would I? All my paperwork is in DC."

"That's a shame," says Danny. "I'm afraid I'm gonna need to confiscate your sidearm."

"That's a mistake," says Alex.

Danny's expression darkens. "No, Doc. I think *you* made the mistake. You invaded a private place of business and threatened four innocent men with a loaded weapon."

Alex feels the rage building in his chest. "These men know something about my son!"

"They say otherwise. You got a wallet, Dr. Cross?"

Alex pulls out his billfold and hands it over.

Danny flips through it and pulls out all the cash, four twenty-dollar bills. He pockets them. "This'll defray the cost for damage you caused." He tosses the wallet back to Alex, then gestures to the door with the barrel of his pistol. "Now, get off my property and out of my town."

Alex realizes he has no play here. Not now. He waves his hands in surrender and heads out. "Okay. You win."

As he steps into the parking lot, he hears Brett say from behind him, "Good luck finding your little chocolate drop!"

Larry adds, "He's probably in an alley somewhere with a needle full of junk in his arm."

Alex sets his jaw, swallows his fury, and just keeps walking.

CHAPTER 74

Sampson

I'M AT DC METRO POLICE headquarters, calling my seventh contact of the evening, one of the names I got from CIA agent Tom Walsh. At my elbow is a stack of personnel files that were couriered over from Langley.

The man I just called is Quint Spooner, a former U.S. Army Ranger now living in Arapahoe, South Dakota. According to the files, Spooner served in the army with Aiden Phillips, and I have a lot of questions for him. He picks up the phone, and after the introductions and a little small talk about South Dakota winters, I get right to it.

"What was Phillips like in the field?"

"What was he like?" Spooner repeats, his voice a little raspy. "He was a lot of things. Depended on the time of day and what kind of mood he was in. But one thing was for sure. He was a stone-cold killer."

I've got the phone on speaker and I'm tapping notes into my laptop as we talk. "Can you give me any examples?"

Spooner coughs. Sounds like a smoker. "Sorry. Those missions are still classified."

"Okay. How about examples of something that is *not* mission-related."

There's a long pause on the other end of the line. Then it starts coming out in a flood.

"Okay. This one time, we were in the mountains, high up and isolated. The Taliban were up there too, harassing us and any villagers they thought were loyal to the Kabul government. We had local scouts and informers feeding us intelligence. But we heard through our interpreters that the adversary thought we were weak, too in love with our creature comforts. They didn't think we had true killer instincts."

I'm typing as fast as I can, trying to get everything down verbatim. My spelling sucks, but I'll fix that later. "Keep going. I'm listening."

"Phillips resented the shit about how soft we were. One night he said he was going out to check the perimeter. Then he just disappeared. No radio contact. After a few hours, we sent out a search team, but we couldn't find any trace of him.

"Two nights later, a bunch of us were sitting around a campfire when Phillips showed up. He was holding a cloth bag. He tossed the bag in front of the Afghans on our team and headed back to his hooch."

"What was in the bag?" I ask.

"One of the scouts picked it up and turned it upside down. A guy's head fell out."

I stop typing. "Jesus! *Whose* head?"

"The Taliban leader from up in the mountains, the guy in charge of the crew that had been giving us trouble."

"So what happened then? Did you report it?"

"Nah. Nobody reported shit. We burned the head in the fire and buried the skull. After that, things quieted right down. And the Afghans on our team started showing us mad respect."

I start typing again. I'm still catching up when Spooner puts a button on the story.

"Say what you want about Phillips. He got the job done."

CHAPTER 75

Cross

ALEX CROSS CROUCHES BEHIND a wall in a sheltered area across the street from the Bracken Motel. He's been there for hours, ever since the sheriff sent him on his way.

He watches as a compact sedan rolls into the parking lot and stops in front of room 101. A young man in a baseball cap gets out of the driver's side. He stumbles around the front of the car as the passenger door opens, and a young woman in tight jeans, halter top, bare midriff slides out. They start kissing and pawing at each other as they head toward the motel room, then disappear inside.

Over in room 105, somebody has wrestled the busted door back into place. Alex can see movement through the windows.

Finally, the damaged door swings open, and the five men file out, laughing and shoving one another as they head for their vehicles. Their body language suggests that they all have a couple beers on board—probably more than a couple.

The sheriff is the first to leave. Larry is carrying the duffels. He tosses them in the back of a Jeep and leaves next. Then the two other guys drive off, swerving as they go.

Brett, the one in the NRA T-shirt, is the last one left. He leans against his pickup and polishes off a beer, then walks back to the rear tire, unzips his jeans, and pisses on the pavement. His buddies are long gone when he opens the door and starts the car.

By then, Alex has moved across the road and is crouched down below the open passenger window. He's holding the SIG nine-millimeter mini he retrieved from his glove compartment. Sampson calls it a popgun, but at close range, it might as well be a howitzer.

The second Brett turns his headlights on, Alex yanks open the door of the truck and slides in. Brett turns his head and finds the short barrel of Alex's gun pointing at his mouth.

"Sit on your hands," says Alex.

Brett mumbles, "Okay, okay." He jams his hands under his substantial ass. He's breathing heavy through his nose.

"Where's my gun?" asks Alex. "My real one."

Brett shakes his head. "Larry took it."

"That's okay," says Alex. "This one works fine. Same size hole." He wiggles the barrel against Brett's teeth. "You know something about guns, right, Brett?"

Brett nods slightly, his eyes wide.

"This little pistol has a trigger pull of about five point five pounds. I'm guessing that right now, I'm pulling about three. Just two and a half pounds more, and I'll blow your skull apart. The lovebirds in that motel room over there might hear the shot, but by the time they get their pants on, I'll be gone—just like the back of your head. Do I have your total attention?"

Brett nods. Very slowly. He's starting to drool out of one side of his mouth.

Alex pulls the pistol away and wipes the saliva off on Brett's shirt. He slides back against the passenger door and points the gun at Brett's temple. "Now, let's have another talk about my son."

Brett is twitching in his seat. He takes a few deep breaths, then turns his head slightly toward Alex. "It was just a joke, that's all. Just a little fun."

"Who was there?"

"Just me and Larry."

"Tell me what happened. Tell me exactly what you did."

Brett shifts awkwardly on his hands. "We were driving up near the preserve early one morning last week, and we saw this twenty-something kid on his bike. Nice bike. And Larry's egging me on, saying he must've stolen it. So I come up right behind him and give his rear tire a little love tap with my bumper. Just a nudge. And the guy goes flying."

"Was he hurt? Was he unconscious?"

"Nah, he just ended up in a drainage ditch. He was fine. A little banged up, maybe. He got up right away. He was shouting at us. Swearin' pretty good."

"Then what?"

"Then Larry puts on his gloves, jumps out, and grabs the bike. He tossed it in the back of my pickup. As soon as we pulled away, the kid started chasing us." Brett winces a little. "Like I said, we were just foolin' around. I...I messed with him a bit, like I'd slow down a little and let him get close, then speed up again. But then we left him in the dust and went up to the trailhead. Larry took the bike down the trail and dumped it."

Alex moves the gun closer to Brett's temple. "What else?"

"Larry found a cell phone and a laptop in the bike pouch, and he took 'em too."

"What did you do with his phone and laptop?"

"We tossed 'em both into a creek."

Alex rams the butt of his pistol against Brett's cheekbone, drawing blood.

"Fuck!" Brett shouts.

"My son! What happened to him?"

"I don't know, man. When we got back down to the main road, he was gone."

"You didn't beat him up? You didn't kill him?"

"Nah, like I said, we just gave him a little workout."

Alex reaches over, turns off the car, and palms the key fob. He reaches into Brett's pocket and pulls out his phone.

"I'm getting out now," he tells Brett. "You're going to keep your hands where they are. You're not going to say a word about this to your buddies or the sheriff or anybody else. And you better pray hard that we find my son safe and healthy and that he confirms your story. If not, we'll meet again."

Alex slides out of the truck and slams the door.

"Hey!" shouts Brett. "My keys! My phone! I live ten miles from here!"

Alex stuffs the keys and phone in his pocket and keeps the gun pointed through the window as he backs away.

"Perfect. Sounds like a good workout for you."

CHAPTER 76

Sampson

ENOUGH.

I made ten more calls after I talked to Quint Spooner, but all were nonstarters. Either no one answered or the people I got were unwilling to talk. Now I shuffle through the pile again and look up at the clock on the wall.

Okay. I have time for one more call.

I look for a number with a West Coast area code, since it's not too late there.

Here we go: Rick Bannon, resident of Eugene, Oregon.

I dial the number and mumble to myself, "Pick up, pick up, pick up…"

He does.

"Rick, my name is John Sampson. I'm a detective with the Metro Police in DC."

"Okay, John, how can I help you?" Bannon sounds bright, alert, articulate.

"I understand you served with a man named Aiden Phillips when you were in the army. Is that right?"

I hear a low whistle on the other end, then: "Is this about the DC bombings? What took you guys so long?"

I sit up straighter. I don't want to give too much away. "Just tell me about Phillips. How well did you know him?"

"Maybe too damn well," says Bannon. "Enough to have reasonable worry that if the freak finds out I've been talking to you, he might blow up my car for giggles."

This stops me for a second. "Why would you say that?"

"Because explosives were his thing."

"Did you consider him a threat?"

"To me? Nah. Just to people who pissed him off."

"For example?"

Bannon is quiet for a moment. "Okay," he says, "here's one. We'd been deployed for six months. We were at an FOB up in the hills, at least ten klicks from any other unit. We were trying to blend in with the locals — we had beards, long hair, tunic shirts, the works. Then out of nowhere, a couple of regular army platoons came in and set up camp nearby.

"A few of the spit-and-polish officers started ragging on us, telling us that we needed to clean up. Phillips mouthed off, told them they didn't know shit about blending in."

"Let me guess. The officers told him to shut up and follow orders."

Bannon laughs. "So you were in the service?"

"Army. Then police department. The brass never change. So how did Phillips react?"

"Unofficially?"

Bannon seems like a straight-up guy. But I'm tired and I need to cut to the chase. "Rick, I'm not looking to jam you up for anything. I've seen your file. You did three tours. You've got a Purple Heart and a Distinguished Service Medal. I'm only interested in what Phillips did. Or what you *think* he did."

"Okay," says Bannon, "I'll tell you. So, these asshole officers had six up-armored Humvees they kept in a guarded barbed-wire compound. One morning, they were getting ready to make a run to a village down in the valley. They all piled into a convoy. When the drivers started up the Humvees, a blast went off under every single one. White smoke and flames shot out from underneath. Scared the shit out of everybody."

"Anyone injured?"

"Not a scratch," says Bannon. "Turns out the charges were only about the size of an M80. So it was like a kid's prank."

"Or a warning?"

"You said it, not me. But, yeah, the officers stopped bothering us. When I talked to Phillips about it, at first he just kind of smiled."

"He didn't say anything?"

"Not then, but he did eventually."

"What did he say?"

"He told me that if you want to get somebody's attention, explosives are the way to do it."

CHAPTER 77

BY THE TIME I get off the phone with Rick Bannon, I'm the only person left in the office. Time to go; I have plans later tonight. I pack up my stuff and head for the door. My finger is on the light switch when I see the elevator door open across the hall.

Shit.

Perkins and Walsh. The two people I least want to see.

The CIA agents make their way through the cubicle maze and stroll into my office. They grab the two chairs in front of my desk and sit down.

"Don't you guys ever call first?" I ask.

"We were in the neighborhood," says Perkins.

No hellos. No explanations. No apologies.

Walsh points at the pile of confidential files on my desk. "What have you found?"

I sit down at my desk. Clearly, I'm not going anywhere for a while. I tap the files. "I talked to about half a dozen vets from your list so far."

"What are you hearing?" asks Perkins.

"Mostly, a lot of complaints about the VA."

"Not our department," says Walsh dismissively. "What have you heard about Phillips?"

"There's a definite pattern to what people remember. Phillips had their backs in the field, but he enjoyed killing a little too much—and blowing stuff up. Nobody I talked to has kept in touch with him, but no one was surprised to hear we're looking into him for the bombings. Several say he seems like the type."

"So this contradicts what you heard from the wife and Florence Nightingale," Perkins states.

I nod. "That's right. Both of them are of the opinion that Phillips is a damaged guy with PTSD but claim he'd never kill innocent people."

"Bullshit," says Walsh. "Ladies always let emotions cloud their judgment. Biggest mistake this country ever made was passing the Nineteenth Amendment."

I just stare at him. "I guess you skipped sensitivity training."

"I did," says Walsh. He forms a pistol with his thumb and index finger. "I was on the shooting range."

I focus on Perkins, who seems to be the more reasonable of the pair. "This is supposed to be a two-way street. Anything from your end?"

"It's hard to pull any info out of Afghanistan these days," says Perkins. "The people we still have over there need to be very careful about who they talk to."

Walsh makes a slicing motion around his neck. "Or else…"

For a second I think about telling them about Phillips beheading the tribal leader, but then I decide to keep that tidbit to myself for now.

Perkins leans forward in his chair. "When Phillips went on his unauthorized missions to bring out friendlies, we know he had contacts with officers he had trained for the Afghan National Army."

"Those guys are all underground now," says Walsh. "Or dead."

Perkins continues. "We're trying to run down whether the C-4 used in the DC explosions was under the control of those officers."

"How long will that take?" I ask.

"As long as it takes," says Walsh.

Enough of this; I'm tired. I stand up, go around my desk, and start gathering my stuff again. "Look, you guys can stay all night if you want. But if you don't mind, I'm heading out."

I keep my back turned until I hear the elevator doors ding closed. Just as I'm once again reaching for the switch to turn off the lights, my phone rings.

Anna Rizzo. We made plans earlier to go to her favorite Spanish restaurant for a late dinner. I'm really looking forward to it.

I accept the call. "Hi there."

"Hi, yourself. How goes the hunt?"

"I learned some interesting facts about our boy Aiden Phillips. And I just talked to the two spooks. But listen, we can talk about everything over dinner."

"Sorry, John, that's actually why I'm calling. My abuela is fighting a nasty cold, so it looks like she can't hang with my kids tonight."

For some reason, this disappoints me more than it should. Then in a flash, I come up with a solution.

"Hold on, Anna. Do your kids like barbecue?"

"Hell yes! Who doesn't like barbecue?"

"Okay. Dinner's still on. You, me, and the kids. Change of venue."

CHAPTER 78

Cross

AN HOUR AFTER ALEX CROSS stranded Brett in his truck, his adrenaline is still pumping. Now he knows more about what happened to Damon that morning: He was riding his bike near the reserve and got chased and harassed by two rednecks in a pickup. They stole his bike, phone, and laptop, then ditched his bike in the reserve and tossed his phone and laptop in a creek somewhere.

But where did Damon go from there? Where did he end up? How could he have simply vanished?

Think!

Maybe Damon followed the truck up to the trailhead and went looking for his bike after the two goons left. Maybe he got lost or hurt.

Just because the search teams haven't found him doesn't mean he's not out there.

Alex makes a hard turn on a dark street and heads for someplace even darker.

Fifteen minutes later, he's driving back up to the trailhead in the Mason Farm Biological Reserve. With every turn in the road, his headlight beams rake across the dense woods and underbrush.

At night, the place looks haunted. It makes no sense to be here. But Alex can't rest. Not now.

He parks the car. His heart is going a hundred beats a minute. He steps out, pats the gun in his pocket, and shines the flashlight of his cell phone around.

There must be another trail here. Another way down. There has to be.

Twenty minutes later, his heart leaps when his hunch is proved right. Not far from the trailhead but far enough that you'd miss it, especially with the other two trails so clearly marked, is another path, an older trail obscured by a tangle of dead branches. When Alex shoves aside the fallen branches, he sees a well-beaten footpath leading down the slope. Narrow, but passable.

He holds his light at hip level and plunges in.

It's not easy in the dark. He keeps getting hooked on briars and whacked by small branches. He waves his light from side to side, looking for clothing, scraps of paper, any trace of a human being.

Suddenly, the trail pitches down at a steep angle. Alex feels his feet slipping out from underneath him. He grabs a branch, but it snaps off in his hand. A split second later, he's on his back, rocks jabbing into his spine. His phone is somewhere in the bushes. Alex is breathing heavy, his chest heaving. He looks up through the foliage to the sky dotted with stars.

He closes his eyes and cries out, "Damon! Where are you?"

A few seconds later, he hears a voice call from below, weak and distant.

"Hello?"

CHAPTER 79

ALEX SCRAMBLES TO HIS feet and regains his balance. He reaches through a patch of thorns and retrieves the phone, not even feeling the stabs. He half slides, half stumbles the rest of the way down the trail to where it opens up onto a patch of high grass.

He hears voices ahead and spots a flickering glow through a stand of trees.

It would be easier to go around the trees, but he doesn't; he picks his way straight through, aiming directly for the sound.

Half a minute later, he bursts into a small clearing with a stream winding through it.

Three young women are sitting in low folding chairs around a campfire. They all leap to their feet at the sight of Alex. One of the women grabs a long stick from near the fire. The other two cower behind her.

Alex is panting from exertion and covered with dirt and sweat. He holds his hands up. "It's okay! Don't worry! I'm with the FBI!"

As soon as he says it, he realizes how outlandish it sounds. He reaches into his pocket for his ID and tosses it to the women. "It's true. Go ahead. Look."

The young woman with the stick stoops to pick up the leather case. She opens it and shows it to the others. She lowers the stick. "Was that you we heard shouting?"

Alex approaches slowly. "Yes. I was up on the trail. I'm looking for my son. Damon Cross. He's a graduate student at Chapel Hill. He disappeared around here a few days ago."

One of the other women reaches into a cooler and holds out a bottle of water. "We haven't seen anybody," she says. "Here. You look like you could use some hydration."

Alex walks the last few yards to the campsite. Now he notices a small tent pitched in the shadows with a neat row of backpacks alongside. He grabs the water and unscrews the cap, then takes a long, deep gulp. He puts the bottle down and wipes his lips. "Thank you. My name is Alex."

The woman with the stick hands him back his ID. "Yup, Alex Cross. It says so right there." She points to the other two women. "This is Nell. This is Diana. And I'm Leigh."

Alex nods to the group. Leigh is tall, blond, and athletic-looking. Willa is shorter, rounder, and Black. Diana is Asian, with long hair falling to her waist.

"You know you shouldn't have a fire out here," says Alex. "It's a nature preserve."

"We just do it once a year," says Diana. "We're careful."

"Don't tell me you're gonna arrest us," says Nell.

"I won't tell a soul, I promise. Are you guys students?"

Leigh shakes her head. "Nurses. We work at the UNC Medical Center. Once a year, we hike the reserve and camp out for a few days. It's our little tradition."

"We've been coming to this same spot for years," says Diana.

"How did you get here?" asks Alex. "The trail I took was a little rough."

Nell points in the opposite direction. "We came in from the east. There's an old utility road."

"What makes you think your son is out here?" asks Leigh.

"We know he was somewhere on the road below the park entrance before he disappeared, and we found his bike in the reserve."

"Wouldn't it make more sense to look in the daylight?" asks Diana.

"We did," says Alex. "But even so, we missed the trail I came down just now. I'm looking for anything that stands out. A piece of clothing, a shoe, a credit card..."

"Sorry. We haven't noticed anything. But we haven't really been looking." Leigh shrugs.

"We're just here to relax," says Nell. "Do some stargazing."

"And a little drinking," Diana adds.

"Yeah," says Nell. "That too."

Suddenly, Alex hears the crack of gunfire. Not too near, but close enough to make him flinch. "What the hell was that?"

"Oh, yeah," says Nell, rolling her eyes. "That happens every night."

"We've gotten used to it," says Diana.

"Where's it coming from?" asks Alex.

Diana points across the clearing toward a low hill, a dark ripple against the sky. "About a half a mile away," she says. "There's an old farmhouse off the utility road. Big yard. Barbed wire all around it."

"We passed it on our way in," says Leigh. "Probably some survivalist or doomsdayer. I guess he likes to do target practice at night."

"Did you see anybody?" asks Alex.

"No, nobody was around when we passed it during the day."

Another volley of shots rings out, echoing against the hills and trees.

"That's a military rifle," says Alex. "Full auto." He tries to triangulate the source. "Which way is the farmhouse?"

"Just follow the curve of the stream and go over the hill," says Leigh, pointing into the distance.

"You can't miss the place," says Diana.

"That's for sure," says Nell. "Whoever he is, I bet he's the whitest white man for miles around."

"Why do you say that?" Alex asks.

Nell shrugs. "You'll see."

CHAPTER 80

Sampson

OVER THE YEARS, I'VE discussed criminal cases in my downtown office, at FBI headquarters, in police stations, on airplanes, and at murder scenes.

I like my backyard better.

Especially when I'm in good company.

I'm sitting next to Anna Rizzo at my redwood picnic table, while my daughter, Willow, and Rizzo's kids, Juan and Tina, run around. They're playing a game they call Disintegrator Man. It's like hide-and-seek but with a flashlight. If the beam hits you—*poof!*—you're disintegrated, which means you have to fall on the ground and pretend to vaporize. Squealing is encouraged.

The grill is cooling down, and the paper plates have all been stuffed in the trash. Everybody's full and happy. Rizzo and I are enjoying a couple of cold beers from my cooler. It's a little late for the kids to be up, but Rizzo doesn't mind making an exception, and neither do I.

Rizzo sips her beer and thumbs through the pile of manila folders on the picnic table. At her request, it's a working dinner. She's wearing a gray U.S. Army T-shirt and khaki shorts. On one arm is the tattoo I saw earlier, the one from her time in the service. On her other arm is another kind of marker—a shiny patch of scar tissue.

Rizzo sees me checking it out. She takes another sip of her beer and taps her scar with the neck of the bottle. "Purple Heart number one," she says. "Got too close to a booby-trapped door."

"Number one? You mean there's another?"

"You bet there is," she says with a smile. "But you'll never see it—unless you get lucky."

I smile back. I'm not sure if she's flirting or just joking. I realize that I would very much like to get lucky with Anna Rizzo.

"That was some of the best barbecue I've ever had," she says, patting her stomach. "Nicely done, John."

"Don't thank me, thank Nana Mama. It's her recipe."

"Nana Mama? Who's that?"

"She's my friend Alex Cross's grandmother. Mine too, in a way."

"How so?" asks Rizzo.

"I met Alex when I was about the same age as our guys here," I say, waving my beer in the direction of the kids running around. "He'd just moved to DC to live with his grandmother. Alex's mom had died, and mine was caught up in drugs. Neither of our dads was in the picture by then. I was basically fending for myself. Alex and I quickly became best friends, and Nana Mama took me under her wing. She saved my life."

"Sounds like a great lady," says Rizzo.

"She is. And she's still helping me out. Willow's been staying with her since the first bomb went off. But I think I'll let my girl sleep in her own bed tonight."

The kids make another loop around the picnic table, wide-eyed and giggling. Rizzo waits for them to run off again, then pats the folders. "I got more info from Langley."

"About the C-4?"

She nods. "There's only one manufacturer of C-4 in the United States, the Holston Army Ammunition Plant in Tennessee. The taggants I located in the residue from all three bombings came from a shipment sent several years ago to a unit in the Afghan National Army. When the government collapsed, this shipment apparently headed north with what was left of the ANA."

"Makes sense," I tell her. "Perkins and Walsh think Phillips was in contact with those ANA remnants when he was doing cross-border incursions to rescue allies."

"Any hard evidence that that's where he secured the C-4?" she asks.

"Of course not. With CIA, it's all smoke and mirrors."

"I thought it was cloak-and-dagger," says Rizzo, smiling. Then she gets serious again. "C-4 isn't something you just toss into a rucksack and bring home like some battlefield souvenir. There are detection devices everywhere—on civilian and military aircraft, at border crossings, customs stations. And the CIA wants us to believe that Phillips had the desire, know-how, and technical means to smuggle C-4 from Afghanistan? And not just a sample—enough to blow up two city streets and an office building? I'm starting to wonder if the spooks are feeding us specific intel," says Rizzo, "while they keep tabs on our side of the investigation."

"You think we're being watched?" I ask. "I mean us, personally?"

"I have no doubt about it. They want to keep ahead of what we're doing so they can feed us information and details that support their narrative."

"Which might or might not be the truth."

Rizzo slides closer to me and lowers her voice: "From now on, let's limit electronic communication between the two of us. No emails. No details on the phone. Face-to-face conversations as much as possible."

I nod. "You keep working the technical side. I'll keep working the people."

Willow runs up to me. "Hey, Daddy?"

"Hey, Willow. Having fun?"

"*So* much fun! Can Juan and Tina come over to play again?"

I look at Rizzo. "If their mom says it's okay."

Rizzo's hip is almost touching mine on the bench. I feel her hand slide over under the table and give my thigh a quick squeeze.

"I think we can work that out," she says.

CHAPTER 81

Cross

ALEX CROSS LEAVES THE nurses' campsite, and twenty minutes later, their fire is just a shimmering dot in the distance. He's half a mile away, heading up the hill that separates the preserve from whatever lies beyond.

He keeps his light trained on the ground, hoping against hope that maybe Damon came this way too, looking for his bike. Or maybe just trying to avoid running into the rednecks again.

But if there are any clues here, they're hidden in the dark.

After about ten more minutes of climbing, Alex reaches the crest of the hill. It flattens out for about fifty yards before descending into the valley on the other side. Standing at the lip of the drop-off, he can see the glow of towns in the distance and the bright patterns of roads miles away.

But directly below, there's only one light. It beams from a white clapboard farmhouse, illuminating a bare expanse of farmyard and scrubby grass.

Alex realizes that he's already walked much farther tonight than he anticipated, and he's feeling it. His lungs burn. His legs ache.

And it's probably all for nothing.

He slips and stumbles down the wooded slope toward the house. When he's about twenty yards away, his right foot slides into a wooden post.

He shines his light back and forth.

The beam catches closely stacked rows of barbed wire rising about twelve feet high. A few yards down, he spots the first of a series of hand-painted signs: NO TRESPASSING. OWNER IS ARMED.

Alex looks closer. Running through the barbed wire are narrow-gauge wires strung through ceramic guides on each post.

Damn! The fence isn't just barbed. It's electrified.

Alex crouches down beside the post. He can see the main house, a small barn, and two outbuildings that look like storage sheds. He moves around the perimeter of the fence looking for an opening, but the only gate he sees is directly in the beam of the house light. And it's secured with heavy chains.

To one side of the gate, there's a wooden platform littered with pierced cans and shattered bottles. The edge of the platform is pocked by bullet holes.

The shooting range.

Alex keeps going, staying low, until he's facing the gate and target platform. He shines his light on the trees around him. Some of the trunks are splintered. Smaller trees have been sheared off about five feet from the ground. Serious ammo. Large caliber.

Alex looks toward the house. The door appears to be solid metal, and the windows are barred. As the wind shifts, he picks up a distinct barnyard odor. He squints along the side of the barn and sees a large fenced-in pen. From the smells and the sounds, Alex deduces what it is: a pigsty.

One thing is for sure, Alex thinks, *if Damon saw this place, he'd have given it a wide berth.* Because Nurse Nell was right. Flapping from a tall metal pole in the center of the compound is a massive Confederate flag. It's a chilling sight.

Alex takes a step back. Something on the ground catches his eye.

He shines his flashlight directly down and sees a thin strand among the leaves and twigs.

A trip wire.

Alex freezes.

Another inch, and his foot would have caught it.

CHAPTER 82

Sampson

SIX A.M. MY PHONE starts ringing. I roll over in my big empty bed, pick up the phone, and check the screen. Anna Rizzo. I answer.

"Morning," I croak. "How are you?" My voice isn't really working yet.

"I'm good," says Rizzo. Sounds like she's been up for hours. "Thanks again for that barbecue last night. My kids really loved it."

"You're very welcome. Willow loved it too."

"John, I know it's early. Can I come over?"

Something in her tone makes me sit right up.

"Sure. What's going on?"

"I'll explain when I get there," she says. "Face to face from now on, remember?"

"How soon?"

"Ten minutes out."

I throw my covers off and swing my feet onto the floor. "I'll put the coffee on."

After a speed-shower and shave, I get dressed, then walk down the hall to peek into Willow's room. Still asleep, legs dangling over the side of her bed. *Let her sleep.* I'll take her back to the Cross house on my way to work.

I walk downstairs to the kitchen and start up the coffee maker. After a few seconds, it's hissing and gurgling. I inhale the first glorious whiff of dark roast.

I reach into a cabinet, pull out two coffee mugs, and set them down on the counter.

I hear a car turning into my driveway. Then—

Boom!

All I see is a flash of light. I'm thrown across the kitchen and slam into the refrigerator. When I lift my head, there's broken glass everywhere. The coffee mugs are shattered on the floor, and the coffee maker is oozing wet grounds onto the counter. My ears are ringing and I feel blood coming out of my nose.

Smoke fills the kitchen. The smoke detectors are beeping like crazy.

I hear Willow screaming upstairs: *"Daddy! Daddy!"*

I stumble to my feet and wipe my nose on my sleeve.

The door that leads out to my driveway is lying broken on the floor. I can see flames and gray smoke through the opening. I smell burning rubber.

I run upstairs, taking them three steps at a time. Willow is standing next to her bed, trembling in her pajamas. "Daddy! What happened?"

"Don't worry, baby, it's okay." I scoop her up in my arms, not even feeling her weight. I carry her into the bathroom, throw a towel onto the bottom of the tub, and lay her inside.

She's sobbing. I can see the fear on her face.

"Stay right here," I tell her. "Keep your head down. Don't move until I come back."

She nods and shrinks against the curve of the tub, arms clutched around her knees.

I run back into my bedroom and grab my Glock and my Motorola radio. "Dispatch, Dispatch, this is Sampson, D-five!"

I'm already jumping down the stairs, back into the thick of the smoke.

"Sampson, D-five, this is Dispatch, go."

"I need fire and police units at my address. There's been an explosion. Roll a bus too! I'm not sure what we've got!"

"Say again. *Your* address?"

"Yes!" I'm shouting into the mic. "My address! *My damn house!*"

I tuck my pistol in my waistband and grab a small fire extinguisher from a clip near the stove. I step over my broken door and start shooting the foam into the burning shell of a car, which is billowing with smoke; it's so dense that I can hardly see what I'm aiming at. The hood is ripped off and lying in the yard. The windows are shattered. The tires are all blown and burning. I'm choking on the stench.

I can hear sirens in the distance heading this way.

I blast the extinguisher until it runs out. Can't see anybody inside. I toss the extinguisher down and grab the door handle. Scalding hot. I pull on it anyway. The door falls open. I lean into the front seat, feel blindly with my hands.

I feel something solid and wet. The smoke clears just enough to reveal a body. Or what's left of a body. Broken. Bloody. Torn apart.

The sleeve on one arm is blown back.

I see a tattoo, barely scorched.

"Anna!"

Lights and sirens surround me. Firefighters jump off their rigs with huge extinguishers. A paramedic runs over and slings his backpack down alongside the car. He elbows past me. "Out of the way, please!"

I hold him back and shake my head. "No. It's no use. She's DRT."

Dead right there.

CHAPTER 83

I'M SITTING ON MY back steps, holding Willow tight.

She's still in her pj's, her head buried in my chest.

The smoke has mostly cleared. But horrible smells hang in the air. Yellow tape runs all around my yard.

My home, my castle, my refuge.

Now a crime scene.

The street is jammed with fire apparatus, police cruisers, a bomb squad truck, and a bunch of unmarked vehicles with flashing lights in their radiator grilles.

And a coroner's van.

I didn't watch when they took her out of the car. I couldn't.

I'm thinking about the way she was last night. Sitting at the picnic table right over there. Smiling, laughing, watching our kids play.

In a little while, I'll have to go to Anna's house and tell her two beautiful children that their mom isn't coming home. Not ever.

"John! John!"

I look up. Bree Stone is just outside the yellow tape.

I stand up and wave her through. She comes over, gives me a quick hug, then wraps herself around Willow.

"Aunt Bree," Willow says, sobbing. "It was so scary."

Bree squeezes her tight. "I know, I know. But you're safe now. I promise. Why don't you go upstairs, get your clothes and your backpack, and come home with me again, okay? Nana Mama misses you already. Ali and Jannie too."

Willow looks up at me with tears in her eyes. "Is that okay, Daddy?"

I nod. "Absolutely."

An officer comes over and escorts Willow into the house.

Bree gives me another hug, a longer one this time. "Are you okay?"

"I'm fine." Not true. "Thanks for coming over."

"I came the second I heard."

She looks at the mangled mess in my driveway, a charred hulk with a huge hole underneath. "John, what happened here?"

"It was an IED. Planted in the driveway sometime last night. It was meant for me, Bree. I would have tripped it when I backed out of the garage this morning."

"Dear God." We both know this is clearly connected to the other bombings. Bree glances back at the car. "Do you know who the vic is?"

"Anna. Anna Rizzo. She was an investigator with ATF. We've been working closely together, got along really well. She was a good person. Mother of two."

"I'm sorry," says Bree. "Really sorry. Let's get Willow out of here."

"I'm ready, Aunt Bree." Willow walks up, her extra-heavy backpack over her shoulder.

"Okay, sweetheart," says Bree. "Let's go see what Nana Mama has cooked up for breakfast."

Willow steps up and gives me a big hug. "I love you, Daddy."

"I love you too, Willow. More than anything."

I watch the two of them walk off together. Willow gives me one last wave before she disappears behind a fire truck.

I sit back down on my steps and put my head in my hands. Blood from my nose is drying on my shirt. And Anna's blood is still on my fingers.

"Sampson! Hey! Sampson!"

Somebody's shouting at me from the street. A familiar voice.

I look up.

He's coming up the driveway, past the yellow tape.

Shit.

Not him.

Not now.

CHAPTER 84

IT'S ROLAND PERKINS, THE accountant-looking spook.

He picks his way up my driveway, stepping over hoses and equipment. I see him pause beside the wreckage of Anna Rizzo's car. All around the vehicle, forensics techs are starting their work—snapping pictures, taking measurements, scraping charred paint into small plastic evidence bags. Perkins holds up his ID and peeks in through the mangled passenger-side door, then quickly backs away. "Jesus Christ!"

By this point, my neighbors up and down the street are standing outside, cell phones aloft, filming the whole scene. The first news vans are pulling up to the curb. I know it won't be long before a News 4 helicopter is hovering overhead.

Perkins looks a bit shaken when he walks over to me. "This is a tough one, Sampson. Unbelievable. I hear Rizzo was a solid investigator. I recall how much you liked her. I'm really sorry."

I can't tell if Perkins is totally genuine or a really good actor. Since he's career CIA, there's no way to know. But I take his words at face value for the moment. "Yeah. Me too."

"We're assuming you were the target?" he asks, sitting down beside me.

"Must've been. Rizzo told me she was coming over only ten minutes before this happened. Whoever set this couldn't have been expecting her. There wouldn't have been any time to hide a device that strong. So it must've been intended for me, for the next time I backed out of my garage, and…" My throat gets tight. "I could have had my daughter with me."

"Why was Rizzo coming here so early?" Perkins asks. "Her office is in Bethesda."

"She had something to tell me. Said it had to be in person."

"Something about Phillips?"

"Maybe."

"Do you think she talked to anyone in her office?"

"I doubt it. We agreed to keep our circle pretty tight."

"How tight?"

"Just the two of us. Other techs were feeding her data and test results, but she was the only one besides me and you guys who had the whole picture."

Perkins nods. "The whole picture is looking a lot clearer." He glances back at the car wreckage and the workers in hazmat suits. "My bet is they'll find more of that tagged C-4. Phillips did this for sure. He wants to short-circuit the investigation by taking you out."

"Maybe so. But that doesn't get us any closer to finding him. He could be anywhere in the world by now."

"We've got alerts at all the airports. Shipping and cruise companies too."

This almost makes me laugh. "Not much of an obstacle if you know what you're doing. This guy managed to sneak into Afghanistan on a private mission right under the nose of the CIA. He got away clean from four bombings, including this one. I have no doubt he'll be able to sneak through one of our semipermeable borders."

"Unless he's not finished here," says Perkins.

"Right. Unless he's not finished."

"We should get you some protection, John. Let me make a call. I'll assign you a few ex-Blackwater guys."

"No, thanks. I don't travel in packs. Never have."

"Are you sure? They'll turn your place into a fortress overnight."

I stand up. "Right now, I've gotta change my clothes and get to Bethesda. I need to notify Anna Rizzo's family." I flash on Juan and Tina running around my backyard with Willow just twelve hours ago. Amazing how fast life can change—and how goddamn dark it can get.

Perkins reaches for his cell phone. "I'll get you a car and a driver."

"Screw that. Get me a bird and a pilot. I need to beat the press."

CHAPTER 85

Cross

ALEX CROSS STANDS IN front of a large wall map in the Orange County records office. He moves his finger around the outline of the nature reserve and then over the border to the west.

"Can I help you?"

Alex looks up. A sixty-something Black woman in pressed slacks and a burgundy blouse is standing next to him. "You work in property records?" he asks.

"I do. My name is Lola."

"Hi, Lola. I'm Alex. I'm in search of property records for a farm in that area."

"Follow me." Lola turns to a bank of metal file cabinets on the other side of the room. "I was born about a mile from where you're looking. Not many farms left around there. Not working farms, anyway."

Alex waits in front of a long table while Lola pulls open a drawer and runs her hands across rows of well-thumbed files.

"You can't do this digitally?" Alex asks.

"I like to feel it in my fingers," she says. "Pencil marks and all."

Lola returns with a bunch of marked-up property sheets and lays them out on the table. "Most of these parcels have been sold off to developers over the years and rezoned for construction." Lola shakes her head and sighs. "The family farm where I grew up is now a strip mall with a Dollar General smack in the middle."

"I'm looking for a small property," says Alex. "Farmhouse, barn, a few outbuildings. Maybe five acres."

"Okay...how about this parcel?" Lola pushes a sheet in front of him, a survey sketch of a property with borders running to the edge of the nature reserve. "That's not far from where you were pointing on the map," she says. "Seven acres. Water well. Septic system. Pretty self-contained little compound."

"This could be it," says Alex. "Who owns it?"

Lola runs her fingers down a column on the side of the sheet. "Interesting. Looks like it's remained in the same family for over two hundred years." Lola taps her finger on the last entry in the column. "Here you go. Colton Brophy. He's the current owner. It seems he inherited the title from his dad twenty years ago. No easements. No fines. Tax payments are up to date."

"The family must have gotten offers for the property."

"No doubt. But some people have their reasons for holding out. Maybe sentimentality. Or maybe they just don't want to be uprooted."

"Any recent permits?" Alex asks. He doubts he'll find any paperwork for a target range. Or for antipersonnel mines.

"Let me check." Lola flips through some papers attached to the property sheet, then taps another spot. "Excavation and building permit. Ten years ago. Looks like Mr. Brophy was digging a bomb shelter."

CHAPTER 86

Sampson

I HAVE A RULE about not drinking alone.

I'm breaking it.

There's a bottle of Scotch on my table and a half-empty tumbler beside it. I'm already feeling the effects. And it's not helping.

Of all the next-of-kin notifications I've done over the years, this morning's was one of the toughest. It turns out that Anna Rizzo's abuela Marina speaks hardly any English. So after I sat Juan and Tina down and told them what had happened, they had to interpret for her. Marina let out an earsplitting wail, which terrified the kids.

I sat with them in their living room, letting them cry, letting them talk, letting them ask me questions—most of which I couldn't answer or didn't want to.

At one point, Marina handed me a scrapbook. Turning the pages, I saw Rizzo grow from a dark-eyed baby to a skinny kid in soccer gear to a beautiful young woman. I saw pictures of her wedding day, with both bride and groom in dress uniform, walking under an arch of sabers. Then with her babies, Juan, followed by Tina.

After two hours, I hugged them all and left them in the care of a kindly next-door neighbor. Told all of them to call me at any hour. Juan asked me if I'd come to his mom's funeral. That just about broke my heart. I promised I would.

I also promised we'd find whoever did this and bring them to justice.

Which is what I always say. Even when I have my doubts.

By the time I got back home, the wreckage of Rizzo's car had been carried away on a flatbed truck. The bomb squad had checked the garage, and they gave my car the all-clear.

My house still smells like smoke. When I look out through my kitchen window, I can see the hole in my driveway, black and deep, with broken concrete and blasted-out dirt all around it. The yellow tape still winds around my yard, flapping in the breeze.

My gun is on the table right next to the bottle of Scotch and my cell phone. Probably not a good combination.

I hear a sound behind me.

I whip around in my chair, but my reflexes are a touch slow.

A pistol is pressing into my forehead. In a snap, I recognize the man who's holding it.

It's Aiden Phillips.

His left arm snakes around and grabs my Glock off the table. He shoves it into his waistband, then grabs my phone. After that, he backs off.

"Don't worry, John. I don't hurt people. Not the good ones, anyway."

CHAPTER 87

Cross

ALEX CROSS KNOWS HE should have contacted the Chapel Hill PD. Hell, he should have contacted the bomb squad. He should have done a lot of things. But he's so pissed off about their lack of cooperation that he's doing this alone. Even though the only weapon he has is his mini-pistol.

Sometimes, he admits, his pride gets the best of him. Always has.

If there's one person he wishes he had beside him right now, it's John Sampson. But his friend is a world away, with problems of his own.

Alex is standing alone outside the gate of Colton Brophy's compound, just waiting to be seen from inside. A guy with this kind of setup definitely has video surveillance.

In the light of day, it was easy to avoid the trip wire he'd almost stumbled over last night. Under the late-afternoon sun, Alex can see the fenced-in pen clearly. He was right, the pen is indeed filled with pigs — a few big sows and a bunch of snorting piglets rooting around in the straw-covered dirt and dunking their snouts into a long metal water trough.

The front door to the house swings open. Alex tightens his grip on his gun. A huge man steps out onto the porch. Easily three hundred pounds and wearing... *what?*

Alex blinks and squints to be sure of what he's seeing.

No question. The man is dressed in the gray uniform of a Confederate soldier, from cap to boots.

Only the gun in his hand is a total anachronism. An AR-15.

"Mr. Brophy?" Alex calls out. "Do not shoot!"

"Who's there?" Brophy calls back. "This is private property!"

Alex holds his ID over his head. "Alex Cross, FBI! I want to talk to you about a missing person!"

"Who?" Brophy shouts back. "Who's missing?"

"Open the gate, Mr. Brophy!"

"Hold on," says Brophy. "I need to cut power to the fence." He reaches behind the door. Alex hears a loud click.

Colton Brophy shuffles slowly across the farmyard, a ring of keys dangling from one hand. When he gets to the gate, he slips a key into a thick padlock, opens it, and unwinds the chains holding the gate shut.

"Come on in," he says, swinging it open.

Alex follows him, staying in the big man's footprints. He can hear the rippling fabric of the Stars and Bars overhead. Brophy goes up the weather-beaten porch steps and waves for Alex to follow him into the farmhouse.

The smell inside smacks him in the face. Mold, body odor, and a haze of stale garlic and onion fumes.

Lola at the records office said the house had been in the family for over two centuries. And that's exactly how it looks. The floor is buckled and uneven. The carpet is mottled and stained. The sunken furniture is covered in flowered fabric, faded and threadbare. Naked light bulbs run in a string across the low plaster ceiling. The walls are cracked and yellowed. A wood-burning stove sits in one corner, blackened from decades of use.

And there are more signs of the past.

All around the room, Alex sees Civil War memorabilia—medals, cavalry sabers, Springfield rifles, and sepia photographs of grim-faced Confederate soldiers.

Brophy eases himself down into a cushioned armchair. The wooden legs splay slightly as his weight settles.

"I can see you're a history buff," says Alex. "That explains the flag outside." He needs to get Brophy talking, find some common ground.

"I'm a reenactor," says Brophy. He reaches over to a side table and picks up a small tintype showing a young man in a rebel uniform. "That's my character. My great-great-great-grandfather. Private Calvin Brophy, First Corps, Army of Northern Virginia."

He puts down the photo. "Never would have fit into that uniform. Had to make my own."

"Looks accurate to me," says Alex.

He can see that Brophy appreciates the compliment. "Damn right," he says. "Down to the last brass button. I just got back from a battle reenactment in Manassas."

Alex flashes back to his American history. "Bull Run?"

Brophy nods. "Our finest hour." His automatic rifle is resting against his chair. He stares at Alex, breathing heavily. "So. FBI, you said?"

"That's right. I'm a contractor with them, and my background is police work. I'm looking for my son."

"I grew up wanting to be a cop," says Brophy. "The academy wouldn't take me. Fat boy. Neither would the Marines." He grins, showing mottled teeth, and pats the uniform over his bulging belly. "This is the one army that'll have me."

Alex presses on with his case. "Mr. Brophy, like I said, my son is missing. I've been searching the area. That's how I found your place."

"No idea what happened to him?"

"Still piecing it together," says Alex. "He left on his bike one morning a few days ago. He's a student at Chapel Hill. I know that some men in a truck harassed him on the main road near the entrance to the reserve, then stole his bike and phone. After that, he seems to have just disappeared." Alex pulls a wrinkled flyer from his pocket and holds it up. "This is him. This is my son Damon. Have you seen him?"

Brophy leans forward and takes the flyer in his thick hands. He studies it carefully. "Nope. I don't see much of anybody out here." He folds the flyer in half. "Can I keep this?"

"Sure," says Alex. "That phone number works twenty-four seven. I'll give you this too." He pulls a business card from his wallet and hands it to Brophy. "If you see anything, please call me first."

Brophy stands up, his chair creaking with relief. "Will do."

Alex starts for the door, then stops. "You know, I saw what looked like a trip wire in front of your house. I don't think it's for an animal trap."

"It's for my personal protection."

"Mr. Brophy, you can't just be planting explosives on your property. Somebody could get killed while you're away playing soldier."

Brophy's expression suddenly turns dark. *"Reenacting,"* he says, "not playing."

"No offense meant." As eccentric as Brophy seems, Alex needs him on his side.

Brophy holds the door open. "Walk twenty yards straight out from the gate, then turn east. You'll be fine."

"And you'll keep an eye out for my son?"

"I will," says Brophy. "I promise."

As Alex walks across the yard, he looks up and gets a sick feeling. The flag of the Confederate States waves over his head.

A symbol of the Lost Cause.

He hopes it's not an omen.

CHAPTER 88

Sampson

"**YOUR DAUGHTER IS STAYING** at the Cross house, right?" says Aiden Phillips. He's sitting in a chair across from me, his gun still pointed at my face.

I sit stiff and silent at the table. No way I'm giving him any information about Willow.

"It's okay," says Phillips. "I'm glad she's not here. She's been traumatized enough for one day."

Whatever buzz I had from my Scotch has been flushed away by a surge of adrenaline. I'm sitting on the edge of my chair, calculating what it would take to launch myself across the room and knock the gun out of Phillips's hand.

Not yet.

For now, I just need to keep him talking. Best way to survive.

"You said you don't hurt good people, Aiden. Help me understand."

You killed a very good person this morning. And you've killed dozens of other innocent people across DC. Why?"

Phillips shakes his head. "I had nothing to do with Anna Rizzo's death. Or with those other bombings."

"Sorry, Aiden. You can shoot me in the head, but don't take me for an idiot. We have evidence. We have pictures. The CIA knows all about you."

"CIA?" Phillips curls his lip in contempt. "Don't you understand, John? They're storytellers. That's what they do. They made up a story about me, and you bought it, hook, line, and sinker."

He points out the window to the bomb crater in my driveway. He shakes his head. "She had kids, right?"

I nod. "Yeah. Two of them. Just like you do."

"That's right," says Phillips. "You met my family. What did Lisa say about me?"

I'm wondering how long Phillips has been on my tail. How much he knows about the investigation. "She said you had multiple deployments and that you came back a changed man."

"But you asked her about the bombings, right? And I bet she told you that I could never kill innocent people."

"That's right. She did. But maybe that's because she still loves you."

"Lisa's a good woman, John. She *knows* me."

I think about my conversations with Phillips's fellow soldiers, Quint Spooner and Rick Bannon, the ones who told me about his bursts of violence and his fondness for explosives. They seemed to know him too.

"So why the gun, Aiden? Why sneak into my house like some paid assassin? If you knew we were looking for you, why not just turn yourself in, provide your alibis, and prove that you're not the bomber?"

"I told you. I don't trust the government. I especially don't trust the CIA. They twist things. They fabricate things. They paint people in ways that aren't true."

"You worked for them, Aiden. Maybe it takes one to know one. You're not exactly making yourself look innocent here. You're in my home holding a gun on me."

Phillips waves his pistol. "Do you have any more weapons in the house?"

I don't see any point in lying. If he plans to shoot me, one gun is as good as another. "I've got a Ruger pistol in a safe upstairs."

"Good. We're gonna need it."

"Need it for what?"

Phillips stands up. "You want to catch the real bomber, John? The one who's actually behind all this?"

"You know I do."

"Good. I'll take you right to him."

CHAPTER 89

Cross

ALEX CROSS SHOWERS AS soon as he gets back to his hotel room. He wants to get the smell of Colton Brophy's house out of his nostrils.

He emerges from the steamy bathroom with a towel around his waist and slips on a clean pair of boxers. Even though it's barely dark, he slides under the bedsheets, discouraged and exhausted. A few seconds later, he drifts off into a light sleep, the kind where old memories bubble to the surface:

"Daddy! Watch me!"

Alex holds his arms out as Damon, age seven, heads toward him on the sidewalk outside their house. The training wheels are off the red Schwinn bike, and Damon is wobbling along precariously. He looks like he could topple over any second. Alex is ready to intercept him, grab the handlebars, and give him another push. Then he decides to change tactics.

"Pedal harder!" Alex yells. "The faster you go, the more control you have!"

Damon leans his head forward, his white bike helmet gleaming in the sunlight.

His skinny legs start to pump. The front wheel straightens out. A smile takes over his face. He's speeding toward Alex, ringing the bell as he comes.

"Don't stop me!" he calls out. "I can do it!"

Alex lowers his arms and steps aside as Damon whizzes past him toward a small hill, shouting "Yippee!" at the top of his lungs.

As his son's helmet disappears below the rise, Alex runs to the crest and calls after him. "Damon! Come back! That's far enough!"

But Damon is already turning the corner behind a thick hedge.

In a blink, he's out of sight.

"Damon!"

Alex wakes to the sound of his phone vibrating on the nightstand. He picks it up, still groggy. "Hello? Alex Cross."

"Did I wake you?"

Alex rolls onto his side and holds the phone to his ear. "Bree! How are you, sugar?"

"Tired. Very tired. Did you hear about John?"

Alex sits up against the headboard, his heart racing. He flashes back to when his best friend got shot a while ago. "No. What happened?"

"Don't worry, John's okay. But there was a car bomb. I mean an IED. One of his colleagues was killed. A young woman."

"Who?"

"Her name was Anna Rizzo. She was an ATF investigator."

"Where did it happen?"

"At John's home. In his driveway. Willow was upstairs."

"Willow! Is she—"

"She's okay, Alex. She's with us again. I don't know how much she knows, or what she saw. She asked if she could sleep with

Jannie in her bed tonight. We're going to let her decompress for a few days."

"And Sampson?"

"You know John. He just plows on. He's stubborn that way. Like somebody else I know."

"Bree, listen, I found out some more information about what happened to Damon."

"What is it? What happened?"

"A couple of local rednecks in a truck knocked him off his bike near the nature reserve, then threw his bike down the trail where we found it. Stole his phone and laptop too."

"Did they hurt him?"

"I don't think so. I think he might have just run away. He might still be hiding."

"These men, these rednecks—you don't think they did anything to him?"

"No. I'm pretty sure I scared the truth out of one of them. They're thugs and racists, but I don't think they're killers or kidnappers. I'm a fairly good judge of character—especially rotten ones."

"Speaking of rotten characters, I did some checking into Damon's search history and I found some scary stuff. He's been monitoring some alt-right forums, and I'm worried that they might have traced him," says Bree.

"You think they're that smart?" asks Alex.

"I think they're that hateful. You need to call Melissa and organize another search."

"I will. But it's hard to motivate people when there's nothing new. I followed up on another lead near the preserve today. Didn't get anywhere."

"Alex, tell me you're not running around in the woods all by yourself!"

"Okay. I won't tell you."

"Alex Cross, listen to me. You can't do it alone. I wish I could be there with you, but I can't. Make sure you ask others to help!"

"Okay, I promise I will."

"I love you, Alex."

"Love you more."

Alex puts down his phone and lays his head on the pillow. Just a little more rest.

Then he'll go out again. After dark.

There's more to Colton Brophy than meets the eye.

Alex is sure of it.

CHAPTER 90

Sampson

I'M DRIVING AIDEN PHILLIPS'S Dodge Charger down a dark road. He's in the passenger seat, his pistol resting in his lap. Both of my guns are in the trunk, loaded but way out of reach. I'm behind the wheel, but Phillips is in control.

At least for now.

I swerve around a dead possum in the center of the lane. The car handles like a tank.

"What's wrong with this thing?" I ask. "It feels heavy."

"Armor plating underneath," says Phillips. "Adds a quarter ton or so. I welded it on myself."

That answer matches up with all the weapons and tactical gear I saw in the trunk.

"What are you, Aiden? Some kind of doomsday prepper?"

"No. I'm a survivalist. I believe the government could come after us at any time. When they do, I'll be ready."

We're approaching Reedville, Virginia, a couple hours south of DC, not far from the Chesapeake Bay. It's an isolated area dotted with farmhouses and trailers. Not another car on the road.

We're looking for a man named J. T. Polermo.

Phillips showed me his picture before we left my house. The two of them were together in DC on a two-week leave from Afghanistan, just one block from the Capitol, both in military camo gear, getting ready to join the march that day in January.

According to Phillips, he and Polermo had split a liberated supply of C-4 and smuggled it into the States.

Phillips says that Polermo is behind the bombings. "But I'm the one being framed for it."

For some reason, I believe him.

We've spent most of the ride not speaking, listening to right-wing radio. Phillips's choice. To me, it all sounds like batshit conspiracy theories and white-guy grievances. But I can tell that Phillips is soaking it up, nodding to every word. "Damn straight," he mutters now and then.

I stand the screeds for as long as I can, then reach over and switch off the radio. I expect Phillips to react, but he just stares out the window. I want to get him talking again. Find out what I might be walking into.

"So that's the last time you saw Polermo?" I ask. "At the insurrection?"

"You mean the march for electoral integrity?"

"If you say so." I never argue politics with a man holding a gun.

"Yeah," says Phillips. "I lost track of him after that. We had different ideas about how to get back at the system."

"You mean you wanted to just limit yourself to trashing the People's House?"

I feel Phillips tense up. "I never went inside the building," he claims. "Got pepper-sprayed just the same." He gestures with his pistol barrel. "Take this turn."

I ease off onto a dirt road. I feel the undercarriage scrape. Now we're passing crop rows and farm equipment. In the distance I can make out the glow from a small ranch house. Nothing around it.

"Cut your lights," says Phillips.

I turn them off and follow the road by feel. The high grass brushes the outside mirror, and the tires roll along deep grooves in the dirt. The chassis creaks and rumbles.

I wish we had some backup. But Phillips has my phone. Wouldn't let me make a call. He says he won't trust anybody but me. Not sure why I have that honor, but so far, it seems to be keeping me alive.

"You think Polermo will talk to you?" I ask.

"No, John. I think he'll kill me. Or try to. We need to get the drop on him. And it won't be easy. He was an escape and evasion trainer. He trained me."

"How do you know he's even here?"

"Give me some credit," says Phillips. "Do you think you're the only one I've been tracking?"

My left tire hits a dip in the road. Then...

Bam!

I get slammed against the door as the car flips over, my side down. I see a flash of flames from outside. My ears are ringing.

"IED!" Phillips shouts. "Get out!"

He releases his seat belt and falls on top of me. I unclip my belt and climb out behind him through the broken window, then fall on the ground, scraping my leg on a piece of twisted metal.

"Get the guns!" Phillips shouts. "He's ready for us!"

I crawl around to the back of the car. The trunk is blown open. My Ruger and my Glock are lying against the sidewall, ammo clips scattered all over. There's also two armored vests, cartons of water, and packets of survival food. I grab the guns and a few extra clips, trying to clear my head. Phillips reaches past me and unstraps a rifle case from deep in the trunk. He unzips it and pulls out an M4 carbine. He hands me a ballistic vest and slides the other one over his head.

Thick smoke is billowing from under the car, obscuring my vision. Phillips pulls me away from the vehicle and into the high grass beside the road.

He sticks his pistol in his belt and grips the automatic rifle, tightens the telescopic sight. I jam a clip into my Glock and slide my Ruger under my belt.

Phillips points across the expanse of tall grass. "We need to move fast. He'll be setting up a field of fire."

And just like that, I'm in combat again.

I grab Phillips's sleeve. "Aiden! If this is really the guy, I want him alive."

"Copy that," he says. "But he doesn't feel the same about us."

CHAPTER 91

Polermo

INSIDE THE RENTED SINGLE-STORY house, former army lieutenant J. T. Polermo assembles his arsenal and plans another getaway. He doesn't know if the burning car in the approach road was a lone invader or the scout for a larger assault team, but he can't take any chances.

He peeks through his living-room window with a night-vision spotting scope and sees two figures moving away from the burning vehicle. One he recognizes. The other, a very tall Black man, he does not. But he has a feeling about who sent them.

He lowers the top frame on a double-hung window and knocks out the screen, then shoulders an automatic rifle and rests it on the frame. He fires off a quick burst and watches the men drop. He waits for return fire.

Nothing.

Polermo hurries into a vestibule, pulls out a camo duffel, and removes a brick of C-4, one of many in his collection. He slings the bag and his rifle over his shoulder, goes to the kitchen, unwinds a length of det cord, and sticks the end into the C-4. He opens the stove and puts the explosive inside, then turns all the gas valves to high. The room fills with the odor of mercaptan.

Polermo unspools the det cord and trails it behind him to the back door. There, he pulls out a Bic lighter and holds the flame to the end of the det cord until it starts to sizzle. Then he shoves the back door open and heads for the woods.

Escape and evade.

CHAPTER 92

Sampson

I'M ON MY BELLY, hugging the ground in the tall grass. Aiden Phillips is a few yards away. As soon as the volley raked over our heads, I wanted to return fire—but Phillips said to hold up. "Let him think he hit us."

We advance like crabs through the grass toward the house. I've got my pistol in one hand as I dig in with my elbows to pull myself forward. I can see the grass moving alongside me as Phillips crawls along on a parallel path.

Twenty yards from the house, the tall grass gives way to a roughly mowed yard. No more cover. No way to rush the place without being exposed on open ground. A frontal assault on a fixed position would be insane. Especially for a two-man infantry unit.

I dig in and sight along my pistol barrel from window to window. Then…

Boom!

The house explodes in a ball of flame and smoke!

I cover my head against the blast. Shingles and siding rain down around me in flaming chunks. When I look up, black smoke is belching out through a hole in the roof.

Phillips shouts, *"Let's go,"* and heads toward the house, gun raised.

"Aiden! Stop! No way he survived that!"

Phillips turns and shouts back over the roar of the fire, "I know J.T.! That wasn't suicide! That was a diversion!"

CHAPTER 93

Cross

ALEX CROSS PICKS HIS way carefully around the perimeter of the fence on Colton Brophy's property. He now knows to look for trip wires and step around them. Even in the dark.

When he reaches the main gate, Alex settles in beside a post and watches the house through a pair of mini-binoculars. The lights are on, and he can see movement inside. Every few minutes, Brophy's bulky shape is framed behind one of the barred windows.

Suddenly, the front door opens. Brophy emerges wearing a pair of denim overalls, like a farmer's. In his hands, he's carrying a steaming metal pot. He walks across the scrubby yard of the compound toward the barn. He stops at the wooden gate to the pigsty and lifts a latch. A few of the pigs move toward him, expecting a meal. Brophy kicks them away.

Halfway across the pen, he puts the pot on the ground and reaches down. He grabs a metal bar and pries under the straw.

Alex hears the scrape of metal on metal. Brophy lifts one edge of a thick panel, grabs it in both hands, and pulls it up until it locks into position at a forty-five-degree angle.

Some kind of hatch!

Brophy picks up the pot, then turns around and lowers himself down into the opening. When only his head is showing, he shuts the hatch. The pigs shuffle across the closed cover, spreading straw and shit as they go — almost like they're part of the Houdini act.

Is this the bomb shelter Brophy got approval for years back? Alex wonders. *And what's he doing down there with a cooking pot?*

One thing's for sure: Brophy didn't come to feed the hogs.

Alex presses himself closer to the ground and waits for the hatch to open again. Two minutes. Three. He looks up at the thick chain holding the gate shut and at the high-voltage line running through the barbed wire.

I need a way in. But how?

Maybe it's time to call for reinforcements. He pulls his phone out of his pocket.

A twig snaps. Alex flinches. He turns his head.

A boot kicks his phone away, and his cheek touches the cold end of a shotgun barrel.

CHAPTER 94

Sampson

I FOLLOW AIDEN PHILLIPS past the burning house toward the woods out back. Smoke is everywhere. My lungs are burning. I stop to peek into a gray Ford pickup truck parked on a concrete slab. I point my gun into the passenger compartment, then into the cargo bed.

Both empty.

I can hear Phillips picking his way through the underbrush ahead of me. I take a position a few yards to his left and start moving with him.

The only light comes from the fire behind us. It's enough to see only about twenty feet ahead. Beyond that, it's pitch-black. Phillips stops behind a tree to peer through his telescopic sight. He points to the left and motions me forward.

I hear footsteps crunching in the distance. Phillips takes off past me in pursuit. I swing wide and get stuck from the knees down in a patch of brambles. As I try to twist free, my Glock falls out of my hand. I reach for it and hear a crack reverberate through the woods.

I look up. No Phillips.

I hear a groan from up ahead.

"Aiden?"

I yank my gun out of the briars and run in a crouch toward the sound. I find him behind a downed tree, curled into a ball, his rifle off to the side.

"I'm hit," he croaks through gritted teeth.

I drop my gun and run my hands over his shoulders and arms. Clean. I roll him onto his back. That's when I see it. A purplish slice in the flesh of his right thigh. A crimson stain is spreading through his jeans across his groin and legs.

I lean in close, tug at the hole in the denim. I'm hoping not to see a rhythmic spurt from a vessel in his inner thigh. I see only oozing, pooling blood.

"You're in luck," I tell him. "It missed the femoral."

Phillips reaches into his pocket and pulls out a folding knife. "Cut my sleeve off," he says. "Wrap it."

I open the knife and jab the point into his work shirt over his biceps, then slice it until the sleeve comes off, leaving his arm bare. I wrap the cloth around his bloody thigh.

"Tighter!" He groans.

I've done plenty of field dressings in my life, but nothing this primitive. I add another twist and secure it the best I can.

"Can you walk?" I ask him.

He grimaces with pain. "I dunno. Maybe." I put his arm around my shoulders and pull him upright. He takes one step on his bloodied leg and falters. "Maybe not." He groans again.

"Hold on." I reach for his rifle and sling it over my right shoulder, bend my knees, and grab his arms. Then I do a dead lift. Lucky for me, he's a relative lightweight, probably a hundred and seventy pounds, fully dressed. Still, it's more weight than I've lugged since my army days. I stagger back through the trees with Phillips over my shoulders. I'm running on pure adrenaline, just like in a hundred other firefights. I'm waiting for the shot that takes me down.

By now, the flames have engulfed the whole house. One side is buckling outward, leaning toward the pickup.

I say a little prayer that Polermo isn't the type to worry about auto theft. When we get to the driver's side of the truck, I lower Phillips to the ground and reach in through the open passenger-side window.

I yank down the visor. *Yes!* The keys drop onto the seat. I drag Phillips around to the other side. I can feel the fire at my back as I open the passenger door and lift him onto the seat. He lets out a grunt. I check the makeshift bandage. Still in place. The bleeding has slowed, but he's looking pale. I know the signs. Shock is setting in.

I fasten his seat belt, then grab my cell phone out of his pocket. I open Google Maps. "The nearest hospital is in Kilmarnock. Twenty miles."

I turn the key in the ignition and put the truck in gear. Phillips reaches over and grabs my arm. "John, wait," he says. "Listen to me..."

CHAPTER 95

Maine

GINA MAINE PUTS HER last dirty plate in the dishwasher and starts it. She wipes her hands on a towel, then bends over the sink and splashes some water on her face. She's so exhausted from her shift at the VA hospital that she hasn't even bothered to change out of her scrubs yet. But now it's time for bed, and she really needs a shower.

She's halfway down the hall when she hears banging on her front door, followed by a quick series of dings on her doorbell. Gina's heart pounds as she heads through her living room. She keeps the chain lock fastened when she opens the door a crack to look out.

"Yes? Can I—" She stops.

On her porch, a huge man is supporting the weight of a smaller man, hanging limp at his side. In a split second, Gina recognizes them both. It's that detective who questioned her at the hospital. John Sampson.

The man he's holding is Aiden Phillips.

"Open the door, Gina," says Sampson. "He needs help."

She closes the door just enough to unclasp the chain. When she opens the door wide, she can see dark spots speckling her front step.

Blood.

CHAPTER 96

Cross

ALEX CROSS FEELS THE shotgun at his back as Colton Brophy nudges him across the scrubby farmyard. Alex's pistol is now in Brophy's pocket along with his ID and cell phone.

Next to the barn, the pigs are rooting and squealing in their pen. Alex is mentally kicking himself for not realizing that the bomb shelter might have another exit. He'd been too busy looking ahead to check his flank. Stupid mistake. Careless. Possibly fatal.

Brophy marches Alex into the pen, then grabs his shoulder and pulls him to a stop. "Face down, arms out."

Alex slowly drops to the ground. The shit-and-ammonia odor here is almost overwhelming. His eyes start to water. He's heard of bodies being fed to pigs. He's seen the results on forensics videos. Nothing left but dentures. Alex has all his natural teeth.

He turns his head in the dirt and sees Brophy again lifting the metal hatch with one hand, shotgun tucked under the other arm.

"You're making a big mistake," says Alex. "I'm with the FBI."

"I know. You told me. You gave me your card, remember? Psychologist. I checked into you. You're some kind of expert on the criminal mind."

"That's right. Which means people will be looking for me."

"Maybe you should have brought them along."

Alex feels the barrel in his side as Brophy prods him to his feet. But this is as far as Alex plans to go. He knows the stats. Resistance is his best chance. Maybe his *only* chance.

As he pushes himself to his feet, he curls his right fingers into his palm, gathering a fistful of loose dirt and straw.

Brophy gestures toward the hatch opening. Alex can make out a dim light below. Stepping closer, he sees a metal ladder that looks like something repurposed from a manhole.

"Turn around," says Brophy. "Back down."

Alex turns his back to the hatch, facing Brophy. He lunges forward, whipping the dirt into Brophy's face, then plows his shoulder into his midsection. Brophy just grunts. It's like trying to topple a statue. He shoves Alex back by the shoulders and thrusts the shotgun barrel into his solar plexus. *Hard.*

Alex crumples, then staggers back, breathless and off balance.

He feels himself falling into the pit. He hears the pigs squealing.

His head strikes something hard.

A stunning pain.

And he's out.

CHAPTER 97

Sampson

I'M LEANING AGAINST Gina Maine's kitchen counter, watching her drop another pair of surgical gloves into the trash. Her scrubs are streaked with blood. She's glaring at me.

"You did a good job," I tell her.

She's in no mood for compliments. "Look, Detective, I haven't treated a wound like that since I was fresh out of nursing school. I stopped the bleeding and cleaned up the leg, but he needs serious medical attention. I'm not sure my dressing will hold. You shouldn't have come here."

"I had no choice."

"Why?"

"You'll have to ask him."

Aiden Phillips had given me the location of Gina's house, about halfway between Reedville and Richmond. He insisted that he couldn't go to the hospital. The authorities would turn him in, he said. And once he was in the system, he'd never get out alive. There were people who would make sure of that, he said.

Before I could ask him who he was talking about, he passed out in the car. But I had more immediate worries. I was afraid he'd bleed out.

Now he's wrapped in a blanket in Gina's guest room. The wound was through-and-through the muscle. Anybody who's been in combat will tell you that if you have to get shot, that's the best way to do it. Clear entry and exit points. No bullet left in the body.

From what I could see as Gina worked, Phillips was hit in his topmost right quad. The bullet had grazed his other leg on the way out but left only a scratch. No vital organs or structures touched. Manhood intact.

Gina storms past me now and heads down the hall to check on Phillips again. I grab a roll of paper towels from the counter and start to wipe the blood off her tile floor. When I turn around, Gina is holding up her cell phone.

"I don't care what you say. I'm calling 911. If he goes into shock and dies in my bedroom, I could lose my job. My nursing license. I could be arrested. You know this is not a first aid situation. He needs medical treatment. There's a firehouse five minutes away."

I could stop her. But I don't. Because she's right. Phillips should go to the hospital. I'll make sure he doesn't get lost in the system. At this point, I think I've earned that kind of clout. Gina dials and puts the phone on speaker.

The dispatcher picks up. "This is 911. What's your emergency?"

Gina's tone is calm and precise. She gives her address and says, "I need an ambulance here. Adult male, GSW to the upper leg."

"Is he breathing?"

"Yes. I'm an RN. He's breathing and his vitals are within normal limits. But he needs transport ASAP."

"I'm rolling the unit right now. Do you want me to stay on the phone with you until they arrive?"

"No. I'm good. Thanks. Just...tell them to hurry."

Gina hangs up, tosses her phone onto a table, and slumps down in a chair. She stares at me. "So are you going to tell me who the hell shot him?"

"Gina, you can't be involved in this."

"*Involved?* I just had my hand inside that man's leg!"

"I don't want to tell you anything that would jam you up later. The less you know, the better."

"Jam me up how?"

"I can't explain. Look, Aiden trusted you enough to make me drive him here. Now you need to trust me. I'll handle the paramedics when they get here, and I'll ride in the bus with Aiden. I'm not letting him out of my sight. If anybody gives you a hard time about this, I promise, I'll have your back."

"You damn well better."

I can already hear the whine of sirens in the distance. Gina gets up, opens her front door, and holds it open with a brick. Then she goes back into the kitchen and grabs her blood pressure monitor. "I'm checking him once more before they take him."

She heads down the hall.

Two seconds later I hear "Goddamn it, Aiden!"

I run to the bedroom. The covers are thrown back. Blood has soaked through the medical pad all the way to the mattress. The window is open.

Aiden Phillips is gone.

CHAPTER 98

THE TRUCK! THE RIFLE! *My guns!*

I run back through the living room and out through the wide-open front door just in time to see the taillights of the pickup disappearing down the road. Passing it in the other direction are two sets of flashing lights—a police car followed by a box-type ambulance, sirens wailing. A few seconds later, the high beams of the patrol car hit me square in the face.

Gina rushes out the front door and stops at my side as the first responders arrive. "Remember," I tell her, "I'll handle this."

"No shit you will."

The cop jumps out of his vehicle as the ambulance pulls up right behind him. A pair of paramedics, a male and a female, climb down out of the cab and grab their gear.

I meet the cop halfway to the door, shoving my badge in his

face. "John Sampson, DC Metro Police!" I point down the road. "We need an APB on that truck you just passed!"

The paramedics are already pushing past me into the house. The cop looks confused.

"Truck? What truck? We're responding to a medical emergency." He points to the house. "Is this your residence?"

I nod to Gina, standing on the front step. "No, it's hers. She placed the 911."

The cop walks up to her. "What's your name, miss?"

"Maine. Gina Maine."

The female paramedic is back already, poking her head out of the door. She calls out to the cop. "Hey. There's nobody here. But there's fresh blood on one of the beds."

The cop turns to me. "What the hell is going on here? We got a call about a gunshot victim. Where is he?"

I try my best to hold it together. Keeping my tone low and reasonable, I say, "That's what I'm telling you. He's gone. He drove off as you were coming in."

The cop scratches his ear. "Drove off? With a bullet wound?"

Both paramedics are now standing in the doorway, staring at me like I'm crazy. I pull Gina over. "Ms. Maine is a nurse. I brought the victim to her and she gave him emergency treatment. After she called it in, he escaped."

"Escaped?"

"He's wanted for questioning in a federal case. The DC bombings."

"He's a suspect?"

"The evidence points that way. All I know is, we need to find him."

The cop turns to Gina. "Did you know you were harboring a fugitive?"

She jerks her thumb at me. "Talk to him."

"What's this mystery man's name?" asks the cop.

"His name is Aiden Phillips," I say. "He's a veteran. And he's got some serious issues."

"You mean beyond the bullet in his leg?"

I glance at the cop's name tag: A. F. Neal. "Look, Officer Neal. This case involves DC Metro, CIA, FBI. It's about national security. And what I need right now is an alert on a gray 2015 Ford Ranger with Delaware plates!"

Neal pushes past the paramedics. "Show me the bed."

"We're wasting time here!"

Neal ignores me. The paramedics lead him to the guest bedroom, with me and Gina right behind. We all crowd through the narrow doorway. Neal steps to the far side of the bed and bends down to look at the bloodstains. He presses his shoulder mic. "Unit fifty-five, requesting backup at—"

I grab his arm. "No! You don't need backup! You need to find Phillips!"

Neal makes a pushing motion to nudge everybody into the hall. "I'm securing this room. My sergeant will be here in five minutes. Until we sort this out, nobody's leaving."

I'm out of options, so I try pulling rank. "Goddamn it, Officer! I'm a detective grade one!"

Neal shakes his head. "Not here in the Commonwealth of Virginia."

He's right. I'm not the boss of him.

CHAPTER 99

Cross

"DAD! OH MY GOD! DAD!"

Alex Cross is face down on a cold concrete floor. His ribs feel bruised. His back feels twisted. And his ears must be playing tricks on him.

"Dad!"

He feels hands on him, rolling him over. He blinks in the glare of an overhead light. A figure is hovering over him. Alex shades his eyes with one hand.

"Damon?"

Alex's heart is racing. He tries to lift himself up. Can't do it. Hurts too much.

"Dad, don't move!"

Dazed and disoriented, Alex manages to turn his head to one side. The walls are cinder block. The ceiling is steel. The stench is horrific. Pain shoots through his body. He squeezes his eyes shut, praying that he's not hallucinating. "Damon! Is that really you?"

He feels a hand squeezing his. "Yes, Dad! It's me! I'm okay."

Alex opens his eyes again and grabs his son's arm. "The men! The rednecks. The ones who took your bike—"

"How do you know about them?" asks Damon.

"Never mind," says Alex. "Did they hurt you? Are they the ones who brought you here?"

Damon shakes his head. "No. They chased me on the main road. I felt too exposed staying there, so I went into the reserve and stayed there all day, until dark. Then I tried going home, but I couldn't find my way back to the main road. I was too turned around. I finally saw some lights from a farmhouse, so I headed that way. Before I even got there, I was whacked on the head and dumped into this goddamn pit."

"Brophy," says Alex.

"Who?"

"Colton Brophy. The guy who owns this place. That's his name. He's some kind of Confederate fanboy Civil War reenactor." Alex sits up with a groan. He touches his belt, feeling for his gun. Nothing but the empty holster. "Damn it! Brophy has my gun. My phone and badge too."

"You've talked to him?" Damon asks.

Alex nods. "Earlier today. I was in his house up top. I showed him your picture. Asked for his help. But something didn't feel right, so I came back tonight. I got careless, and he caught me. Nobody knows I'm here."

Alex feels like an idiot. It's not the first time his independent nature has gotten him in trouble or put him in danger. He should know better by now.

He flinches when he sees movement in the shadows behind his son.

Damon turns and beckons two people over. "Guys, this is my father, Dr. Alex Cross. Dad, this is Professor Lucas and Amy Tyne."

Holy shit.

Darius Lucas is a slim, serious-looking Black man. Amy Tyne is petite and pale with a short, elfin haircut. "Sorry to meet you this way, Dr. Cross," she says. She kneels alongside Alex and runs her hands over his legs. "Can you feel this?"

Alex nods.

She places her hands around his ankles and wiggles them. "How about this?"

"Yes," says Alex impatiently. "I'm fine!"

Amy looks over at Damon. "I think your dad's okay. He's just shaken up."

Alex looks at Lucas and Tyne. "How long have you two…"

"We're not sure," says Lucas. "We think we were here for a week before the guy brought Damon down."

"What about your research trip? Your department head told me—"

"We never left," says Amy. "Never made the plane."

"Do you mind telling me where you were going?" asks Alex.

Tyne glances at Lucas, clearly not sure if she should speak.

"Gambia," says Lucas. "We're investigating the slave trade to North Carolina in the mid-1700s. We think it was more extensive than previously reported."

"Gambia was one of the main ports of embarkation," says Tyne.

Lucas nods. "We're looking for the names of ship captains, manifests, and the names of North Carolina traders and slaveholders."

No wonder Reuben Chase wanted to keep this research under

wraps. "I can understand why your department head was so secretive."

"Roots can get really tangled when you go back that far," says Lucas. "But we're just looking for the truth."

"Right," says Tyne. "But Chase also wants to be sure that nothing we uncover will embarrass the state or the university. Or the donors."

"So what happened to you?" asks Alex.

Lucas answers. "We went hiking in the reserve the day before we were scheduled to leave. We spotted a huge Confederate flag through the trees and decided to investigate. But someone must've come up behind us and knocked us out when we got close to the fence."

"When we came to," says Tyne, "we were down here."

"You're lucky you weren't blown to bits," says Alex. "Brophy's got the whole place mined. He's stuck in his own little paramilitary world and seems to think the Confederacy was on the right side of history."

Damon leans in close, his hands on Alex's shoulders. "Dad, does he know about Melissa?"

"What do you mean?"

Damon's voice is pinched and anxious. "He must've checked my socials once he knew my name." Alex sees a flash of fear cross Damon's face. "When he came down here earlier, that guy told me my girlfriend and I would be reunited soon. And for good."

CHAPTER 100

Sampson

IT TOOK ME ANOTHER half an hour to pry myself out of Gina Maine's house.

It wasn't easy.

When the supervising sergeant first arrived, he was just as suspicious as Officer Neal was. It took an encrypted call to Ned Mahoney at home to convince the sergeant that I knew what I was talking about and that we had a serious fugitive situation on our hands. Two fugitive situations, counting J. T. Polermo. Both men armed and dangerous.

By the time Neal put out the APB for Polermo's truck, the Virginia State Police had already found it. It was abandoned near a water tower in Stratford, about halfway back to DC. No sign of Aiden Phillips. No weapons in the vehicle. Just some bloodstains on the driver's seat.

Either Phillips is on foot or he's found alternate transportation—probably by stealing a vehicle. We know that he's highly trained and heavily armed.

He could also be bleeding to death.

Once the cops were convinced that Gina had been nothing more than a Good Samaritan, she let me borrow her Subaru to join the search. Before I got into the car, she grabbed my arm. "Find him," she said. "Don't kill him."

I told her I'd do my best.

Two and a half hours later, I'm driving through a residential neighborhood just outside of Georgetown. The street is lined with pole lights that look like nineteenth-century gas lamps. The houses are sturdy brick Colonials with huge yards, separated from one another by thick hedges. The cars in the driveways are Mercedes, Audis, and BMWs. It's the kind of enclave where well-paid government workers raise their kids and enjoy their cocktails. A bedroom community, sleepy and secure.

I'd gotten the address from Mahoney. He'd asked if I wanted help. I told him I'd call if I needed it. For now, I told him, I was just looking for a conversation.

What I really want is some answers. If Polermo is the real bomber, then somebody framed Phillips—and did a good job of it.

Sure fooled me.

I lean out the window and scan for the house number. *There!* I pull up in front of an elegant residence with a red door and white shutters. I wasn't expecting a senior CIA officer to have his name plastered on his mailbox, but there it is, plain as day: R. PERKINS.

It's time for a one-on-one with my supposed partner at Langley.

If Phillips is right, the CIA is wrong.

About everything.

CHAPTER 101

Melissa

"AMERICA HAS ALLOWED ITSELF to become contaminated and degraded! Our national identity is being corroded from within! Before long, we won't even know who we are as a people! And here in the South, our cultural integrity is under threat again."

Michaelson Woods has been speaking for nearly an hour. He's a handsome young man, tall and preppy with wavy blond hair. What's more, he has an electrifying presence, and he's a galvanizing speaker, even with a mostly hostile audience in front of him. In fact, he seems energized by the catcalls and chants that follow almost every pronouncement he makes.

"Nazi, go home!"

"Fascist!"

"I hear you!" Woods shouts back. "But I'm right. And America knows it!"

Behind him on the outdoor podium, white men in black

uniforms and domino masks stand at attention. A long line of them. Below, in front of the stage, a cordon of Chapel Hill police stand facing the audience.

Woods is lit from below by a bright spotlight that casts a huge shadow across a long row of American flags. Here and there in the audience, red, white, and blue glow lights flicker in the dark.

Melissa Lange and Nia Williams are watching from the left side of the huge gathering, angry and disgusted. Woods's voice blasts from PA speakers at deafening levels. Melissa leans toward Nia's ear and shouts over the ranting, *"Do you believe this shit?"*

Cold fury shows in Nia's eyes. She shakes her head. *"No, I don't!"* she yells back. *"I thought the country was past this!"*

The two of them are packed in with other anti-Woods protesters, barricaded in a makeshift corral, most holding handmade signs and banners. Melissa carries a placard that says FREE SPEECH, NOT HATE SPEECH! At the end of every one of Woods's inflammatory catchphrases, she thrusts the sign up and waves it over her head. In response, counterprotesters on the opposite side of the park hoist signs of their own.

AMERICA FOR AMERICANS!

DILUTION IS POLLUTION!

ONE COLOR, ONE COUNTRY!

After a last high-pitched harangue, Woods starts wrapping up. Melissa has watched him do this same finale dozens of times. Always the same closing. "To all true citizens, remember — legacy Americans are the heart and soul of this nation! We will not be removed, we will not be replaced, we will not be forgotten! This is still our country! But only if we fight to keep it as it was meant to be. Pure! Strong! And righteous!"

Nia cups her hands around her mouth and shouts toward the

stage, "You mean *white*!" But her voice is lost in the mixture of boos and cheers that accompany Woods's final fist pump.

As he exits the stage, the PA system starts blasting "This Land Is Your Land." Not the Woody Guthrie folk-anthem version. This one was recorded by a student choir at a Christian university. Combined with the visual of Woods's uniformed acolytes, the lyrics take on a whole different meaning.

"They're co-opting *this* song?" Nia shouts in disgust. *"Really?"*

She and Melissa are jostled from side to side as the crowd disperses.

Melissa drops her sign into a huge trash barrel and wipes her eyes.

"What's wrong?" asks Nia. "What's going on?"

"Damon should be here," Melissa says. "He would have jumped right up on that stage and grabbed the microphone. He would have shut Woods down and made a speech of his own!"

Nia opens her arms and brings Melissa in for a long hug. "I know, I know." She pats Melissa's head gently. "We'll find him. I know we will."

When Melissa pulls away, her eyes are red. "I'm not sure anymore, Nia. I'm losing hope. I'm not sure I'll ever see him again."

Nia wraps her arm around Melissa's shoulders. "Stop it. Don't talk like that. Tell you what — come back to my house. We'll crash on my sofa, drink some cheap wine, and" — she shouts toward the stage — *"forget about all this bullshit!"*

Melissa shakes her head. "Thanks, Nia, but I'm tired. I just want to go home. You need a lift?"

Nia thinks for a second. "Nah. I think I'll just wander around the park for a while, see if I can get into a fistfight with a racist."

They hug again. Melissa walks down the barricade line toward the parking lot, now a tangle of exiting vehicles, honking and inching along, bumper to bumper.

Since the lot was already filled to overflowing by the time she arrived that evening, Melissa had parked in a small cul-de-sac at the edge of campus. It was a reserved faculty space, but she'd grabbed it anyway. Hopefully, she won't find a ticket from campus security under her wiper blade.

Melissa walks up the small grassy rise that separates the parking lot from a cluster of academic buildings. Most of the crowd is behind her now, moving in the other direction. When she looks over her shoulder, she can still see the brightly lit flags behind the stage. The music is still pumping.

Where's Michaelson Woods right now? she wonders. *Probably in his armored SUV heading to his next rally to give his next dog-whistle speech.*

Melissa is still simmering with anger, and not just about what Woods said. Maybe without all the disruption and conflict caused by his visit, the Chapel Hill police could have focused on finding the man she loves.

She passes a group of students heading in the other direction, male and female, all giggling and clinging to one another. Melissa can smell the pot fumes in the air. One of the white girls is locked in a kiss with a Black kid.

Melissa wipes her eyes again. *Damn it, Damon! Where are you?*

Her Kia is just ahead, sitting alone by the curb. Lucky for her, no ticket. Melissa pulls her key fob from her bag and clicks the button. Her car cheeps and the parking lights flash. The building behind the car is mostly dark, just a few scattered offices lit up on the top floor.

It was smart to park here. I can avoid the bottlenecks at the parking-lot exits and cruise home in no time. All she wants to do now is take a hot shower and forget every hateful word Michaelson Woods just spewed.

She reaches for the door handle.

Suddenly, something thick and dank is pulled over her head and down to her shoulders. A hand clamps over her mouth through the covering. Her car keys are ripped from her hand.

Melissa twists and kicks. She slams her feet toward the car door, trying to set off the alarm. *"Stop! Let me go!"*

No use. Her voice is muffled beneath the covering. Her feet flail in midair.

Whoever's holding her is a lot stronger than she is — and more than twice her size.

CHAPTER 102

Sampson

ROLAND PERKINS LEADS ME into his home office. A thinking man's man cave, the kind they show in architectural magazines demonstrating classic Georgetown style. Floor-to-ceiling bookshelves. Oriental carpet centered on a dark hardwood floor. Warm, cozy lighting from a brass lamp on a sturdy oak desk.

Perkins sits down stiffly on one of his matching leather sofas. "You should have called," he says.

"Surprise visits are best," I tell him. "Something I learned from my old friend Alex Cross. That way, people don't have time to rehearse their stories."

I can tell that Perkins is peeved that I'm here. Also nervous. There's a sheen of sweat on his forehead.

It's just the two of us. Perkins lives alone. Divorced. Kids on alternate weekends. That much I got from Ned Mahoney.

"What's this about, Sampson? Is it about Anna Rizzo? Because—"

I hold up my hand to interrupt him. "Quiet. The reason I'm here is that I found Aiden Phillips. Actually, he found me."

Perkins blinks and shifts on the sofa. "Then I'm surprised you're still alive. What happened?"

"He got away. He's wounded."

"You shot him?"

"No. Somebody else did."

"Did you interrogate him?"

"Not really. I mostly listened. And from what he told me, I believe he's innocent. Look, I know what he did in the past. He's got a lot of darkness in him, for sure. But I don't think he's our bomber."

Perkins is silent. Only his eyes shift. Not the reaction I expected. I hear a rustle behind me, then a voice.

"Finally. I just wanted to hear somebody say it out loud."

No need to turn around. I already know who it is.

Aiden Phillips.

I look at Perkins. "How long has he been here?"

"Since before you arrived. Nothing I could do. He's had a gun on us the whole time."

Phillips moves around to the center of the room, pointing his pistol back and forth between us. He's limping, favoring his wounded leg. He's wearing the same jeans he was shot in. The blood has crusted and dried around the tear. I can see Gina's dressing through the hole. Phillips is pale and sweaty, but he seems sharp and in command.

He grabs the landline off the desk and plops it in Perkins's lap. "Call Walsh," he orders. "Put it on speaker. And no coded shit. All you say is 'I need you here now. It's important.' Then hang up."

Perkins picks up the handset and I hear a sequence of beeping tones as he enters the number.

Two rings. Then a pickup.

"Perkins! What's up?"

"I need you here now," says Perkins. "It's important." He hangs up.

I look over at Phillips. "Have you thought this through? What if Walsh brings an army with him?"

"He won't," says Phillips. "He and Perkins go way back. There's stuff they don't want anybody else to be in on. He'll come by himself." Phillips checks his watch. "He won't be long. Only lives five blocks away. Same kind of cozy little cocoon."

Perkins turns to me. "Why the hell do you believe this guy? You know he's a rogue operator. You heard what he did in Afghanistan. He's a stone-cold killer."

"I was a soldier," says Phillips. "Well trained. By the United States government."

"You did those missions over the border on your own!" says Perkins. "Those were your own personal black ops!"

"That's right. I did it to save some of the people this country left behind. The Afghans who risked everything for us. The people who guys like you ignored."

Perkins shakes his head. "You knew we couldn't get everybody out. That was never a possibility."

"What about Polermo?" I ask. "Was he one of yours? Were you running him too?"

Perkins looks blank. "Who the hell is Polermo?"

"First Lieutenant J. T. Polermo," says Phillips. "We deployed together."

"I don't know any Polermo," says Perkins.

I hear a car pulling into the driveway.

Phillips looks out the window. "That's okay. Walsh does."

CHAPTER 103

Cross

ALEX CROSS HAS SPENT the past hour looking for a pole, a brick, a nail—anything. But the tiny underground enclosure is bare except for a bolted-down chemical toilet, a couple of filthy mattresses, and the cooking pot, which Alex can see is half filled with soup. The door to the rear exit is locked. Solid steel. A single industrial bulb glares down. The only other break in the ceiling is an air-vent grate, welded on.

"We need some kind of tool," says Alex. "Some kind of weapon..."

"Forget it," says Damon. "We've searched every inch of this place."

"One night," says Amy, "I thought about grabbing the soup pot and hitting the fat fuck in the head with it. But he always keeps one hand on his gun."

"No sense in shouting from down here," says Lucas. "The walls are too thick."

"Right," says Alex. "It's bombproof. And we're about twelve feet down. Under a pigsty."

"Is that what we're smelling?" asks Lucas.

"That — and ourselves," says Damon.

Damon is right. The air is ripe with body odor and the emissions from the toilet in the corner. The pungent smell, the head injury, and the lack of oxygen all combine to make Alex feel dizzy.

Think, Cross, think!

Suddenly, the hatch creaks and a shaft of light shoots down the ladder. Alex can hear snorting pigs and footsteps rustling in the straw overhead. A few clumps of dirt and manure drop onto the ladder steps.

Kicking feet appear in the opening.

Not Brophy's.

Alex, Damon, Lucas, and Tyne rush to the bottom of the ladder and look up.

"Back away!" Brophy's voice from above. "Make room!"

The figure coming down feetfirst is female. As she descends, she thrashes her legs, feeling for support. *"Stop! Where are you taking me?"* Her voice is muffled by a thick canvas hood draped over her head and shoulders. She sounds terrified.

"Shut up!" Brophy's voice again. Now the barrel of his shotgun is pointing down into the space, almost touching the woman's head. As soon as she clears the first two rungs, his booted feet come down behind her.

When the woman reaches the third rung from the bottom, she almost slips off the ladder. Damon grabs her around the waist and sets her feet on the floor.

"*Take your hands off me!*" she screams, twisting and throwing her elbows.

"Melissa?" Damon yanks the hood off her head.

Melissa blinks. "Damon!" She throws her arms around him, tears streaming down her face. "Oh my God—Damon!"

"Move back, all of you!" Brophy stops midway down the ladder. He holds a shotgun in one hand. With the other, he reaches up and pulls down the hatch. It closes with a solid thunk, sealing the dank room shut with all six of them inside the small space.

Damon moves toward Brophy. "Did you hurt her? Did you touch her? I'll kill you!"

Melissa pulls him back. "Damon! I'm okay!" It's only then that she notices the others in the room. Her eyes go wide. "Dr. Cross! Professor Lucas! Amy!"

Melissa whirls on Brophy. "Who are you, you sick bastard?"

Brophy slowly descends the rest of the way down the ladder and pokes Melissa in the belly with the barrel of his gun. "You're the sick one," he says. "All of you. Sick. You goddamn *mixers*." His tone is low, deliberate, menacing.

Alex is kicking himself for not recognizing the extent of Brophy's troubled mind sooner. When he talked to Brophy earlier, he thought the man was merely compulsive, maybe a little delusional or dissociative.

Wrong. He's a raging psychopath.

"Colton, let's calm down," says Alex. "Nobody needs to get hurt. Why are you so angry? What's the reason for all this?"

Brophy waves his gun at Lucas and Amy. "Ask those two," he says. "Then ask your boy and his white trophy girlfriend."

Damon balls his fists. "What did we ever do to you, asshole?"

"Damon, stop it!" says Alex. "Let Colton talk. We're in his world right now, and he deserves to be heard."

Brophy grunts. "Damn right I do."

He rubs his hand over his stubble and leans back against the ladder, resting his bulky backside on one of the middle rungs.

"This country had it right for so many years," he says, shaking his head. "Two races, segregated. No mixing of the bloodlines. White on white. Black on Black. The way nature intended. The way *God* intended."

"Are you talking about Jim Crow?" asks Lucas. "For Christ's sake, there was no *end* of mixing! Usually by rape on the part of the white men in power!"

"Not now, Professor," says Alex.

Brophy juts his jaw toward Lucas, then points to Amy. "How old is she? Your little white concubine. How long did it take you to seduce her?"

Amy clasps her short-cropped hair as if she's trying to pull it out. "I've told you a dozen times! This is my boss! My mentor! I am not his girlfriend!"

"I don't believe you," says Brophy. "You were holding hands when I caught you!"

"I was helping her step over a log!" says Lucas. "You're *crazy*!"

"Now, now," says Alex, trying to defuse the tension. "Not crazy. Colton just has different opinions. A different view of the world. Isn't that right, Colton? Those feelings run deep in your family. They go back for hundreds of years, don't they?"

Brophy nods. "Yeah. They do."

"And they're very important to you."

"Damn straight."

"I understand," says Alex. "When I was in your home earlier today, I could see how much you honor your ancestors and how you're trying to keep their values alive."

Alex is winging it, pouring on the empathy. Over the years, he's used the same technique to build bridges with serial murderers, family annihilators, and even men who've tried to kill him personally. Sometimes it works. Sometimes it doesn't.

Now Melissa speaks up. "Sweet Jesus, I can't believe this." She's calmed down. Her voice is gentle and measured. She shakes Damon off and takes a step toward Brophy.

Good, thinks Alex. *She's picking up on my tone. Smart girl.*

"Believe what?" says Brophy.

"I can't believe it's taken me this long to wake up." Melissa glances at Alex. "Michaelson Woods was right."

Damon grabs her arm. "Melissa!"

She pulls away. "Don't touch me!" She moves closer to Brophy. "Don't let him touch me, Colton! Not ever again!"

Brophy grins and raises his gun toward Damon. Melissa pushes it down. "No. Not yet. He needs to hear me first." She turns on Damon. "I don't know what I was thinking! How could I have ever wanted your Black hands on my body! What did you do to me? Did you hypnotize me? Work some jungle voodoo?"

Damon just stands there, dumbfounded.

"I know what I need now," says Melissa. "And it sure as hell isn't down here with you perverts." She looks at Brophy. "I was scared when you took me tonight. I admit it. But now I'm glad. It's about time I saw the truth." She moves another step closer. "I'm right, aren't I? Tell me I'm right!"

"Yes, little girl," says Brophy, "you sure are."

Melissa turns back toward Damon and spits in his face.

Brophy's grin gets wider. The shotgun droops lower…

Now! Alex lunges for the barrel. The gun goes off, blowing a huge divot in the floor. Brophy jerks back, thrown off balance by the recoil.

Melissa whirls around and kicks Brophy straight in the balls.

CHAPTER 104

Sampson

"PERKINS! WHERE ARE YOU?"

I can hear Tom Walsh calling from the entryway. When nobody answered his knock, he pushed in through the unlocked door.

Aiden Phillips is hidden beside the office door. He aims his pistol at Perkins and opens and closes his hand to mimic talking.

"In here, Tom!" Roland Perkins calls out.

I'm standing at the side of the sofa, wondering if there's a way to take Phillips down. Should I warn Walsh or just let things play out? Phillips had a dozen chances to kill me tonight, and I'm still standing. For some reason, he wants me alive as a witness.

What is it he wants me to hear from these two spooks?

Walsh walks into the office and stops short, clearly startled to see me there. He takes a few tentative steps farther into the room. "John Sampson? What's going on? What are you doing here?"

"He's with me," says Phillips, stepping up behind him.

Walsh freezes when he feels the pistol at the nape of his neck. Then he raises his hands slowly. "Let's be cool here."

"Okay," says Phillips. "I'm cool. You can turn around. Slowly."

Walsh pivots until they're face to face. "Phillips! *Jesus fucking Christ!*"

"Now, back up," says Phillips, nudging Walsh toward the sofa. "Take a seat."

Walsh settles nervously on the opposite side of the sofa from Perkins. As Phillips limps out of the shadow, Walsh glances at his bloody leg.

"What happened there?" he asks. "One of your bombs go off in the workshop?"

"No," says Phillips. "Somebody was trying to shut me up. Permanently." Phillips looks at me. "Take his phone."

I move behind Walsh, reach into his jacket pocket, and pull out his iPhone.

Phillips eyes Walsh. "You armed?"

"Armed? This is Georgetown, not the O.K. Corral. See for yourself." Walsh lifts his jacket above his belt and opens the flaps. Then he lifts his pants legs to mid-calf. "You want to see my dick too?"

Phillips takes a step closer. "No. I want to talk about Lieutenant J. T. Polermo."

Walsh has been playing it tough. Now I actually see him flinch. For a guy who's been trained his whole career not to give anything away, it's a pretty big tell.

"Polermo? What about him? I haven't seen him since we got back."

"How about the others?"

"What others?"

"The others who knew about your little business operation in Pakistan."

Perkins turns to Walsh. "Tom, what the hell is he talking about?"

"Quiet," says Phillips, shutting him down. "While you were sitting stateside with your cushy desk job, me and Walsh and Polermo were in the thick of it over there. We all had our little side projects. But only Walsh violated title eighteen, paragraph twenty-three eighty-one."

Perkins sits up straight. "Treason?"

"Good for you," says Phillips. "You know your criminal codes."

On the other end of the sofa, Walsh is turning red. "Phillips. Shut the fuck up."

But I can tell that Aiden is just getting started. "Before we pulled out of Afghanistan," he says, "our people destroyed a lot of equipment so the Taliban couldn't use it. We disabled tons of Humvees and helicopters. And when the Taliban located our advanced missile-defense systems, they figured out that the hardware was useless without the software and codes."

Walsh is squirming now. "Phillips! We can talk about this! You and me."

Phillips leans toward him. "No. I've waited a long time for this. I prefer an audience." He turns back to Perkins. "The Taliban tried to find the software on the black market, but it was all outdated or corrupted. So they came looking for an inside source. They learned that the classified software and codes were being held in a secret base in Pakistan near Guldara Baghicha. The base was run by the army, but the CIA was in charge of classified military materials. One paramilitary officer in particular."

Perkins looks at Walsh.

"Bullshit," says Walsh. "I didn't have access to those codes."

"Of course not," says Phillips. "You couldn't do it alone. Those systems required multilevel authorization. It took four other people. Four enlisted soldiers who must have suspected that you were doing business with the Taliban. J. T. Polermo was one of them."

Walsh jabs a finger at Phillips. "You're out of your mind, son!" He turns to Perkins. "You've seen this guy's file! You know what Sampson found out about him. He's a loose cannon! He should be in a psych ward!"

Phillips stays calm. "So what happened, Walsh? Did you get nervous? Did you worry that one of them would talk? Is that why you hired Polermo as your cleanup man?" Phillips pulls a slip of paper out of his pocket and walks toward Perkins. "You want the other names? I've got 'em right here—"

Walsh stands up and grabs for the paper. Perkins jumps in front of him and snatches it first.

I hear a loud pop.

It's the sound of Perkins's head exploding.

CHAPTER 105

I HIT THE FLOOR, belly-first. "Shooter! Twelve o'clock!"

Roland Perkins is lying on the carpet a few feet away, skull splintered, brains and gore oozing out in a gleaming wet mass. I grab the blood-spattered paper and stick it in my pocket. Phillips is on the floor too, covering Walsh with his body. He looks over at me. "It's Polermo!"

Phillips reaches over and yanks the desk lamp down by its cord. The bulb shatters when it hits the floor. The room goes dark except for the glow of the streetlamps through the windows.

I crawl toward Phillips. "Give me a gun! You're in no shape for this!"

He reaches into his rear waistband and pulls out my Glock. He tosses it to me. "Full clip."

Walsh lifts his head and shouts, "Polermo! It's Walsh! Don't shoot!"

Phillips rams Walsh's head into the floor, stunning him. He pulls a few long black zip ties from under his belt and slides them over to me. "Get him secured and under cover!" He stands up and limps to the front window, pistol raised, hiding himself behind the thick curtain.

Walsh is half conscious, bleeding from the nose. I pull off his necktie and put it between his teeth, then tie the ends tight behind his neck. I zip-tie his ankles, then his wrists. I grab him by the belt and drag him past Perkins's bloody body and under the desk. He starts mumbling through the gag. I point the pistol at his forehead.

"Keep quiet and don't move or I'll shoot you myself!"

I'm still not clear on what the whole story is, but I don't have time to find out. What I know for sure is that there's a trained vet with a high-powered rifle outside. The second he spots a helicopter or hears a siren, he'll be gone again. Maybe for good.

I can't call for help. And I can't hide.

All I can do is fight.

CHAPTER 106

I GRAB MY PISTOL and crawl across the floor to the window behind the desk. One of the panes has a hole in it surrounded by spider-web cracks. I peek over the windowsill.

Another shot pierces the pane above me and slams into the wall across the room.

I call out to Phillips, "Behind the hedge! About twenty yards!"

He nods. "I'll take the front. You flank him."

"Phillips! You can hardly walk! You're an easy target!"

"I'm fine." He ducks behind the sofa and comes up with his M4 rifle. He points at a door on the other side of the office. "There's a patio through there. Stay low."

Am I really taking orders from this guy? I guess so. He knows the enemy. And he's got a bigger gun.

Phillips goes through the office door toward the main entrance. I dash for the other exit. Outside the office is a short hall lined with windows. I drop and crawl below them until I get to the patio door. Through the lattice panes, I see a stone terrace with cushioned outdoor furniture and a huge gas grill. Accent lights run across the base of a low stone wall that separates the patio from the lawn.

I shove the door open and crawl across the cold stone until I'm against the wall with my head just below the top. I poke my head up, just barely to eye level. *Bam!* The wall cap is blasted into pieces a few inches away, stinging my cheek with stone fragments.

I see movement behind the hedge. I aim my pistol and get off five quick rounds—suppressing fire. I need to give Phillips time to maneuver. I jump over the wall, crouch down low, and head for a stand of tall trees in the backyard. I hear a burst of automatic fire to my left. I can see Phillips moving across the lawn in silhouette, firing as he goes. I crouch behind a tree trunk and mentally count my rounds. Ten left.

Phillips drops when a burst of fire comes from the hedge, closer to the road.

Polermo is on the move! I don't have a clear shot from here. I sprint across the open lawn to the far end of the hedge. It's about two feet thick, trimmed square on both sides—a solid wall of foliage. Can't walk through it, only around it.

I look back to where I saw Phillips last. He's gone. Then I see a flash of movement behind a parked car at the edge of the lawn. Phillips is taking cover, hardly moving. Shit! His leg probably gave out.

Suddenly the windshield buckles and cracks. The car alarm starts blaring. I run down the hedge toward the street. I see a shape moving toward the car, all in black, rifle raised. I see Phillips inching along the side of the car, cradling his rifle. For a few seconds, he's outlined against the white door. A perfect target.

The black shape advances and fires. Bullet holes pock the door above Phillips's head as he flattens himself on the pavement. As I come around the end of the hedge, I've got a clear shot at the shooter from the rear. Head or body. My choice. I drop my pistol and shout, "Polermo!"

He wheels around. I'm right there to meet him. Before he can bring his barrel up, I deliver a hard uppercut to his jaw. He's a big guy, but I'm bigger.

My punch lifts him right off the ground.

He's out before he hits the lawn.

CHAPTER 107

Cross

IT TAKES BOTH ALEX and Damon using all their strength to push the metal hatch open. They manage it on the fourth try. When they emerge into the stinking pigsty above, Alex Cross can see flashlights approaching Brophy's front gate. Lots of them.

He found his phone in Brophy's pocket, and his call obviously got some attention.

Alex hurries across the yard to the main house and pulls the switch to cut power to the fence.

"All clear!" he shouts.

He sees a flash of gunfire and metal sparks as somebody shoots the lock apart.

When the gate swings open, a dozen cops in tac gear pour through under the moonlight. Probably the entire Chapel Hill police force.

Alex hurries back to Damon in the middle of the yard. "Put

your hands up and stand still," he says. He knows how trigger-happy cops can get. This is no time for mistakes.

Then he hears a familiar voice. "Hold your fire! Eyes on the hostages!"

It's Gail Bailey. She's the last one through the gate. No full tac, just a ballistic vest over a polo shirt and jeans. She shines a flashlight in Alex's face. "You can put your hands down, Dr. Cross," she calls.

Bailey walks across the farmyard. "You must be Damon."

"Yes, ma'am," he replies.

Bailey turns to Alex. "Better-looking than his picture. Good manners too. I can see you raised him well."

"Damon," says Alex, "this is Detective Gail Bailey, Chapel Hill police. She's been helping me look for you."

"I'm sorry it took this long," says Bailey. "Are you okay?"

"Yes, ma'am. Thank you."

Bailey turns back to Alex. "I appreciate your talking us through the minefield out there. I'll get some ordnance experts out here in the morning to defuse the place."

"Damon!" Melissa's voice.

Alex turns as a couple of cops lift her out of the hatch. She runs over to Damon and wraps herself around him. A few seconds later, Lucas and Amy get pulled up. A paramedic leads them over to the front porch. Another paramedic walks up to Damon and Melissa, who are still clinging to each other. "Let's get you guys checked out, okay?"

"We're fine," says Damon, hugging Melissa even tighter.

Alex taps Damon on the shoulder. "Go with the medics, son. They're here to help."

Damon keeps one arm tight around Melissa's waist as they walk off.

"Detective!" one of the cops calls from the opening of the hatch.

Bailey walks over. Alex follows her.

They both look down into the pit. Colton Brophy is on the floor at the base of the ladder, squirming and cursing, his hands tied firmly behind his back with Alex's belt.

Bailey looks at Alex. "You want to read him his rights?"

"No, thanks," says Alex. "Your town, your collar."

Bailey tells the cop, "Get a couple of our biggest guys and haul him up."

"Copy that, Detective."

When Bailey turns around, Alex catches her eye and looks up at the Confederate flag, lit from below by a floodlight, rippling against the night sky.

Bailey turns back to the cop and points to the flag. "But first, tear that damn thing down."

CHAPTER 108

Sampson

One week later...

I HAVEN'T WORN MY dress uniform in two years. Not since the last funeral I attended, somewhere in New Jersey. I didn't know the officer, just knew that he'd been killed in the line of duty. So a lot of us showed up from all over, like we always do.

Today is different.

Today I'm in Arlington National Cemetery, and this place carries a lot of weight. White headstones everywhere, as far as the eye can see. I feel like I'm surrounded by duty and sacrifice. Whenever I'm here, I get a strong feeling of survivor's guilt.

Today that feeling is stronger than ever.

Today we're burying Anna Rizzo.

Willow is at my side, wearing a black dress that Jannie Cross found for her.

Rizzo's flag-draped coffin is suspended over the open hole in the ground. The chaplain has given his remarks and recited that psalm, the one about walking through the valley of the shadow of death and fearing no evil.

Amen.

Off to the side, a line of seven soldiers in dress uniform point their rifles and fire off seven shots in unison.

Then seven more.

Then seven more.

A bugler blows taps—a call I've heard way too many times in my life, in too many places.

The uniformed pallbearers lift the flag from the coffin, pull it tight, then fold it into a progressive series of triangles, smaller and smaller, thicker and thicker, until only a section of the blue field and white stars is showing.

The officer in charge takes the folded flag and carries it in a slow march to the front row, where Marina, Tina, and Juan are sitting, dressed in their Sunday best. The sergeant hands the flag to Marina, then kneels in front of her and says a few sentences in Spanish. Marina nods, dabbing her eyes with a tissue. She lifts the flag from her lap and cradles it against her chest.

The officer places a white-gloved hand on Tina's shoulder, then Juan's. He says a few words to each of them. Then he stands up, snaps to attention, and salutes.

Willow pulls away from me and goes over to Juan and Tina. She hugs them both. I give them a moment, then follow. All the mourners are standing now—cops, friends, FBI agents. Ned Mahoney and Dennis Chan are in the back row next to a group of techs from Rizzo's ATF office. Marina is speaking in Spanish to a relative. Willow walks over to place a single flower on the casket, then hangs her head.

I stoop down and gather Tina and Juan in my arms. I press their heads against my shoulders so they can't see my face. Nobody wants to see a guy my size crying.

My throat is burning, and it takes me a few seconds to find my voice.

"Your mother was a hero," I whisper. "I know you'll always love her. I know you'll always be proud of her, and I know that you'll never, ever forget her."

Neither will I.

Rest in peace, Anna.

CHAPTER 109

Two days later...

IT'S A CLOSED-DOOR CONGRESSIONAL hearing, and I've got a front-row seat. Actually, a side-row seat. Right next to Aiden Phillips.

CIA director Alvin Crowell played the national security card to keep the proceedings under wraps. I can't blame him. He's trying his best to protect the Company—and his own job. Nobody at Langley wants this mess aired in public.

Fortunately for Crowell, he has a friend in Representative James Halpin of Missouri, the chairman of the House Intelligence Committee, who agreed to the secret fact-finding session.

Everybody here, from the recording clerks on up, is sworn to secrecy. Including me. I can't tell anybody what happens here. Not even my best friend, Alex Cross. Not ever.

The conference room we're in has none of the pomp of the

House chamber. No walnut paneling or marble sculptures here. Just rows of standard-issue meeting-room furniture, with armed guards outside the doors.

No unauthorized spectators. No press. We're two hundred feet underground, sheltered by walls designed to withstand a nuclear blast.

Phillips and I have both given our testimonies under oath. Now it's J. T. Polermo's turn. The prime witness. The whistleblower of all whistleblowers. He's sitting at the center of the table in a civilian suit. His lower jaw is still a bit purple. My knuckles are still a bit sore.

It's a good hurt.

Polermo will be indicted for the murders of Roland Perkins and Anna Rizzo as well as the other victims killed in the DC bombings. But that's not what this is about. This inquiry is about Polermo providing testimony against a career CIA officer.

His old handler, former station chief Tom Walsh.

Walsh sits at the far end of the table, glowering. His attorney, a balding guy with a walrus mustache, is beside him.

The preliminaries are out of the way. Polermo has been sworn in. Junior committee lawyers have put his résumé on the record: Dates of service and promotions. Deployments and duties. Medals and commendations. The picture of a perfect soldier. At least on paper.

Now Halpin steps up. He doesn't waste any time.

"How long after you returned to civilian life were you contacted by Mr. Walsh?" Halpin asks in his down-home Missouri accent. His reading glasses rest halfway down his prominent nose.

"About two years," says Polermo.

"You were adjusting well at that time?" asks Halpin.

"I had some bumps," says Polermo, "but I guess I was doing about as well as could be expected."

I suspect that Polermo is sugarcoating the past. Like a lot of vets, he probably doesn't want to talk in public about the nightmares or the flashbacks. I'm pretty sure he has them. Most of us do, whether we admit it or not.

"You saw a lot of action during your deployments," says Halpin.

"Yeah. I did."

"And when did you first meet Tom Walsh?"

"Not until after the airlift in August 2021."

"And where did you meet?"

"We were assigned to the same unit in Pakistan."

"The secret base in Guldara Baghicha."

Polermo looks at his lawyer, who gives him a slight nod. "That's correct," says Polermo, turning back to Halpin.

"Did you expect to hear from Mr. Walsh again after you left Pakistan?"

"No. I had no interest in hearing from him again. I thought we were done. I figured what was in the past was in the past."

"What did Mr. Walsh say to you when he contacted you?"

"He said we had unfinished business to take care of. For both of our sakes."

"Did you understand what he meant by that?"

I see Polermo stiffen in his chair. "I did."

"And what did he mean?"

"He meant that the Pakistan operation had to be locked down once and for all. Nobody could ever know that he'd supplied military intelligence to the Taliban."

"And were there others who knew that secret?"

"Yes. There were three others who knew, not counting myself."

A clerk puts an image up on the large screen at the front of the room. It shows the piece of paper Phillips had been about to hand to Perkins—the one I'd stuffed into my pocket after he was shot.

The paper is wrinkled and spattered with dark brown spots. On it are three handwritten names. Beside the image of the paper on the screen are three photos. Two men, one woman. All in their early twenties. All posed in their official military portraits, in dress uniform, in front of the American flag, looking proud and determined. Ready to take on the world.

The same way I looked right after basic.

"Are you familiar with these individuals, Mr. Polermo?"

"I am. I served with all of them."

"Right," says Halpin. "And then you killed them."

Polermo sets his jaw and stares straight ahead. "Yes."

"You killed them with bombs you set in Washington, DC."

"That's correct."

"You killed them to protect Tom Walsh's secret."

Walsh's lawyer stands up. "We object, Mr. Chairman!"

"Save your objections, Counselor," Halpin drawls. "This isn't a trial. It's a fact-finding session."

Walsh and his lawyer put their heads together and mumble out of mic range. Polermo turns to face front again.

"Walsh knew that I'd smuggled home a supply of C-4. And I knew that he could hang me up with that. I also knew that he could probably have me killed, no questions asked."

"So you weren't just saving Tom Walsh," says Halpin. "You were saving yourself."

"That's what I believed, yes."

From one chair away, I can feel Aiden Phillips tense. Halpin looks over at the screen and reads off the three names.

"Former army corporal Ray Kilbourne, twenty-six, killed in the Thirteenth Street bombing. Former army sergeant Stacy Fine, twenty-eight, killed in the Vietnam Veterans Memorial bombing. Former army specialist Jean Baptiste, thirty, killed in the Montgomery building bombing."

Halpin turns his gaze from the screen to the witness table. "Can you tell us what all these bombing victims had in common, Mr. Polermo?"

"They all worked at the base in Guldara Baghicha."

"And all three had TS/SCI clearances?" asks Halpin.

"Correct."

"Meaning that, like you, they had access to confidential weapons system codes and operating software."

"Yes."

"Information that Tom Walsh was selling to Taliban operatives for his own profit."

"Yes."

I've heard all this before, during Phillips's questioning. But hearing it from Polermo's mouth—straight from the killer himself—makes me furious all over again.

The Washington, DC, bombings were not terrorist attacks after all. They were disguised assassinations, aimed at just three people. The other victims were all collateral damage—a smoke screen of human carnage. With the troubled vet sitting beside me framed for all of it.

None of us focused on the individual victims killed in the bombings. That three working-class military folk were killed in three separate explosions hadn't raised any immediate red flags. Veterans are everywhere in DC—in government offices, hospitals, businesses, stores, restaurants. It was the perfect cover.

Nobody had made the connection. Not me. Not Ned Mahoney. Not Roland Perkins.

Nobody but Aiden Phillips.

And then Anna Rizzo had too. According to Phillips, that's what she'd been coming to my house to tell me.

Halpin puts down his notes and pulls his glasses off. He rubs his face and stares at the witness table. "You were a U.S. Army soldier, Mr. Polermo. A decorated combat veteran. And you killed three of your own, along with a lot of other innocent people, in your nation's capital and framed another decorated vet for your crimes. Do you have any regrets about what you did?"

"Yeah, I do," he says. Polermo's lawyer puts his hand over the mic. Polermo shoves it away and leans forward.

"I should have just blown up Tom Walsh."

CHAPTER 110

I'M WALKING WITH Aiden Phillips along the pathway that circles the Ellipse. Today, the Ellipse is pretty much empty. We're both glad to be back aboveground and in the fresh air.

"What are the odds they'll execute Walsh for treason?" asks Phillips.

I shake my head. "Zero. The last man this country executed for treason was Bill Mumford."

"Never heard of him. What did he do?"

"He tore down an American flag over New Orleans during the Civil War."

"So after all this, you think Walsh will walk?"

"My guess is they'll ship him to a remote post in the Middle East and keep him under wraps. He'll help them target the weapons systems that he made operational. A few drone strikes, maybe some ground-level sabotage. Walsh is sixty. No wife. No kids. No family. He'll stay quiet, but I doubt he'll be allowed to set foot in this country again."

"That's it? The perp goes down and the mastermind goes free?"

"Not the first time, and it won't be the last. Remember Iran-Contra?"

"Not really. Happened before I was born."

"They didn't make you study it in school? Well, allow me to enlighten you. In 1986, thirteen people in the U.S. government were involved in a plot to sell weapons to Iran and use the money to fund right-wing rebels in Nicaragua. The scheme went all the way up to the secretary of defense. Know who served time for it?"

Phillips shakes his head. "I'm guessing not the SecDef."

"One guy. Tom Clines. A ground-level CIA operative. He did sixteen months."

"And Langley doesn't want to be embarrassed again."

"That's correct. They control the narrative. You said it yourself—they're storytellers."

"But won't it all come out in Polermo's murder trials?"

"There won't be any murder trials, Aiden. No doubt Polermo will take a plea before it gets that far. Same with his domestic terrorism charge. He'll serve his time in a supermax in protective isolation. In a few years, nobody will remember his name. If you're lucky, nobody will ever know yours."

"So, that's the end? I'm done?"

"You'll need to sign some papers. They'll be classified top secret and locked away in a vault for fifty years. By then, the press will have plenty of other stuff to focus on." I grab Phillips by the shoulder and turn him to face me. "Aiden, my advice to you is go home to Lisa and your kids. Go back into counseling. Get the help you need. And if you ever run into any red tape at the VA, call me. Trust me, I know people."

Phillips lets out a long breath. "I've done bad things, John. Really bad things."

"That's true. We all have. But you've also done good things. You saved a lot of Afghan informants and interpreters from falling into the hands of the Taliban. And you led me to capture a serial bomber."

Phillips gives me a tight smile. "Almost got you killed in the process."

"No harm, no foul."

He reaches out to shake my hand. "I owe you, John. For believing me."

"You're a good fighter, Aiden. But your war is over. Now it's time to fight for yourself and your family."

"Yes, sir."

"And take care of that damn leg."

"Copy that."

Phillips turns and heads off toward the Washington Monument.

He's still limping—but he's walking tall.

CHAPTER 111

THE CROSS HOUSE IS a madhouse tonight—just the way I like it. Growing up here, Alex and I were the wild kids. Now we're the patriarchs, sitting in our easy chairs sipping our beers while the chaos swirls around us.

Alex tips the neck of his bottle toward me. "Glad you're here, Sampson."

I clink his bottle with mine. "Glad you're here too, sugar." I'm the only one who calls him that. The only one allowed to.

I know Alex is eager to discuss everything that happened over the past few weeks. I am too. At least the parts I can talk about.

But not here. Not tonight. Tonight is all about family.

Pans are banging and cabinets are slamming in the kitchen, where Nana Mama is hard at work. The aromas of fried chicken, buttermilk biscuits, and brown gravy waft through the air, almost thick enough to taste.

Back at my house, the restoration company and contractors are repairing the driveway and getting the smoky smell out of the curtains and carpets. So, for now, Willow and I are bunking here with the Cross family full-time. It's a bit crowded, but nobody minds. For me, it's like coming home again. Same for Willow, in a way.

The doorbell rings. Ali runs to answer it. I hear him squealing "Damon!" and his big brother walks in, holding hands with a pretty blond girl.

Alex and I stand up as they walk into the living room. Damon comes over and gives me a big hug. He pulls the girl forward. "Uncle John, this is my girlfriend, Melissa."

I turn to Alex. "So this is the one who—"

He nods. "One of the gutsiest young ladies I've ever met."

Melissa smiles. "I've heard all about you, Detective Sampson. You're the one who punched out the DC bomber!"

"Right. And you're the one who kicked a kidnapper in the nuts."

"John! Language!" Nana Mama pokes her head out from the kitchen.

"Sorry, Nana Mama."

Damon and Melissa hurry over to hug her. Bree and Jannie emerge from the dining room. They get their hugs too.

The floor vibrates as Willow loops through the living room. "Hi, Damon!" she shouts as she speeds by.

Damon waves at her, then tugs Melissa's arm. "Let's get our stuff out of the car."

Melissa gives me a nod. "So nice to finally meet you, Detective."

"Same here. Call me John."

Alex and I ease back down into our chairs and pick up our beers.

"They seem like a good match," I tell him.

"They are," says Alex. "And even stronger now."

Bree walks over. "Food's almost ready. What are you two scheming about?"

I take another sip of my beer. "I was just wondering if Damon and Melissa might get hitched and go into the family business. You know, crime-fighting, conspiracy-busting, ball-breaking—"

Bree slaps my leg. "For God's sake, John! Give them a little time!"

Alex smiles. "There'll be plenty of opportunities for them to go into the family business if they want to. No shortage of crazies and criminals in this world."

God knows he's right about that. An endless supply.

Damon and Melissa come back with their bags just as Nana Mama pops out of the kitchen holding an empty skillet and a metal spoon. Willow makes another loop through the room and skids to a halt in front of Nana Mama as she bangs the skillet. "Everybody—stop yakking, quit running, and go wash your hands! Supper's on!"

Alex and I jump up like we did when we were youngsters, back when Nana Mama ruled the roost.

Who am I kidding?

She still does.

ABOUT THE AUTHORS

James Patterson is the most popular storyteller of our time and the creator of such unforgettable characters and series as Alex Cross, the Women's Murder Club, Jane Smith, and Maximum Ride. He has coauthored #1 bestselling novels with Bill Clinton, Dolly Parton, and Michael Crichton, as well as collaborated on #1 bestselling nonfiction, including *The Idaho Four, Walk in My Combat Boots,* and *Filthy Rich.* Patterson has told the story of his own life in the #1 bestselling autobiography *James Patterson by James Patterson.* He is the recipient of an Edgar Award, ten Emmy Awards, the Literarian Award from the National Book Foundation, and the National Humanities Medal.

Brian Sitts is an award-winning advertising creative director and television writer. He has collaborated with James Patterson on books for adults and children. He and his wife, Jody, live in Peekskill, New York.

Dear Reader,

My life's work has been to get kids reading. That's because reading saves lives.

Think about this: millions of fourth graders across America—a full 67% of them—read at or below the barest minimum competency level.*

One big reason is because they've never read a single book they've loved.

Reading shouldn't be work. Reading should be play. Reading should be joy.

But it's not the school's job or the library's job to get kids reading. It's our job. It's mothers and fathers and grandparents and aunts and uncles and carers.

You need to read to your kids.

And don't just pick books that you think are good—find books that *they* think are good. Put books in their hands that make them say, "I love that." Ones that make them say, "Give me another book."

For more information, visit **JoinRaisingReaders.com**

*2022 National Assessment of Educational Progress (NAEP) reading assessment: www.nationsreportcard.gov/reading

For a complete list of books by
JAMES PATTERSON

VISIT
JamesPatterson.com

 Follow James Patterson on Facebook
@JamesPatterson

 Follow James Patterson on X
@JP_Books

 Follow James Patterson on Instagram
@jamespattersonbooks

 Follow James Patterson on Substack
jamespatterson.substack.com

 Follow James Patterson on TikTok
@james.patterson.author

Scan here to visit **JamesPatterson.com** and learn about giveaways, sneak peeks, new releases, and more.